DRAGONSEERS AND AUTOMATONS

SECICAO BLIGHT BOOK THREE

CHRIS BEHRSIN

Edited by

WAYNE M. SCACE

To Ola, for being there through the toughest times.

.

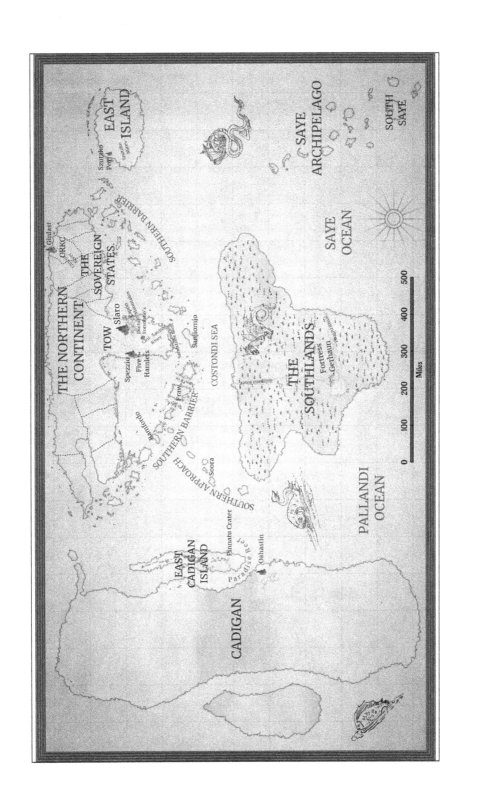

CONTENTS

PART I

TAKA

"From my childhood, I gained a confused sense of identity. Was I a boy, a girl, a dragonseer, or just a normal young soul trying to make sense of a chaotic world?"

— TAKA SAKO

1

J ust as the spider automaton swivelled its turret towards me, I did a forward roll out of the way. It let off a shot at the now absent target. I raised my rifle and fired.

But I hurried it so much that I missed.

"Dragonheats," I muttered under my breath. How had it got here so fast? Faso had undoubtedly worked some of his magic into these things, but I knew this magic was pure unadulterated science.

Taka, my twelve-year-old surrogate son, stood next to me with a smaller custom built rifle in his hands. He turned towards the automaton and fired. The automaton bucked over on its eight legs, let out a sputtering sound, and collapsed to the floor.

"Did you see that, Auntie?" he said. "That's Taka fifteen, Auntie Pontopa, zero."

I clenched my teeth. I was meant to be training the boy today, and he seemed to be better at the task than me. How he'd become such a sharpshooter so quickly, I hadn't the faintest idea.

We were hunting these spider automatons in the secicao jungle. I was trying to train Taka in how to fight against automatons, but he seemed to have it under control. Like me, he wore wellies, as protection against the secicao resin. We also both wore gas masks to guard against the brown acidic secicao clouds all around us, which would suffocate us if we took the masks off. The clamminess of the clouds stung at my skin, adding extra discomfort on top of the sweat.

And my profuse sweatiness wasn't just because of the activity, but also the medicine I was taking – an issue I didn't want to tell Taka about.

I heard a whirring sound, ever so faint in the distance. Another spider automaton. Then I spotted it, glaring at me with its red infernal glowing eyes. This is the one thing about automatons that never changed. Those same red eyes as their dragon-killing war automaton fathers.

The spider automaton turned and swung its turret around to target me. It was perhaps thirty metres away, sandwiched between two thick secicao branches. I raised my rifle and sighted the automaton down the scope. But I was too slow.

A sharp pain lanced in my shoulder and light flashed out from the automaton's stun-cannon, momentarily sending a soft flanging sound into the air.

"Dragonheats," I said. And I clutched my hand to my shoulder. "Did Faso program these things to fire on me alone?"

Taka laughed. "I don't think it's the automatons, Auntie. You have to be stealthy, see?" and he entered a crouch. "Get down low so they can't see you."

I shook my head. "Who's meant to be the teacher here?"

"Gerhaun said experience is the best teacher of them all."

"And you have a long way to go until I'll happily call you experienced."

All of a sudden, a wave of dizziness washed over me. I clutched my hands to my head. It felt like wool, but such a feeling was better than letting Finesia in. If I hadn't taken the medication, she'd take control of my mind, and no one wanted that. I had to stay in control.

"Time for Phase Two," Faso's voice came from a talkie at my hip. He was somewhere nearby, surveying the scene from an airship. But the clouds were so thick I couldn't see his position through the murk. "Are you ready?"

I took hold of the talkie and spoke into it. "Ready as can be. Are you keeping track of the score?"

"Of course," Faso said. "And I can see Taka is winning hands down. What happened to you, Pontopa?"

"The boy's good," I said. In all honesty, if it weren't for the medication, I would have been a lot sharper, a lot faster on my feet, and a lot quicker to react.

"Okay, so I'm calling them in," Faso said. The talkie crackled and then it cut out. This time, Faso would call the spider automatons in, in droves. And so, taking them down wasn't a job for rifles. There was no way that Taka or I, even augmented, could bring down a good dozen of these things with just a few rifle shots before they swamped us.

I waited for a sound, wondering exactly when the automatons would attack. Faso had modified the spider automatons so they could now bury themselves in the soil and jump out and ambush us. For all we knew, they could have been scurrying under our feet right that moment.

"Taka," I said. "Can you sense anything?"

"Negative, Ma'am," he said, with a slight undertone of sarcasm in the word, Ma'am. He was getting close to that sullen teen point of his life. Yet, his transformation had seemed to accelerate the last few months or so. I just hoped that it was natural, and not Finesia trying to take control of him.

"Just keep an eye out. Always be vigilant, Taka; you don't know what lies in wait."

He looked up at me, and I could faintly make out the traces of a smile at the sides of his mask, which had a tube leading from the glass to a tank on his back. But the tank was empty, as Gerhaun and I wanted him to learn how to fight without secicao. His long-gone mother, Sukina, had trained in much the same way. To work on the foundations first, so the skills were even stronger after augmenting.

"Oh yes, wise master," Taka said mockingly in reply. "I'll heed every word you say."

"You can drop that sarcasm immediately, Nephew. It really is the lowest form of wit."

Taka put out his hand to stop me and then turned his head slightly and cupped his hand to his ear. "There, Auntie. Can you hear it?" He pointed out into the distance. But I could see nothing beyond the thick secicao clouds.

"What?"

"Ha ha, made you look."

"Taka, this isn't a joke. You won't have time to fool around like this in true combat situations. Give this one the respect it deserves."

"But this isn't a full combat situation. It's a stupid training drill. And I'll know when they're close."

"But how –"

Taka cut me off by raising a finger to where his lips would be if his mask wasn't in the way. "This time... Really... Can you hear it?"

"Didn't I just say this is no time for jokes?"

Taka ignored me and turned slightly to the right and stretched out his arm and index finger towards the horizon. "Just a few hundred metres away..."

"How could you possibly..."

"The secicao... You can sense it too, right?"

I sighed as I wondered what the dragonheats the boy was talking about. Then I squinted, trying to make out the first sign of the automatons' forms cutting through the secicao clouds. Soon enough, I noticed them, looking kind of spectral in the murk, scampering forward on eight spindly legs.

"Okay, it's time," I said. "Now, which dragonsong are you going to use in this situation, Taka?"

"Oh, there are so many to choose from."

"So pick the first one that seems relevant and give it a try."

"Hmm. How about the one where Varion the Great flies up into the sky and breathes fire on the whole automaton horde?"

"That's not a dragonsong," I replied. "And Varion never did that in your mother's books."

"But wouldn't it be cool if he did?"

"Taka, you should never wish to become a dragon. Those beasts you saw in East Cadigan Island... They weren't like dragons or humans. They weren't even natural, but something else entirely. They aren't things to admire."

"Fine," Taka huffed. "So, I could sing, but I have a better idea." And he cocked his rifle.

The automatons were getting even closer now, and almost in shooting range. Our Pattersonis could reach further than their stun guns, so Taka might take down one. But as for the rest of them...

"Taka, you couldn't possibly get them all. We have dragons nearby. Use them."

"But why should I waste their efforts when I can do it myself?" He took a shot from his rifle, and the gunfire echoed through the jungle, the sound bouncing off the secicao trunks. One of the spider automatons sputtered and fell as its mechanical life was snuffed out of it.

"Pontopa," Faso's voice came from the talkie at my hip, sounding alarmed. "What the dragonheats are you up to? You were meant to call in the dragons..."

"Not my idea... Taka's."

Faso paused a moment, then he spoke a little louder. "Taka, they'll take you down within seconds. You have no chance against a host of automatons with those kinds of tactics. If this were a real army..."

"But it isn't, and they won't." Taka snatched the talkie out of my hand. "Papo, it's time to show you how cool your son has become while you were busy working on your mechanical dragon. Are you watching?"

"Taka... I've spent hours preparing these automatons for this session. If you think I'm going to let such blatant stupidity off so easily, then you've got another thing coming."

The talkie crackled out, and Taka shrugged and threw it on the floor. I made a mental note to have a word with Faso when he came back to Fortress Gerhaun. He didn't seem to care whether or not Taka won. Nor about Taka learning valuable lessons. He just wanted to prove how good his technology was.

There came a screeching sound from a nearby spider automaton, and it scurried into life. This time, it turned its turret on Taka. So, it seemed that Faso had programmed the automatons to target me after all. Another thing I'd have to have a word with him about. Even if the shots were non-lethal, they still bloody hurt.

"Think you can punish me, Papo, with your stupid machines," Taka shot the automaton down before it even had a chance to fire. Up there, Faso was controlling the whole battlefield like it was a game of chess. And Taka seemed to be winning.

Two more automatons came forward in an attempt to flank Taka. One shot, that was what Faso was probably thinking, one non-lethal shot in the chest to teach the boy the value of obedience and following orders.

But Taka raised his nose to the air and regarded both automatons from the bottom of his eyes as they swung their turrets around in sync like clockwork cogs. They fired in unison. But before the shots could hit their target, Taka cartwheeled out of the way with lightning speed and drop-kicked one automaton on its bulbous head. His foot connected with such force that the spider automaton's legs snapped, and it collapsed under its own weight.

"I thought we agreed that you wouldn't augment, Taka," I said. "Where did you get the secicao from?"

"I didn't take secicao, Auntie Pontopa. It's just that I'm awesome. See how awesome I am? I can take them all out. There's only twelve of them."

"Fine," Faso's voice came from the talkie, now on the ground. Naturally, he sounded quite annoyed. "If you're going to practice insolence Taka, then I'll send the rest of them against you as one. You can see how you'll handle an entire force."

And with those words, the rest of the automatons sprang to life. They started sidling around us, while five of them pushed forward with their turrets trained on Taka. The boy watched them with discernment, waiting for the shots to come.

Soon enough, the legs bucked underneath the bodies of the foremost automatons as they fired. Taka rolled forward underneath the shots and he emerged with the rifle against his chest. He shot one automaton and smacked another with the butt of his gun. He then vaulted over two automatons and did a backflip to dodge another barrage of shots.

He then spun around and let off another shot. Somehow, he'd reloaded when he was in the air. The automatons continued to fire at him, but he seemed to see their shots coming in advance, cartwheeling and pinwheeling and somersaulting and returning fire. I even saw him let off a few shots in mid-air, my mouth agape behind my mask.

Around ten minutes later, there remained one boy, and a whole dozen destroyed automatons. Taka took a moment to admire his annihilated prey and then walked back over to me.

What I really should have done, was to sing a dragonsong to call the dragons in and show him how he should have behaved in this situation, stolen away his thunder, and bruised his false pride.

But really, I'd been so completely mesmerised with the way he moved, that I'd forgotten myself. His movements reminded me of his mother. If I could cry, I'm sure it would have brought a tear to my eye. He'd been more remarkable than Sukina had been, and that was saying something. And he'd done all this without augmenting. It was impossible.

Taka dusted off his hands. "See, Auntie. Who needs dragons in a situation like this? If there were a thousand of them, then perhaps I would have sung a song. But these things aren't war automatons, but stupid little toys."

I shook my head. "Taka, you're missing the point here. This was meant to be an exercise in dragonsongs, not in showing off your martial arts abilities." Perhaps I should have given him at least a little praise, but I didn't want his cockiness to become a habit.

"Then you'll have to select a more suitable challenge, Ma'am," and he gave that mock salute again.

2

Taka didn't say much on the journey back to Fortress Gerhaun. And, as soon as we landed on the golden coloured mosaic of Gerhaun, the dragon queen, he stormed out of the courtyard.

Instead of chasing after him, I thought I'd let him stew for a while. I didn't want to encourage him to seek attention when it wasn't due.

I didn't see Gerhaun immediately, nor did she acknowledge me in the collective unconscious when I arrived. She might have even been having a nap, which she'd been doing a lot recently. A couple of hours here and there during the day at random times, instead of sleeping for weeks on end. There was an advantage to this, though. This way, I didn't have to wait ages to wait for her to wake up so I could ask her a question.

But at the same time, her unusual sleeping patterns were making everyone around here anxious, especially the dragons. Longer periods of sleep meant a healthier dragon queen. And shorter ones indicated she might be approaching the end of her long life.

She'd laid the egg of a young dragon queen recently, so fortunately she now had a successor. But it hadn't hatched yet, and without a dragon queen alive, there would be nothing to keep the secicao out of Fortress Gerhaun. Her presence, as a powerful source of the collective unconscious, pushed the clouds away. But when she died, we'd have between around twenty-four and forty-eight hours before the noxious yellow clouds closed in, suffocating any human life in the fortress. Meaning we'd have to vacate fast.

Unfortunately, her frequent calls to rally the other seven dragon queens remained unanswered, and so we didn't know if any of them would grant us refuge.

I had other errands to run, so I pushed my worries aside. My supply of cyagora was almost out, and if I wanted to keep Finesia out of my head, I'd need more.

I walked out of the courtyard, through the musty corridors with tapestries of dragons hanging off hooks nailed into the brick walls. After I turned a few corners, I rapped my knuckles on a heavy oak door.

"Come in," a voice answered after the second knock.

Inside, Doctor Forsolano sat at a desk at one corner of the room. His clinic was spacious, with two patient beds on the right-hand side of it. One of these was a standard adjustable examining bed. The other was a hard-stone table large enough to hold a dragon queen.

A massive canopy spanned over a hole in the ceiling, retractable for those times a dragon needed to enter for treatment. Since moving to the Southlands, Doctor Forsolano had extended his range of expertise as an excellent doctor, to also act as a veterinary surgeon for dragons. You can probably imagine there weren't many of those in the world.

"Ah, Pontopa," he said, and he examined me over the top of his horn-rimmed glasses. He was around five years older than my father, so had wrinkles in a few places, but he still looked pretty healthy. "What can I do for you today?"

"I'm almost out of cyagora," I said. "And I hoped you had access to some more."

He smiled. "Straight to the point, I see. But I didn't realise you were due for a refill? How many have you been taking daily?"

"Enough to keep the voice out of my head."

He frowned and looked down at his notes. "I think... Didn't we say one every three days?"

"Okay, I admit, I took them every day. But I'm a dragonseer and Finesia's voice is strong inside me. If I let her have control, there's a lot more at stake than just my own mind..."

"I see, I see," he said as if not quite believing me. He was a scientist, after all. He opened his desk drawer and rummaged around inside. "We'll need to ration them, unfortunately. The next shipment of cyagora hasn't come in yet, and you can imagine how, in these trying times, supplies are dwindling. There were only two places in the world that cyagora grew and one of them was East Cadigan Island."

I raised an eyebrow. "The other?"

"The Saye Archipelago. But the king's been blockading that shipment route recently. There's a lot of valuable medicine that comes from those islands and King Cini knows this all too well."

"I can find a way to get Velos over there, so I can forage for what you need."

"Can't you employ someone else to do it? Like Mr Gordoni? I'm sure your time here is much more valuable."

I smiled, imagining the conversation I might have with Faso about this.

"I think Faso would see a task like this as far below his station." Although, I thought, if I could convince him that it aided science, maybe he'd be a little more receptive to the idea. Perhaps I could tell him how a new branch of medicine had been discovered over there, and then maybe I could convince him to lead an expedition.

"Very well," Doctor Forsolano said. "But I wouldn't be doing my duty if I didn't say that I don't approve of you taking these at the rate you're taking them. There are other effects, such as on your fertility. I really wish there was another way, Pontopa."

"Believe me, if there was I'd take it. But Finesia is a risk to all of us. Someone needs to make sure Taka stays on the right track to becoming a dragonseer."

Admittedly, with the way he was behaving lately, I was concerned that Finesia might have taken control of his mind. But to force a boy to take such huge tablets would be verging on cruel.

Doctor Forsolano shook the jar for a moment and then he handed it over to me.

"You have thirty tablets, and remember, these are my very last. I'll ask my staff to keep an eye out for merchant traders who are stocking them. But if supplies run out, make sure you wean yourself off them slowly. Don't even go a day without the drug, for now, do you hear? Otherwise, that voice inside your head will be amplified tenfold."

I nodded and took hold of the jar while a wave of dread arose in the pit of my stomach. The drugs weren't pleasant. Each tablet was the size of a small thumb and, if I didn't take it down in one, its effectiveness would be greatly reduced.

They helped stop thoughts running wild inside the head. This kept Finesia, the mad empress of legend who wanted to control my mind and convert me to her cause, away. And listening to her voice could have severe effects.

But the drugs also numbed my connection to the collective unconscious. This meant I couldn't connect to dragons, I couldn't communicate with Taka telepathically, and even Gerhaun's voice came kind of faint inside my head.

"How can I wean myself off them," I asked Doctor Forsolano, "if I can't even go a day without them? Didn't you expect me to take one tablet every three days?"

"That was before I knew you were taking one every day. Now, you'll need to increase the time in between doses by an hour at a time, waking yourself up in the middle of the night if you have to. This stuff is not to be trifled with, Pontopa."

I nodded. "Okay, I understand."

Part of me wasn't listening. I could go a day without the drug, surely, If I had to. But I wasn't planning to anytime soon. Doctors always erred on the side of caution to protect their careers. And I was a dragonseer, not an old woman who needed molly-coddling.

"Thanks," I said. "I'll stick to the same dose for now. By the way, I need to talk to you about Taka. Has he been in for any check-ups lately? He's been acting rather strangely recently."

The doctor tilted his head to the side. "In what way?"

"He has these awesome abilities, but I have no idea where he's getting them from. Could you possibly keep an eye on him? Check out for signs of secicao addiction?"

That was the thing people rarely mentioned about secicao. You could get addicted to it. The hot cups of the beverage widely distributed in secicao houses around the world weren't so dangerous. But secicao was when it was in its most concentrated form as oil.

This was why King Cini only allowed access of secicao oil to his military. Otherwise, he'd risk a nation going riot after the stuff.

Also, if the citizens of the Northern Continent consumed the stuff in such concentrated quantities, the secicao in their urine would leach into the soil, acidifying it and creating conditions perfect for secicao and no other life to grow. This was already happening with the massive consumption of secicao by the cup. But everyone drinking the oil would accelerate the process even more.

secicao's ultimate goal was to spread across the planet and destroy all other life except the immortal dragonpeople who thrived on it. And Finesia lived inside the secicao and had a similar goal.

Due to recent circumstances, both Taka and I had become more susceptible to her will. I was already a dragonwoman and could transform into an almost impervious dragon if I so wished. But to do so would be to tap into one of Finesia's 'gifts', which would surrender part of my soul. Piece by piece, she'd gradually take control of my mind.

All this is why it was so important for Taka to behave himself and to follow orders. Finesia had found a way inside his head through a mind-altering drug named Exalmpora that had been forced on him at a young age. If Finesia took control of his mind, then I wouldn't only have to battle Alsie Fioreletta – Finesia's ruthless right hand – but also Taka.

Doctor Forsolano studied me through his glasses for a moment, his hand on his chin.

"Very well. I'll keep an eye on the boy. I've not seen much of him lately, admittedly. He's always keeping to himself is that young man."

I smiled. "Thank you, Doctor." I stood up to leave.

"Try to get me a new shipment."

"Affirmative," I said. And I made a mental note that I'd have to get more cyagora before those thirty days were up. There was no way I was letting Finesia back in my head. Not after I'd seen what had happened to Charth...

AFTER VISITING DOCTOR FORSOLANO, I went to visit my oldest friend in the whole wide world – Velos. I'd vouched to spend more time with my dragon recently. For a while, after the fall of East Cadigan Island, we'd kind of drifted apart.

I found Velos in his stable, tucking into a trough of secicao. Over his natural coat of blue scales, he wore his dragon armour, which didn't have its usual shine to it. Instead, it looked grimy, as if it hadn't been tended to for weeks.

The armour itself was a combination of plates arranged on top of each other. It had hard metal seats on top for seating three riders. Two Gatling turrets jutted out from either side, which could target enemies with pinpoint precision. A more recent addition was a large slot underneath Velos' belly that could house a twelve-foot cannon, but this wasn't connected right now and instead lay on the floor to one side of the stable. This cannon could bring down an automaton in one shot, searing a hole right through it. The disadvantage was that it was incredibly slow to charge.

Velos didn't even turn to me as I approached. There was once a time he'd at least heed my footfalls and raise his head to me and croon. But he kept his snout in the trough, munching down on the food as if there was nothing else more important in the world.

I sat down next to him and stroked the scales on the back of his neck, but I received no response. I tried singing a dragonsong, but it came out flat. Defeated, I let out a lengthy sigh, which caused Velos to finally turn his head and look at me. But his expression seemed to say, 'why the dragonheats are you disturbing me from my meal?'.

"It's not my fault I became a dragonwoman." I felt at the bullet scar on my belly. "It was either that or die. And it's not my fault that Finesia is now in my head and I need to block her."

Part of me wanted to cry. But, because of the numbing effects of the drugs, no tears flowed to my eyes.

Velos lowered his head to me as if he understood. But did he, really? I couldn't sense what he was feeling anymore, and he couldn't sense what I was feeling either. Our link was broken, and this left me with a sense of emptiness. I'd grown up with Velos, and now circumstances had forced me to push him away.

"You know, there's another way." The voice of Gerhaun Forsi, my dragon queen and long-time mentor resounded in my head. *"You can learn to control it without the drugs. It just takes discipline."*

Her voice was ever so faint, but still strong enough to make out the words. But I could only hear her because she was such a powerful source of the collective unconscious. And I worried that if the effect of the medications got much worse, or perhaps as she edged closer to death, I wouldn't be able to hear her in my head at all.

Then, they might as well stop calling me a dragonseer, because I'd be useless. All my latent abilities stripped away because of some stupid drug. A drug I had to take – I had no choice.

"Gerhaun," I replied. *"We've been through this. I can't be trusted. We thought we could trust Charth, didn't we? I don't want to turn out like him."*

"Charth had continually and stubbornly tapped into Finesia's gifts, despite me advising him not to," Gerhaun pointed out. *"You have already proven your strength at East Cadigan Island. You can resist her charms, Dragonseer Wells. You have the ability."*

I shook my head. *"We think that now. But who knows how I'll behave in the future. No, as much as I hate this, it's what I have to do."*

"But I've not got long left in this world, and I worry that I won't pass on all that I can. While I'm still here, I can help you master your mind. You can't keep taking these medications forever."

"And why not?" I shot back.

"Because the world needs you to be strong, Dragonseer Wells."

I snorted and kicked at some dirt in the ground, creating a shallow hole. Then, I felt guilty for marring Velos' stable, and I filled the hole back in using the side of my foot as we continued the conversation.

"Gerhaun, we've not seen action for two years. The immortal dragons are doing their own thing in East Cadigan Island and haven't been seen since our last battle. And who knows what King Cini is up to right now."

"But these forces shall rise again. After grand battles, fleets and armies need time to build. We can never assume we're safe forever."

"The world doesn't need me. They need dragons and soldiers and sailors, the brave souls who fight for us. We have General Sako, and Admiral Sandao. And we have other excellent military personnel like Lieutenant Talato. Why the dragonheats do you need me?"

"Do you really need me to answer that question?" Gerhaun asked. *"As one of the few in this world with the power to control dragons, you underestimate yourself."*

"BUT IF THE cost of me being at my best is to turn the dragons against us..." I trailed off. *"What if I did something that got them all killed, Gerhaun? What if I destroyed them all?"*

"Which is exactly why you should train to prevent that. Strengthen yourself while you have time."

"No," I said. *"I should prevent Finesia from ever reaching me. It's the safest way."*

There was a long pause. I took some time to look up at the sky, and the secicao clouds rolling in. When I'd arrived at Fortress Gerhaun, you couldn't really smell them here. But now, their sulphuric tang permeated the air.

Because I'd become a dragonwoman, I could probably breathe the gas without dying. If the clouds closed in, I might be the only human that survived. Taka might also survive if he'd passed further over to Finesia's side than we realised. But that would probably involve accepting her gifts and losing control of our minds.

"You know I can't force you against your will," Gerhaun said. *"But that*

doesn't mean I won't stop trying to convince you. I just hope you see sense before it's too late."

I'd had similar conversations with Gerhaun many times before. And I knew, as if with a nagging grandmother, I'd have it many times again. And every day, I'd reserve the right to change the subject.

"How's the little one?" I asked.

"Getting closer to hatching every day. And her father keeps coming to visit, laying branches of secicao in offering at the egg's base, which I have to keep cleaning up. I can't have them spoiling my treasure room."

I laughed. Anyone who didn't know Gerhaun might wonder why she needed to protect her treasures so meticulously. But the trove she guarded funded entire military operations, which, in turn, helped us win battles.

"He certainly knows how to keep a lady happy." I looked up at Velos, kind of hoping for at least a croon. But without the connection to my feelings in the collective unconscious, there was no way he could understand any of this.

"I worry," Gerhaun said. *"I want the egg to hatch before I pass on. But you know it's only a matter of time."*

"You're not gone yet. Doctor Forsolano still says you have plenty of time ahead of you."

"Doctor Forsolano is new to dragon medicine, and he's never treated a dragon queen before me."

I sighed. I really didn't want to be hearing how my mentor and recent benefactor would soon leave this world. What would we do here without her? What would I do? Meanwhile, some children giggled outside the doorway to the stables. They pinwheeled flamboyantly through the corridors as they passed. I turned away from them, trying not to think of how having to vacate might suddenly affect their lives.

"Everything will be okay," I said. I had to believe it. *"You'll see."*

"It will happen eventually," Gerhaun said. *"And when it does, you'll need to be prepared. I had a think who to seek refuge with. And you might want to try Castlonth."*

Castlonth was one of the seven other dragon queens. Gerhaun had mentioned her name a few times.

"But how would I go about doing that?" I asked.

"When the time comes, you will find a way."

And my heart felt heavy in my chest. Gerhaun was the kind who didn't provide answers to puzzles, but gave hints to help solve them at propitious times. Usually, her approach worked. But it didn't make it any easier to be constantly confused.

"I guess I'll have to," I replied.

"Trust me, you will." Gerhaun said. *"Now, if you excuse me, I need to be taking a nap."*

"But you've only just woken up," I said worriedly.

She didn't hear me. Because, just like that, her voice cut out of the collective unconscious.

I sighed, then looked up at Velos. But he turned away, as if I'd disappointed him, and returned to his food. I felt so alone here now. Missing not only the natural connection to my dragon, but a healthy state of mind.

But in all honesty, the medications also helped me forget who I'd lost...

Sukina, a good friend and mentor who'd taught me so much about what it is to be a dragonseer. She'd sacrificed herself at King Cini's palace to Alsie Fioreletta, so Taka, Faso and I could escape.

Then there was Francoiso, who was also killed by Alsie Fioreletta. I was forced into a betrothal to him, and he hadn't been a good man until his very last moment, when he also helped Taka and me escape.

And Charth. Dear old Charth, Sukina's betrothed. He had survived much longer, tapping into the power of Finesia whenever he needed to protect us. Until Finesia ended up taking his soul. Alsie Fioreletta again had coerced him into using the ultimate gift that caused Charth to lose his mind.

Alsie – always there to stir up trouble; always there to make things worse.

A commotion coming from the doorway interrupted me from my train of thoughts.

"Pontopa, Pontopa, come quick". Faso came flailing through the door, his arms aflutter, his face red and his rich pinstripe suit looking kind of crumpled. On his shoulder stood Ratter, his six-legged ferret automaton that glared at me with unsettling red glowing eyes.

"What's the hurry?" I replied.

"It's Taka, you'll never believe what he's just gone and done. Come quickly."

And before I could get another word in, he was rushing back out of the room.

I sighed and then turned back to Velos. "I'm sorry, old friend," I said. "But I'm afraid that I'll have to help my other comrade, Faso. Although I still much prefer you."

And Velos didn't even turn his head to see me go.

3

Taka was waiting in the courtyard, Faso towering above him, glaring down at the boy. Six armed guards in olive-coloured uniforms surrounded the boy. Whatever this was about, I hadn't expected it to be a military matter.

As I approached, I noticed two automatons on the floor. One of them was Ratter, stalking in a circular motion around the second machine. This was a disabled Hummingbird – an airborne common-place automaton used for a variety of tasks from reconnaissance to stunning dragons in flight, hence removing them from the sky.

I hoped that I hadn't been summoned to endure another of Faso's lectures on the benefits of technology. I walked over to the Humming-bird and kicked it gently with my toe to check whether there was any life in it. But it was like kicking a rock.

"What the dragonheats is this about?" I asked.

Faso reached into the inside pocket of his suit and took out a small vial of green liquid, with black speckles of something swimming within. "I found Taka taking this off the automaton here. If it weren't for Ratter, the thing would have got away."

I turned to Taka, who averted his gaze as soon as I met it.

"Taka... Look at me when I'm talking to you.... What is this?"

The boy gazed upwards through red-rimmed eyes, and a tear fell from his cheek.

"Faso, let me have a look at that." I snatched the vial out of the inventor's hand. It was warm, and black speckles danced within and glowed slightly in response to my touch. "Taka, answer me. What is this?"

Taka, now staring at the floor, said nothing.

I folded my arms. I couldn't say I was angry as such. With the cyagora numbing my emotions, I rarely had the capability for anger. But I knew how to fake it when I had to.

"Fine," I said. "Going to give me the silent treatment. So, at least tell me this. How long have you been taking it?"

Still not a word.

"Suit yourself. Then I shall destroy this and every vial that comes through from this day. And you'll remain grounded until you're ready to talk."

I looked over to one guard as if to indicate I was about to give an order. Then, I pulled back my arm and prepared to smash the vial on the floor. Out of the corner of my eye, I saw Faso flinch, but he didn't step forward.

"Wait," Taka said. "Auntie Pontopa, it's…"

I turned my head to Taka slowly and kept my hand hovering in the air. "I'm waiting."

"It's…. I don't know. This automaton… It put me in touch with a man called Travast Indorm. He said he had something that would make me powerful and help me save the world. That's what *Chantell* wanted, right? To save the world?" *Chantell* was Sukina's and Taka's native word for mother.

I raised an eyebrow "He what? Taka… How long's this been going on?"

"I just want to help, Auntie. I can see that you've not got your strength lately. Something's happened to you… Someone needs to be a dragonseer here."

I wanted to reach out and ask Gerhaun if she knew anything about this, but she was fast asleep. Meanwhile, Faso let out a quick whistle, and Ratter scurried up the inventor's shoulder, along his arm, and buried himself in Faso's widened left sleeve.

I wasn't going to let me or the boy get distracted. I turned back to Taka.

"Taka, do you know what addiction is?"

"Uh huh. I'm not a toddler, you know...."

I frowned. "But you don't really know it until you've admitted to yourself you have a problem. And Taka, whatever this stuff is, it sounds like you're addicted to it."

"I'm not, I can come off it at any time."

"Fine. Then you won't mind if I just destroy this then."

I pulled the vial back even further and this time I really wanted to smash it on the floor. Faso took a step forward, but honestly there would be no way for him to make it in time to stop me. But Taka moved at lightning speed and pinwheeled forward, catching my arm in his hands before I had even moved it an inch.

Taka's block wasn't supple, but as hard as wood. He had a hunger in his wide eyes that I recognised all too well. I'd felt the same hunger for Exalmpora multiple times. A hunger to hear the voice of Finesia and tap into her powers. "No, Auntie Pontopa. I need that."

I snatched back my arm, and Taka didn't stop me, although I guessed whatever was in this concoction gave him the strength to do so.

"Taka," I said again. "What is this stuff? You shouldn't be able to move this way."

"I don't know, Auntie Pontopa. I just know it makes me feel good..."

I sighed, and then I handed the vial to Faso. "Take it to Winda and find out what it is."

Faso nodded, checked the stopper on the vial, and then put it in his inside pocket. "I intend to do just that."

"And don't destroy it," I said. "Make sure your tests don't alter that stuff. We might need it." I gave Taka a curt nod.

Faso put the vial in his pocket and folded his arms. "Why the dragonheats would I destroy something that could be of valuable scientific importance?"

I ignored him and turned back to the boy.

"Young man, you must trust us." I took hold of his hand. "Now come, we must go and see Doctor Forsolano."

"I'm coming too," Faso said. And somehow, I knew already that the boy wouldn't like that idea. Faso wasn't a dragonseer, and he'd dismiss many of Doctor Forsolano's theories as mumbo jumbo, just because he didn't understand we were physiologically different to normal humans.

"I think you've got your work cut out for you, Faso," I said. "Plus, this is something I think Taka and I should handle alone. It's a dragonseer matter."

He crossed his arms. "Fine. I guess I want to know what's in this stuff as quickly as possible." And he stormed off towards the lab.

Meanwhile, Taka was looking up at me with wide eyes beneath his sandy haircut. Something certainly seemed different about the boy. If this drug was the same Exalmpora that had been forced upon me multiple times, it could alter his physicality even further than merely changing his sex. We had to do something, and we had to do it fast.

WE REACHED Doctor Forsolano's clinic a couple of minutes later. Taka had surprisingly come without resistance. Which suggested he might not be as far gone as it had first seemed. Maybe he realised that we were less likely to destroy the drug if he could demonstrate that he could live without it. Taka was a smart boy, after all.

I knocked on the door, and Doctor Forsolano called us in. I opened it and led the child inside.

"Ah, Pontopa," the doctor said "Twice in one day. What can I do for you this afternoon?"

I didn't hesitate to get to the point. "Doctor, you know that checkup we talked about for Taka? I think we need to do it much sooner than I'd thought."

Doctor Forsolano smiled, and then when he noticed the boy's eyes, his expression changed to one of concern. "This redness isn't from tears," he said, and he walked forward to examine the skin around Taka's eyes.

Taka flinched a little, but otherwise kept still.

"We caught him with a drug in a vial," I explained. "It looked like secicao oil, but it had something else floating inside it. Taka's been taking it for a while, and we need to check that he's okay. Faso, Winda, and their scientists are running tests on the drug as I speak."

"I understand. Taka, if you would please lie down over there." The doctor pointed to the smaller bed, which had a white cloth lain over it.

But Taka didn't move at first until I stared daggers at him. If anything, he knew he didn't want to be angering his Auntie Pontopa, so he complied.

Once the child was in place, Doctor Forsolano rummaged around in a cupboard under his desk, and took out a needle, a set of electro-cardiogram sensors, and various other medical equipment. He took off Taka's shirt, attached the contacts to the boy's chest and then stuck the needle in Taka's arm.

Taka's blood filled the ampoule – black as coal. I gasped.

"Exalmpora? Taka?"

"Travast told me it isn't Exalmpora," the boy replied.

Doctor Forsolano raised an eyebrow to me. "Who's Travast?"

"I don't know," I growled. "But I intend to find out."

Doctor Forsolano plugged the other end of the electrocardiogram equipment into a steam-powered plotter. He turned it on and put some coal in the burner underneath. After he'd lit it up, the machine whirred away. A long stream of paper passed through a roller, whilst several needles plotted out several thin and sinuous lines on it, bobbing up and down in a steady rhythmic pattern.

"Everything seems normal," Doctor Forsolano said. "Except for the fact your heart is beating at two-hundred beats per minute. Even if you're only young, that's abnormal for a resting state."

But the increased rate did make a lot of sense. In most cases, depending on the blend, secicao oil would cause the blood to pump faster. This often caused increased anxiety in those that used it.

"We must take him off the drug, immediately," I said.

"Not so fast," Doctor Forsolano said. "Remember what I told you before about weaning yourself –" He stopped himself just before he broke patient confidentiality about the cyagora. "I... er.... need to run some tests."

He took out the needle, detached the ampoule of blood, and carried this back to his desk. He then selected a few small brown bottles out of the cupboard behind him, as well as several empty petri dishes. These he placed on the desk and proceeded to distribute a few globules of Taka's blackened blood into each dish. He added drops of the various liquids to each sample. In one, nothing happened. Another turned red, another green, another transparent. In the last one, the blood glowed ever so faintly.

"This one," Doctor Forsolano picked up that very petri dish and squinted at it. "I've seen nothing like it. Taka, where did you get this drug from?"

Again, the boy said nothing.

"Taka, answer the man for wellies' sake. He has your best interest at heart."

The boy huffed and then turned to the doctor. "I got it from Travast Indorm."

"Ah, so you mean the king's scientist?" Doctor Forsolano asked.

"Yes," Taka said. "The king's scientist." Taka hadn't told me he knew this man. But at this point in time, I didn't think I'd get much information out of him.

I turned to Doctor Forsolano instead. "You know him?"

"I've heard his name. He used to serve under the king around the time Faso Gordoni became famous. He worked as a basic lab scientist, just there to perform basic tests and hand reports up to his superiors. Faso might know of him."

"He didn't seem to," I said. He would have mentioned something otherwise.

Doctor Forsolano scratched his chin. "Perhaps he doesn't

remember him," he said. "But I heard rumours that after Faso left, Mr Indorm climbed the ranks fast."

Come to think of it, the three old men that I'd met in the cave inside the Pinnatu crater had mentioned that an eminent scientist was now among the king's ranks.

"Can we cut him off the drug immediately?" I asked.

Doctor Forsolano shook his head. "I wouldn't recommend it. From the blood test and my examinations, it's clear the drug has a strong impact on his physiology. If we stopped it just like that, the effects would be unpredictable."

"Then we need to find out where this man is sourcing the stuff from and what his intentions are."

"I think so. But I don't understand –" Doctor Forsolano glanced over at Taka, "– how did Travast Indorm get past our guards?"

"Somehow, a Hummingbird automaton got through," I said. "But it would have needed someone controlling it for it to sneak past the guards so well."

Doctor Forsolano cocked his head. "You think he's nearby?"

"It's possible. We should probably send out scouts looking for him."

And out of the corner of my eye I saw Taka grimace. Whoever Travast Indorm was, the boy didn't seem to like the implication that we'd need to take the man hostage.

"I don't like the sound of this," Doctor Forsolano said.

"Neither do I," I replied. "Neither do I."

Doctor Forsolano continued to run tests on Taka, and after we'd finished, I dismissed the boy and sent him to his room. I waited for him to leave, and then I thanked Doctor Forsolano and walked out the door.

AFTER WE'D CLOSED Taka in his room and I'd posted some guards outside, I went to find Faso. I had a bone to pick with him, and it wasn't only about how he'd evidently programmed the automatons to target me during the training exercise before.

All this time, he'd promised to spend more time with his son, instead of endlessly tinkering with his machines. If he'd occasionally diverted attention away from his pet project – his dragon automaton and made sure that Taka got the care he needed, maybe none of this would have happened.

But somehow, he just seemed to expect that my parents and I should assume parental duties, while he focused on his 'work'.

As usual, I found him crouched down in the courtyard, applying some changes to the dragon automaton that he had set up in one corner. He was focusing on a hatch on the dragon's neck where he'd probably later insert a power core.

The machine had come on quite a way, admittedly, since Faso had started working on it. It wasn't quite the size of Velos, but roughly the size of a Grey. And it looked even more complex than Velos' armour, with all its fancy plates and greebles. I couldn't help but wonder if any of this served any functional purpose, or if Faso had just designed it that way to make it look impressive.

I took a deep breath, not quite appreciating the eggy smell of secicao on the air. I approached Faso, kicking up some dust on the way, and stood over him with my hands on my hips. I waited for him to acknowledge me but, much like Velos, he showed no sign of even realising I was there.

So I interrupted him with a loud cough. "Faso," I said. "A word, please. I've not been impressed with your behaviour recently."

Faso looked up at me disdainfully, but he otherwise didn't budge. "Nothing new there. When are you ever happy with me, Pontopa?"

"On those rare moments when you're actually showing respect for other people and you're not solely concerned about yourself."

That caused Faso to put down his screwdriver, stand up on his two feet, and look me straight in the eye. Ratter ran out of the flared sleeve on his pinstripe suit and took a perch on Faso's shoulder. It glared at me with those red menacing glowing eyes.

"I'll have you know," Faso said, "that everything I do has a selfless objective. I work for the advancement of science, so that we may win the war against King Cini or Alsie Fioreletta, whichever one we'll end up fighting first. It's only a matter of time until one of them attacks, you know, and we can't be sitting on idle thumbs."

I shook my head. "That's not all of it, admit it. You don't want to have to deal with people. Especially your son. You're always shirking off your own responsibility onto other people's shoulders."

He puffed out his cheeks. "That's not true at all. I do care about people and I reserve a suitable hour for Taka every day. But I need time to focus on my work, or it will never get done."

"An hour a day? A boy should have more time with his father than that."

"I've offered to spend more time with him, so long as he works with me on the automatons, but he doesn't seem to want to."

"He's not interested in the automatons, Faso. He wants to forge his own path, and it's your responsibility to help him find a good one. Now, because of you neglecting him, he's had to go and find entertainment of his own."

"Oh, so that's what all this is about. And next you're going to say that it's my fault that Taka ended up taking those drugs. Dragonheats, he's almost a teenager, and he'll end up doing things like this, no matter how much you try to stop him."

"And so you just accept that and refuse to keep an eye on him? That's the point of parenting, you're meant to help him learn what's good for him and what's bad for him."

"But you're saying all this, Pontopa, while being rather hypocritical yourself. You're his guardian too. And if you hadn't been sleeping all the time, then maybe you would have noticed him wandering off where he shouldn't on your watch. Isn't that meant to be your job? Guarding the castle and looking out for everyone here..."

"No," I said. "I can't keep my eye on everyone at once. He's your son, for wellies' sake, Faso. By blood..."

And I tried not to let the heavy guilt sink down that I'd been spending half the day sleeping. This was one of the side effects of the cyagora. If Faso knew, then maybe he would understand, being a man of science himself. But there was no way I would tell him. There was no way he'd believe that a mad empress was living in my head, and he'd deem me just as bad as Taka – addicted to a drug I shouldn't be taking.

Of course, it wasn't that clear-cut.

"Just admit it," I said. "You're addicted to your work, and you can't put it down. That's why you slave for twelve hours a day and hardly have time to at least read Taka a bedtime story."

"Oh, he's a little too old for bedtime stories, don't you think? He's now in his exploring phase." Faso turned up his nose. "Of course, you wouldn't know about that, being a woman."

"And you would know. You know better than anyone, being Faso Gordoni, inventor extraordinaire." I mirrored the exact same voice he'd used when he met me, at the time trying to impress me with empty shenanigans.

Faso paused for a moment, and his face went red. Then he turned timid all of a sudden. You kind of knew when you hurt this man's feelings – he was incredibly sensitive underneath it all, despite seeming so bull-headed

"Look, I don't know what this is about," he said after a moment, "but you seem to be having another one of your mood swings. You don't seem to realise how important my work is. Once we finish this dragon, then we might have something that can oust Alsie's dragonmen in battle. And what about you... While I'm here slaving away, what are you doing all day? Addicted to work? You seem to be addicted to doing nothing. Why aren't you spending time with Taka?"

I put my hands on my hips. "I spend a few hours training with him every day."

"Doing what? Knitting jumpers while he takes swigs of that drug behind your back?"

I felt the blood rush to my cheeks. "That was uncalled for, Faso."

"And you criticising my parenting methods wasn't? Just let me get back to my work."

"Faso, you listen to me." I pointed a finger at his chest.

Faso scowled. "You're just getting annoying now, Pontopa. I should get Ratter to sedate you, that would shut you up."

"Do that and you'll spend a week in the cells."

Faso chuckled to himself. "What difference would it make, anyway? You'll probably be asleep in a couple of hours." He turned back to the dragon automaton, crouched down, and continued to focus on screwing the hatch in place.

I waited for a while, wanting to say something else. But nothing came of value. If I walked over to thump him, his automaton would probably turn on me. It was there to be Faso's bodyguard after all. And, as I waited, it glared back with those red infernal eyes.

"This isn't over, Faso," I said.

And I stormed off into Fortress Gerhaun's corridors. But I had to stop at the first corner to break into tears. And this wasn't so much because Faso had hurt me. But more, because this was the first time in a long time I'd felt anything at all.

But it didn't last long...

Soon enough the emptiness sank back into my chest and I could cry no more.

4

When she arrived in Fortress Gerhaun, and for a while after, my mother had found herself unoccupied, much to her frustration. To combat this, she'd set up a tearoom for the troops and inhabitants of the fortress. Secicao – or at least the type you get served in cups – was banned here for good reasons.

It would be hypocritical for Gerhaun to write books about how the stuff was destroying the planet and then allow its consumption within her fortress' very walls. But even so, everyone missed having a warm drink, and the tea reminded them of the secicao they used to drink from their home countries. So my mother acquired as many varieties of tea as possible and started serving it strained out in delicate china cups.

I entered through the double doors of the refurbished canteen, and took a deep breath of the heady aroma, clearing my lungs somewhat. This was one of the few places in Fortress Gerhaun you could escape from the stench of the secicao clouds, and perhaps the only place where it would be replaced by a pleasant smell.

Mamo had set up several round teak tables at the door-side corner of the room. She stood behind the bar, cleaning its surface with a soft cloth. A few troops in olive-coloured uniforms sat around one of the tables. They were playing cards and one of them smoked a cigar, adding an extra homely scent to the room.

Papo, my father, sat at another table reading a magazine.

"Oh, Pontopa, dear," My mother said as she saw me come in. "I haven't seen you at all today. How are you?"

I shrugged. "Same as always. Bored out of my mind."

She lifted the hatch on the bar and walked over to me. "Why don't you take Velos out flying? I hear he's not had a chance to stretch his wings for a while."

"Oh, he goes out by himself without needing me."

Mamo's expression changed to one of alarm. "Whatever's the matter, dear? I remember the days in the Five Hamlets, that you would take any opportunity you could to fly him out in the open. What happened to those?"

I shook my head. "I don't know," I said. I hadn't yet told them about my medication, and fortunately Doctor Forsolano respected patient confidentiality well enough that they'd never find out from him. "Things are just a little different now."

"Whatever it is, you know you can talk, right? We're here to help."

"I know", I said. And I reached out so my mother could give me a hug.

I held it a moment, appreciating the warmth. Then I broke it off. "Come on, let's sit down. We have a little to catch up on… It's been a whole day." There was a certain lack of enthusiasm behind my words, I have to admit.

But still, my mother laughed – probably not so much because of the joke but how dryly I'd delivered it. "It's good that we didn't end up getting stuck back in the Five Hamlets while you were grounded here. You know, our old home was beautiful and all that, but I must say, I'm starting to prefer this place."

I raised an eyebrow... "Really?"

"It's about the people. They're much friendlier here. In the Five Hamlets, the folks had too much money. And well, although we had Mayor Sandorini and a few other good men and women. I just found most a little stuck up. But here, I guess everyone just feels a little more human…"

Part of me felt I should smile at that comment. But the emotion didn't come, and I didn't want to fake it.

"Go on," my mother said. "Take a seat and keep your father company. I'll bring some tea over."

I nodded and then I sauntered over to where my father sat at the table and pulled up a seat.

"Why hello, Pontopa," Papo looked up from his magazine. "Fancy seeing you here."

I shrugged. "It's not like I have much else to do."

Papo smiled. "Plenty of magazines to read here. You know, life has been so much easier since I got hold of the Tow Observer. It's important to keep up with what's going on in your homeland, don't you think?"

The Tow Observer was one the major publications in my home country of Tow. Highly censored by King Cini, of course.

Back home, Papo would read it from cover to cover every day. But after the move, he had to put up with the Fortress Digest, a smaller magazine which told of the goings-on in Fortress Gerhaun. And in all honesty, with so little happening here, it was hard to fill a whole paper with decent news.

But fortunately, for Papo, our good friend and merchant trader, Candalmo Segora, had established a trading route between Tow and the Southlands. He wouldn't smuggle anything that could get him into trouble. But he could bring a copy or two of the Tow Observer and supplies of dried tea leaves.

So long as he returned with tons of harvested secicao, King Cini wouldn't even bat an eyelid about the exported tea. We had a mutual agreement with Candalmo not to send out Greys to disrupt his harvesting procedures. Which meant Candalmo didn't have to spend as much on defences and could travel deeper into The Southlands to gain richer secicao. This kept his prices low, his quality high, and made him one of the most sought-after merchant traders in the whole of Tow.

"So what's the news?" I asked my father.

"Oh, not much. Still pretty uneventful. There are rumours of a new factory up north. Ginlast... Say, wasn't that where Sukina and General Sako are from?"

"Yeah," I said. "What of it?"

"There's an article in here about the king's personal scientist and how he has built the most advanced technology ever seen."

I snorted. "Yeah, we've all heard that one before." Every day, in fact, from our resident inventor genius, Faso Gordoni.

"Ah, but this is different," Papo continued. "The scientist designed a factory that can produce automatons all by itself. An automaton that produces automatons, which might eventually become automatons that can also produce automatons, so the factory is a self-replicating machine that builds itself up over time. Isn't that fascinating? Why hasn't Faso created anything like it?"

I nodded. "I'm sure if Faso had all the resources, he could do this too." And in a way I hoped he didn't see the article, because this might put ideas into his head. But given my father and Faso were such good comrades, no doubt the inventor would soon hear about it.

"Does it say what kind of automatons they're creating?" I asked.

"Oh, the usual: war automatons, Hummingbirds. Perhaps even some automatons of which we've never seen the likes of before. But the details are highly secret."

My heart fluttered in my chest, and I put my hand to it. Increased war automatons would mean increased attacks from the king down here in the south. As soon as Gerhaun awoke, I'd have to make her aware of the matter. And we might see ourselves going into battle sooner than I'd first thought.

"Anything else?" I asked Papo.

Just before Papo replied, my mother placed three teacups down on the table, and I lifted the cup to my nose to relish the aroma and warmth. She sat down on the stool next to Papo.

"There's also news of increased convictions in Tow and other countries of the Northern Continent," Papo said. "The Observer says the king's ruthlessly cracking down on even the pettiest of crimes.

There's even a central feature article with mugshots of a hundred of the most wanted that have been caught and sent to prison."

He turned the paper around to show me the photos, all in sepia monochrome, and everyone looking at the camera with angry eyes. I didn't recognise any of them, but then why would I? I hadn't lived in Tow for a while and I didn't really keep track of what was happening up there. In all honesty, I hadn't kept abreast of things so much while living there either. But I did hear a lot of the news from my father.

"I wonder where he's keeping them."

"Beats me," Papo said. "But if he arrests too many people, he'll reduce the number of blue-collar workers in the cities, and then there'll be a problem."

"It's all speculation, dear," Mamo said. "By the way, Pontopa, how's the tea? Candalmo brought a new strain from the mountains just southwest of Ginlast."

I took a sip. It had a certain smokiness in it I'd never tasted in tea before.

"Pretty good," I said. "Unusual. Although, it has a pretty acidic taste as well."

Papo took a sniff of his tea, then a short sip, and placed the cup back down on the table. "I can't help but miss secicao."

"Papo, we've been through this thousands of times. Secicao is destroying the planet. To drink the stuff would be to support a habit that will see the destruction of this world in thirty years if we're not careful. That's what we're fighting for, remember?"

"But what does it matter here?" Papo said. And every time he'd say the same thing. "The soil is already dead here and the only thing that grows is secicao. It can't spread any more on this continent."

"That's not the point, Papo, and you know it. It's the principle that counts, the morale behind the troops. Plus, we don't want anyone getting addicted to the stuff." And I thought once again of Taka. "Speaking of which..." I turned to Mamo.

"What is it, dear?" she looked up from her teacup.

"We need to watch Taka," I said. "Ratter caught him taking a vial of a drug off an automaton. It looked like some kind of secicao oil, although Winda is still running tests to discover what it is. We suspect Taka has been taking it every day."

"Some kind?" Papo raised an eyebrow.

"It had something else in it. It was strange. It reacted to me touching it through the glass. Anyway, the point is he's addicted."

"Did you take him to see Doctor Forsolano about it?" Mamo asked.

"Of course. Whatever it is, Doctor Forsolano realises it's strong stuff. We need to wean him off it slowly, otherwise it could have unpredictable effects."

Mamo nodded. "I'll look out for him," she said. "Poor child. Losing his mother at such an early age. It can't have been easy for him."

This caused a slight pang of sadness to rise inside me, although ever so faint as the rest of the emotion was tamped down by the drug. "Yes," I said. "It's been tough for him..." Particularly when his father didn't even seem to care.

I opened my mouth to say something else, forgot completely what it was, and so I lowered my head and took another sip of the tea. It wasn't long before we heard a commotion coming from the doorway.

Lieutenant Gereve Talato came in, the woman I had promoted to replace Lieutenant Wiggea as my personal dragonelite bodyguard, after her bravery helping Velos and I survive a superstorm. The short, stout woman looked great in her olive drab uniform, and she had an expression of concern plastered all over her face.

"Dragonseer Wells," she said. "You must come quickly. General Sako has ordered an emergency briefing."

I stood up quickly. "What's it about Lieutenant?"

"We've sighted a sizeable battalion of automatons approaching. Mammoths, war automatons, Rocs, Hummingbirds and these great mechanical flying zeppelins. They're heading right for us."

"Dragonheats! Then we must take action at once. Mamo, Papo, wait here."

But Papo had already stood up. "If there's a battle out there, I want to be fighting too."

"I don't have time for this, Papo. You're needed here, and I don't want you slowing us down."

And Mamo stood up and pushed him back down into his seat by his shoulders. I nodded to thank her, and I rushed out into the corridor.

I was surprised to find Taka approaching as soon as I stepped out of the door, trailed by two rather alarmed looking guards, one of whom was Lieutenant Candiorno – perhaps General Sako's most trusted officer.

"Lieutenant Candiorno, I thought we told you not to let Taka out of the room?"

"It's not as if we can shoot him, Ma'am, and General Sako would kill us if we caused any physical damage to the boy."

"But wasn't the door meant to be locked?"

"He needs toilet breaks..."

I nodded, biting my tongue. "Taka, what is it?"

"Auntie Pontopa," he looked kind of excited. "I felt them coming. There's a battle, isn't there? I want to join in."

"But you're far too young to be going out on the field. And how the dragonheats could you know what our scouts detected several miles away." I guessed it would be another side effect of the drug, but I wanted confirmation.

"I told you, I sensed them. They're powered by secicao, aren't they?"

"Sensed them? Taka, what's this about?"

He said nothing.

I huffed. "We'll talk about this later." I turned to the guards. "Take him back to his room and make sure he doesn't go anywhere."

Candiorno leaned in to grab Taka. But the boy pirouetted out of the way, ducking underneath the officer's grasp like an agile monkey. He scampered off down the corridor.

"We need to make sure he stays here safe and sound," I said with a sigh as I watched him go. "Do what you can to make it so."

And I left him to act on my orders as I picked up pace towards the courtyard.

PART II

GENERAL SAKO

"Blunders happen when leaders don't pay attention."

— GENERAL ORGATI SAKO

5

"Blunders and Dragonheats," General Sako's voice bawled out into the corridor, before I'd even entered the courtyard. "What's the boy doing here? Candiorno, I thought you were meant to be keeping him under guard?"

Candiorno trailed out after me and saluted his superior. "I'm sorry, sir. The boy proved rather elusive."

"You can say that again," the ruddy-faced moustachioed general said. "Taka, go back to your room at once."

Instead, the boy skipped down the side of the rows of seats and he took a place next to a female soldier with long black hair. She looked at him with raised eyebrows, seemingly unsure what to do.

"I'm part of this all," Taka said. "And I'll have to fight them some day. Don't you think it's better that I can at least see what's happening?"

General Sako paused a moment and stared at the boy. Everyone fell silent, as if wondering if Taka's grandfather would lash out. But the boy didn't seem afraid, and it was General Sako who eventually conceded.

"Fine," he said. "It will do you good to see what we're up against and time is of the essence. Dragonseer Wells, sit down please. Faso, I see you've finally managed to get here, late as usual."

Faso and his assistant and girlfriend, Asinal Winda, came out of a door at the opposite end of the courtyard and placed themselves on the back row. We called her just Winda, not out of rudeness, but because she'd told us her surname was also her childhood nickname, and so she preferred it.

Ratter scurried off of Faso's shoulder and onto a tall table behind the two scientists. The automaton opened his mouth to reveal a projection lens. The machine whirred, and the lens extended to twice its length, before Ratter clasped his jaw around it. It lit up to display some images on the screen at the front.

I hurried over to my place on the front row and folded one leg over the other when I sat down next to Lieutenant Talato, my dragonelite bodyguard. She turned to me and smiled, then turned back to the screen.

Talato hadn't been kidding when she'd described what we were up against. Indeed, the battalion was sizeable and comprised of an impressive array of different types of automatons. It would take an enormous flock of dragons to oust them in combat, and we also didn't know what was lurking beneath them in the soil.

"How long ago was this taken?" I asked.

"Hold your horses, Dragonseer Wells," General Sako replied. "I haven't even started the briefing yet, and you're downright asking questions."

I stood up. "We have no time for delay. I need to know the information quickly so I can act as fast as possible."

A cough came from the back and I turned around to see Faso had stood up again. "She's right, you know, General. We must spring into action at once."

"Gordoni boy," General Sako replied, his face red, "what would you know about military tactics?"

"I know danger when I see it. And, of course, I shall accompany your soldiers into battle. I could learn a thing or two from observing these Roc automatons."

Through the masses of heads, I just caught sight of Asinal Winda's expression. No woman wants their boyfriend to be charging out into battle at the first opportunity. She wore glasses, grey hair, and a meek demeanour that didn't quite bring out her looks. She was also now Faso's girlfriend. She was therefore one of the few around here who could settle the inventor's renegade spirits. But this time, she did nothing to stop him.

"Okay, okay," General Sako said. "You've all made your point. I'll keep this brief. The automatons are about a couple of hours from here. If we let them carry on their path, they'll take down Fortress Gerhaun, and you already know this place wasn't built to weather a siege."

That was true. For generations, no one would have expected for anyone to close in on the fortress. It wasn't until we invented gas masks that humans could live down here, although the dragons had always been capable of breathing the thick secicao air.

"Gordoni boy," General Sako said. "I hear your dragon automaton is nearly ready for battle. Is this true?"

"Not yet," Faso said. "We still need to make a few minor modifications."

"And how long will that take?"

"I don't know… Around an hour or two, give or take."

"Then, blunders and dragonheats, why are you here and not over there tinkering? It could help us win the battle."

"Fine," Faso said. "Then I'll just get back to work then. I guess you won't be needing me here."

Winda stood up and trailed Faso towards the back of the courtyard where the nearly-completed dragon automaton lay splayed out on the floor.

"Taka, boy," General Sako said. "Join your father over there and help him complete the automaton."

"No," Taka said. "I'm going into battle with my auntie here."

I turned over my shoulder to scowl at the boy. "Taka, you know full well this is a serious military matter. You will do as your grandfather and our well-respected general says."

"You'll have to catch me first." Taka sprang off his seat and sprinted towards the stables at a surprising speed.

"Taka!" I shouted, and I took off after him.

I didn't know quite where he had gone, and I couldn't detect him in the collective unconscious. My best bet was Velos' stables, and so I sprinted towards there.

But once I reached them, he wasn't there, and Velos lay asleep on the hay on the floor. I stopped to catch my breath, and then a roar came from the sky so loud it both shook my bones and caused Velos to jerk upright. I craned my head to see hundreds of Greys rising into the sky.

Soon enough, I heard the faint calls of a dragonsong in the collective unconscious, Taka's voice behind it. Taka sat astride one dragon, a gas mask pressed against his face and his little legs dangling from the sides.

"Are you coming, Auntie?" he said in the collective unconscious. "We don't need the soldiers. Travast tells me the dragons will be enough."

I wasn't sure what I was more surprised by – seeing him fly away or the fact I could hear his voice in the collective unconscious when I was under the effects of cyagora. But I didn't have time to dwell on it.

"Dragonheats, Taka," I replied. "You can't trust this man. He works for King Cini."

"No, Auntie, there's more to it than that."

"What the dragonheats are you talking about?"

"You'll see… You'll see."

The dragons disappeared behind the thick clouds. I tried to sing a song to call them back, but with the cyagora inside me, I couldn't even sense them. Lieutenant Gereve Talato had chased after me and was already standing beside me. I turned to her.

"Come with me, Lieutenant. We must follow the boy on Velos."

"Affirmative, Ma'am."

We both ran towards the dragon. I scrambled up the ladder on the armour, sweating and unnaturally out of breath whilst Talato ran up Velos' tail towards the back seat.

Just as we were ready to take off, General Sako barrelled into the room.

"I'm sorry about this, General," I shouted down to him – I felt partially responsible, really. "But we still have plenty of Greys. Get as many troops on dragonback as you can muster and follow me out."

"I guess we have no choice," General Sako said, and he looked up into the sky, astonishment evident in his wide eyes.

I pulled back on Velos' steering fin, and he roared in response before flying into the sky. It wasn't a roar of anger, but rather excitement. For Velos hadn't tasted battle for a long, long time.

6

We were soon neck to neck with Taka; me sitting at the front and Lieutenant Talato sitting at the back with one hand on the modified control panel that could now control the whole armour. We didn't have as much control as Faso would when he had Ratter there to scurry around operating things. But Talato knew enough to turn the Gatling guns on and off and augment Velos with secicao.

Taka held onto his Grey's steering fin, a rictus of pleasure on his face and his eyes set dead ahead. Both Taka and Talato wore gas masks, as the air wasn't breathable up here.

Instead, I wore my bit-and-clip device, pretty much the same as what divers used with a peg over the nose so I didn't accidently breathe through it. I found this much more comfortable than a clammy mask.

"Taka," I screamed, as we were too far away from Gerhaun to talk in the collective unconscious, "what in the dragonheats do you think you're doing?"

Once, I'd found it difficult to project my voice with my teeth clenched around a bit. But I'd now perfected this skill to an art.

His high-pitched voice came out muffled behind his mask, but still loud enough to hear. "You said before it was urgent. So I thought we should get into battle as quickly as possible. If you let Grandfather take charge, we'd be there all day."

"But that's foolish. We need time to gather our forces. And you're far too young for battle."

"Oh, we won't need more dragons. Travast has told me what we have is enough."

"See, that's it again. Travast works for King Cini, Taka, and he got you addicted to that drug. What makes you think you can trust him?"

"Auntie, please. I know what I'm doing. Now, I need to concentrate." Taka put his hands to his temples, meaning he had nothing but his thighs to keep his grip on his dragon.

I clenched my teeth even tighter so much I worried that I might break the bit. But we had no choice. I couldn't knock Taka off his perch, and I didn't have the strength of mind right then to overpower his song.

This wasn't Taka's doing, anyway, but the drug that was making him act this way. And I worried that it might have allowed Finesia to take control of his mind.

"Taka, this is stupid," I said again – I had to at least try. "We must return home so we can regroup with a larger force." And lock Taka up in the cells until the battle was over, hopefully teaching him a lesson.

"But we'll get there soon, Auntie. Have you not noticed how fast we're going?"

That was true. I'd flown so many times on Velos that I knew how quickly the secicao usually whizzed by beneath us. Taka had something in his song, it seemed, that could hypnotise the Greys into performing far beyond their apparent capabilities. So, while we'd been flying only several minutes, it would probably take General Sako and his forces at least fifteen to reach our current location.

I'd seen an entire flock knocked out in that time.

I didn't quite have my normal connection to Velos and felt a little clumsy flying him. He wasn't heeding my commands all the time either, sometimes flying off to the left or swooping down as if following a mind of his own. But soon after, he'd latch on to something – presumably Taka's dragonsong – and correct himself back on course.

"We're close," Taka said after a couple of minutes. "You might want to augment."

I shrugged, and I took hold of the golden flask at my hip, surprised by how much I shook as I tipped some of it into my mouth. The world soon lit up in speckled green, the outlines of the secicao branches visible below, despite the speed they whizzed by. Though, admittedly, the effect was more muted than usual.

But it was strong enough for the automatons to soon come into view. There were Rocs, war automatons, Hummingbirds, and mechanical hornets. There wasn't a massive amount of them, admittedly, but enough to pose a challenge.

I took hold of a field glass from my bandolier and looked through the eyepiece.

There was a man in the centre of the mechanical battalion, standing on top of a floating platform. He wore a purple bandana over his lower face and had long brown hair that blew behind him in the wind. The platform itself was a mishmash of cogs and gears and floated on two down-turned rapidly whirring propellers. As we sped forwards, the entire battalion of flying and ground-based automatons rotated together around the platform, as if one.

The man cocked his head, almost as if he could see me looking at him through the telescope. He raised a loudspeaker to where his lips would be behind the bandana and spoke into it. The air became laced with a raspy voice.

"Ah, Taka," the man said. Despite his voice's hoarseness, it still carried upon the air a sense of authority. "I see you brought your auntie with you. Dragonseer Wells, it's a pleasure to meet you. I've heard so much about you and your exploits in the royal palace. I'd like to say King Cini misses you, but he's still a little peeved after you kidnapped his nephew."

I tried to ignore these blatant lies. Taka wasn't Cini's nephew but Sukina's daughter, and I had a hunch this man knew this as a fact.

"Is that Travast Indorm?" I hollered over to Taka.

Taka nodded. "That's him."

"You know, it's been years since I've travelled down here to the Southlands." Travast continued. Despite the ugliness of his voice, he seemed to love it far too much. "Meanwhile, I've heard that you've been taking the boy through some rather pointless training regimes. How is he ever going to become great if he receives inadequate tutelage?"

He paused a while, and the air felt stale in his silence.

"Has he told you what he wants?" I shouted over to Taka. The wind had picked up, meaning I needed to raise my voice quite a bit to project it across the ten or so yards between us.

"Exactly what he just said," Taka said. "But don't worry, he won't hurt us. He just wants to show the king how much I've grown."

"But why?"

"It doesn't matter," Taka said, and I could see the determination in his eyes, which were set dead ahead. "We can take them. The king needs to know how powerful we are."

"But that will just convince the king to send more automatons. If rumours about this factory are true…"

Taka was so consumed in his actions, probably still slightly under the effect of his drug, that he didn't seem to be listening. Instead, he entered into a song that caused both the dragons around me and Velos to let out a massive ear-splitting roar. Then, Velos went out of my control, and instead dived into battle under Taka's command. I tried to pull back on Velos' steering fin to reel him back up, but he didn't respond. And my songs came out too weak to have any power over Taka's unwavering voice.

"Taka, stop this," I shouted. But my request was futile. It was as if someone was in control of his mind. Perhaps Travast through the drug. Or perhaps even Finesia.

The war automatons responded to our charge first. The Gatling guns on their arms twisted on their pivots and let out a spray of gunfire. Under Taka's command, the dragons responded by barrel rolling in mid-air. A few got shot out of the sky.

Before I would have felt their deaths in the collective unconscious. But now, I just felt empty, as if they were meaningless drones plummeting to the earth.

The rest of the dragons, including Velos, soon reached the ground-based automatons, and we showered them with fire. It melted the brass on the automatons, and hundreds of them toppled over and collapsed to the floor.

I glanced over my shoulder to see Lieutenant Talato had lifted her rifle off her back and now was tracking Travast through the sights. A loud bang suddenly filled the air, and a shot came from a small gun protruding out of Travast's platform. Talato's rifle spun out of her hand and tumbled through the brown secicao clouds, becoming lost in the thorny foliage below.

Then, while the Greys rose into the air and circled back around, Travast lowered his hand and a ceasefire started. This gave him time to speak.

"Don't think you can best me with your inferior technology," Travast said over his loudspeaker. "The privilege of impressing the king doesn't belong to the lieutenant, but Dragonseer Wells and Taka Sako. Show him what you're made of, because I'm recording this entire scene."

"What are you up to, Travast?" I shouted over to him.

And for a moment he paused, and it seemed that he couldn't hear me. Below, the wind soughed through secicao branches. The acidic clouds became thicker around me, their acetic touch stinging my skin. I could now faintly smell their eggy aroma through the clip on my nose.

"I've already explained enough," Travast bawled through his loudspeaker. "Now, it's time to prove to King Cini that you are a force to be reckoned with, because despite having lived with Alsie Fioreletta all his life, he doesn't quite believe in dragonseer magic."

The surrounding automatons sputtered back into life and their Gatling guns roared into action. I swore and swerved Velos sharply off to the side. I took him down low as some bullets hit the ground in front of us, sending up plumes of ash and dust, and sticky specks of secicao resin.

Taka followed a little off to the right and behind us. "Do you trust him now?" I hollered back to him. But I don't think he heard.

Over to my left, I noticed a war automaton, spouting bullets out of its guns. And I pushed up on Velos's steering fin to compel him towards our target.

"Power them up, Lieutenant," I shouted back behind me. Promptly, the Gatling guns on Velos's flanks rolled into action. Two trails of gunfire homed in on the war automaton. They hit it dead in the chest, and the machine toppled over and crumpled into a heap on the jungle floor. They hit it dead in the chest, and the machine toppled over and crumpled into a heap on the ground.

But we didn't have a chance, because from straight ahead, a swarm of Hummingbirds spun up from the ground and followed a sharp curve to attack us from the right. One bashed into my chest, as I turned Velos towards them. If I hadn't been strapped into Velos's armour, it would have knocked me straight out of my seat.

"Dragonheats," I screamed. "Hold on."

The Hummingbirds sailed past us at speed and regrouped with a huge Roc automaton ahead. I locked eyes on the beast, remembering how a similar automaton had skewered Velos' tail with its pointed beak at the Battle of East Cadigan Island, almost killing him.

That was when the gunfire cut off once again, so Travast could voice his latest speech. I clenched my teeth, feeling insulted. This wasn't a battle at all, but a test.

"This isn't going well at all," he said through his loudspeaker. "Dragonseer Wells, you are meant to have remarkable abilities. And yet you seem to exhibit the skill of a common peon. And Taka, I expected more from you. You showed much better potential back in the palace. Now, I'm just going to have to eliminate you, unfortunately."

I looked back at Taka. I could see in his eyes how much he felt betrayed.

And then, from behind, the swarm of Hummingbirds made chase. They sped right past us, evidently trying to get ahead. Behind them, the huge Roc lumbered forwards a much slower pace. Dragonheats, the Hummingbirds were trying to force us into its path.

"Can we get above them, Ma'am?" Lieutenant Talato asked. Her voice was barely audible over the now roaring wind.

I shook my head. "They're secicao powered," I replied. "They can get just as high as us. We're dead meat."

"Not if I can help it," Faso's voice came out of the right-hand side of Velos's armour.

"What the –" I said.

"Thank me later," Faso said. "Looks like I completed my invention in the nick of time."

"Faso," I shouted. "How did you – Wait… Can you hear me?"

"Loud and clear. I took the liberty of installing speaker technology on your dragon armour so we can talk while you're flying your dragon and I'm flying mine."

I huffed. I would hardly call an automaton a dragon, no matter how much it might look like one. But then, whatever made Faso happy. He was here to help, and that's what mattered.

Soon enough, the inventor came into view, sitting on a mechanical dragon that looked more majestic than I'd expected. What must have been a good two-hundred Greys accompanied him, with olive suited soldiers riding aback them, carrying rifles and wearing masks.

Unlike Velos' armour, Faso's automaton only had two seats, both brass and equally uncomfortable looking as the one on which I sat. Faso had taken the front, Winda sat behind him holding onto the inventor's waist. Her mousey hair streaked out into the wind as the automaton sped forwards. Her eyelids were scrunched, and although I couldn't see her grin of ecstasy underneath her mask, I knew it was there. Really, she was the last person I'd thought would take so much pleasure from flying.

Faso, on the other hand, wore this strange-looking helmet, as well as his mask, making him look a bit ridiculous. The mask looked like some kind of automaton – a sphere masking the crown of his head, with spinning cogs and gears arrayed around it. The helmet covered his ears, and at his temples two hinges supported a curved visor that spanned across his eyes. There was no way he could see through it, but he still seemed to know exactly where he was heading.

In front of Faso, Ratter had curled himself over a set of handlebars, his paws manipulating a control panel containing a complex web of wires. The dragon automaton also sported a gigantic cannon on its underbelly, much more sophisticated than Velos' because of several hollow rods protruding out of the sides of it, which I presumed to be guns. These shifted around tracking the automatons beneath. The dragon automaton also had four Gatling cannons on its flanks as opposed to Velos' two. At the back, above Winda's head, towered a much larger mounted turret, with a triple-layered bullet belt snaking away from it.

As the dragon automaton moved, it glowed bright green, flaring up in my augmented vision.

"My, my," Travast said over his loudspeaker. "If it isn't the great Faso Gordoni."

"And who the dragonheats might you be?" Faso said.

"I'm Travast Indorm, no doubt you've heard the name."

Faso laughed. "I've heard it somewhere."

"So you've not been keeping track of the king's most talented scientists since you left."

"Ha," Faso said. "There has been no one so great as myself in the king's domain since my leaving."

"You know so little about your field for such a 'great' man," Travast replied. "All the latest automatons in the king's arsenal are my invention, including this newfangled factory you've no doubt heard about."

"And such a thing is balderdash. Technology has not yet reached an advanced enough stage to produce itself."

"Well then," Travast replied. "You'll soon learn how mistaken you are. The magnificent machine I've built in Ginlast contains enough automatons to obliterate your entire precious base."

"We shall soon see about that," Faso said. He had now levelled himself out, so he was hovering right besides Velos. He pulled a lever on the left-hand side of the dragon automaton, causing it to let out a huge ear-piercing screech. It was so high pitched that Talato, Taka, and I had to clutch at our ears. The Hummingbirds ahead of us spun into action and readjusted their target to charge at Faso and his dragon automaton.

Then, the guns protruding from the cannon bucked into life. They let off a volley of shots. At once, a whole load of spheres tumbled out of the tight Hummingbird swarm, reducing it by half. The Gatling guns then did their work, pivoting on their great turrets and letting out a loud whirring sound that resonated off the ground. More and more spheres plummeted from the sky until only several remained. Then, Winda took hold of the two handlebars on the overhead gun and she unleashed a final barrage of bullets that eliminated the Hummingbirds from the sky.

Faso took hold of a stumpy stick that jutted out of the handlebar in front of him. He used this to turn the dragon automaton to face the Roc. On the automaton's underbelly, the cannon started to glow white at the front.

"Keep it steady," Winda shouted out. I could only hear what she was saying because Faso hadn't turned off the speaker system.

"I'm doing it," Faso said.

Meanwhile, energy continued to build in the cannon below, which soon became a brilliant beam of light directed straight at the Roc automaton. The massive automaton opened its beak and let out a high-pitched hiss before it plummeted towards the floor.

"This is exactly what I need," Travast shouted through his loudspeaker. "Mr Gordoni, you've surpassed yourself. I've recorded everything, and the king will be most impressed."

"What's he talking about?" Faso asked.

"This was a test," I replied. "He wanted to record us taking down a small force so he could show our power to the king, but he hasn't explained why."

"But why doesn't he just eliminate us here and now if he has the capability?"

"I don't know," I said. "Why don't you ask him?"

But he didn't have a chance, because two obtuse-angled wings shot out of the side of Travast's platform, and the propellers turned to face towards us. They powered up, and the platform jetted off into the distance, a plume of green gas trailing in its wake.

7

General Sako stood waiting for us in Fortress Gerhaun's courtyard, as we came in on our final approach to land. As soon as we touched down, Taka leapt off Velos and ran straight back to his room, without even a glance at his grandfather. Gerhaun was still asleep, so I couldn't reach out to her to tell her what had happened.

I worried that I could be at risk from Finesia. So, without thinking, I took a flask of water from the seat, opened my jar of cyagora and took a pill down in one excruciatingly painful gulp. I scrunched up my eyes as I endured the pain as the tablet worked its way down my throat. Then, I returned my attention to the situation at hand.

I checked whether General Sako might have noticed me taking the pill. But he was staring up at the dragon automaton that Faso had just flown overhead – low enough that we could hear it screeching through the sky, creating a harsh draught. The Greys weren't far behind him, and they each returned to their stables.

Lieutenant Talato dismounted via the ladder, with an agility that belied her stocky build. I followed her down, and then I went to greet General Sako. His breath stank of secicao, which he habitually smoked through a pipe.

"Blunders and dragonheats, you look terrible, Dragonseer Wells. What happened out there?"

I shook my head. "Turns out that Travast's army was much more powerful than it first looked. He rode on this floating platform device that could shoot a rifle right out of Lieutenant Talato's hand from two-hundred yards."

General Sako's moustache twitched. "What did you expect when flying with such a small force? My grandson had a death wish."

"I don't know what he was thinking. But I'll go talk with him right now."

"Maybe you can get through to him. The number of times I've tried to understand that child. But he just has an agenda of his own."

"He's almost a teenager. And I guess he's just going through that phase."

"Aye," General Sako said. "I've raised one myself and know what you mean. Though Taka, he seems much different than Sukina was."

"Boys can be tougher, I hear," I said.

"You can say that again," he grumbled. General Sako had taken a long time to accept that his long-lost granddaughter had been transformed into a boy, and sometimes I didn't think he completely grasped the concept.

"By the way," he continued, "before you go, I've already scheduled a briefing for tomorrow." He pointed to a talkie at his hip. "Faso installed this remarkable technology that allowed me to hear everything. With what Travast Indorm said about the factory, it sounds like we have to act fast."

I nodded an acknowledgement, then I turned on my heel and made my way towards Taka's room.

As I marched through the musty corridors, whizzing past the ornate tapestries of dragons depicted in battles against automatons, I listened out for signs that Gerhaun might have awoken. But still there was no sign of her. When the dragon queen slept, she remained dead to the world.

I soon arrived at Taka's room. Candiorno stood leaning against the wall by the door, one leg crossed over the other, and a trail of smoke rising from the cigarette sandwiched between his lips. I gave him a curt nod and then rapped on the oaken door.

It took Taka a while to respond.

"What do you want?" he asked.

"Taka," I said. "We need to talk."

He paused a while. When his words came, they sounded almost stifled by tears. "When are you going to be yourself again, Auntie Pontopa? You're meant to be the hero here. Someone I can look up to."

A little warmth rushed to my cheeks, and I looked over at Candiorno, feeling slightly abashed. "That's exactly what I want to talk about, Taka. Why don't you open the door?"

Admittedly, I could have just ordered Lieutenant Candiorno to unlock it, since he had the key. But I didn't want to damage my relationship with Taka even more. So, I waited a moment for the boy to respond. Soon enough, the lock clicked, and the door opened to reveal Taka standing with red-rimmed eyes on the other side.

I reached out and put my hand on Taka's shoulder, but he recoiled so I retracted it.

"Are you okay?" I asked.

The boy lowered his head. This time, I didn't chastise him for not answering me, instead waiting patiently for a response.

"I thought I could trust Travast," Taka said eventually. "He told me that he'd make things better. That through him, I could become great. Why did I listen to him, Auntie? I feel like such an idiot."

I shrugged. "I don't know. Why did you listen to him? I mean, did you know he worked for the king?"

"I've known him for a long time. He brought me gifts when I was younger in the palace. But he told me he'd resigned when he learned I wasn't King Cini's nephew. He said he couldn't work for a king who didn't tell him the truth. He was like a father to me, Auntie... And then he went away... Now he's working for the king again. He said he's now a spy and he said he wanted to help us. But I don't believe him anymore, Auntie. He betrayed me."

I raised an eyebrow. "He was more of a father to you than Francoiso and Charth?"

Taka shook his head. "Francoiso was hardly ever there and Charth was always so strict, just like Alsie. But I felt like I could rely on Travast. He was always there to talk about boy stuff when things didn't quite go right. At least at the beginning."

"And so now he brought you the drug and told you it would make things better. Why do you feel you need to change, Taka?"

"Because after what happened at East Cadigan Island, we can't just sit and pretend nothing is happening. A war is coming, Auntie Pontopa, and Alsie Fioreletta and King Cini are just waiting until it's time to attack. Travast told me Fortress Gerhaun would need someone to lead them. Not just Gerhaun, but also a dragonseer. And... I'm sorry Auntie, you just didn't seem up to the task."

He lowered his head to look at the bed beneath him. I wanted to feel sad, I really did. But, the cyagora I had just taken now had started to come into effect.

I felt foolish for taking it when I'd landed. As always, once I'd felt any kind of emotion rising within me, I got scared of Finesia and swallowed down the pill. Now, one thing was for certain. My attempts to keep Finesia out had also ended up pushing Taka away. I hadn't looked after him like I promised Sukina I would.

I took hold of Taka's dry hand and I turned to look out the window for a moment. Like every other room in Fortress Gerhaun, Taka's room was lit by a single tall and narrow window, surrounded by a dusty brick wall. Outside, the secicao clouds were edging ever closer. Gerhaun's influence was getting ever weaker and Taka was right – if we didn't do something soon, the stuff would close in and swallow us, as if punishing us for our inaction. Without us, secicao would take over the world.

Taka eventually broke the silence. "Auntie... There's something I want to tell you."

I turned back to him. He looked at me through wide almond eyes. "What is it?" I asked.

"I've not been completely honest." He let go of my hand, stood up and pulled the bed skirt away from the floor. Underneath, he lifted one of the floorboards and placed it to the side. He then shifted another two floorboards, and then reached into the gap, from which he produced a brass briefcase. He sat back on the bed, placing the briefcase in his lap.

"Taka, what is that?" I asked.

He unclasped the briefcase and opened it. It contained around thirty vials of the drug we'd caught him with, each of them corked by a rubber bung. Like the original vial, these had black specks floating in them, which pushed out to the edge as if attracted to the boy through some magical force.

"I didn't take any after you took the last one off me. I swear."

I looked at the collection, astonished. "How the dragonheats did Travast get that in here?"

Taka pointed to the window. "By Hummingbird."

"But how did it get past the guards?" I was getting a bit worried about our security.

"I don't know," Taka said.

I let out a sigh. "How often were you taking these, Taka?"

"Six times a day. Travast told me I needed to take them that often for it to give me awesome dragonseer abilities. But when you talked to me about addiction, I saw I needed to stop."

I nodded. That explained why, in our recent encounter with Travast, his ability had weakened after only a brief period of time. I reached out for the briefcase, and Taka removed his hand from it. I closed it shut, and he grimaced as he lost sight of the drug, but he did nothing about it.

I locked the briefcase, then stood up with it. "I'll need to take these to the workshop. Whatever Travast was giving you, we need to understand it. Perhaps we can get to the bottom of what he was actually intending here. There's a lot that doesn't make sense."

I turned towards the door and took hold of the handle. The

cyagora affected my sense of hot and cold, and so I couldn't quite feel the metal there. But my skin tingled a little to the touch.

"Auntie," Taka said before I opened the door.

I turned back to him. "What is it, Taka?"

"I just wanted to ask… What are those pills I've seen you taking, Auntie? You seem to want to hide them from everyone. Are you addicted too?"

I cursed under my breath. All this time… "How long have you known?"

"I don't know, Auntie. For a while, I guess."

I stared out into space. "It's just, I need those pills. They help me keep control of my mind."

"Isn't that what addiction is? When you think you need something, but really you don't? That's why I stopped, Auntie Pontopa. Because all of a sudden, you made me realise I didn't need that stuff. Not really."

"My case is different, Taka… You don't understand."

"Then tell me…"

Dragonheats. If he knew, did anyone else? I walked up to him, put my hands square on his shoulders, and looked him straight in the eye.

"Taka, this is important. Have you told anyone about the pills I take?"

"No. Why would I?"

I sighed and then I placed the briefcase on the floor beside the door and went back to sit next to Taka on the bed.

"Taka, I told you how we must not listen to Finesia, right? Do you know what happened to me before the battle of East Cadigan Island? Just before we took down Colas' ship and escaped the volcano…"

"You became a dragonwoman. I felt it." And all this time, I'd hoped he hadn't realised.

"And I changed," I continued, "because I heard Finesia inside my head. You know that's why we lost Charth? Because he listened too long and too often to Finesia. The drug I take is a medication called cyagora that Doctor Forsolano gave me. And the only reason I take it, though it makes me feel unwell to do so, is to keep Finesia's voice away."

"Can't you just push her away, Auntie? Or ignore her? That's what you and Gerhaun have been training me to do, right? Not to let Finesia in."

That caused a very faint feeling of alarm to rise in my chest. Again, it would have been much stronger, were it not for the cyagora. "Taka, do you still hear Finesia in your head?"

"Sometimes… But I'm trying hard not to listen."

"And did the voice get stronger when you took the drug?"

"She's always been there, Auntie. I don't know what you mean by stronger. The voice has always been kind of strong."

"Taka this is important, now. Have you ever done what Finesia asked you to? Have you ever listened to and obeyed what she wanted you to do?"

"No," Taka looked surprised. "Why would I?"

"It's just… Keep it that way, Taka. She is the enemy and we must never let her in."

"You keep saying that, Auntie, and I won't."

"Good," I said. In all honesty, it was my worst fear that Taka would also lose himself to Finesia. "Keep it that way…"

I picked up the briefcase from off the floor and made towards the door.

"I still think you should come off the drug, Auntie," Taka said from behind.

I looked over my shoulder at him. "I'll bear that in mind."

I closed the door behind me and took a deep breath. I felt a bit of a hypocrite, really. I'd gone there to warn Taka off addiction, while I was probably addicted too.

But then what was I addicted to exactly? Was it the drug? Or was it the peace of mind that it stopped Finesia running rampant inside my head? In a way, Taka was right. But then, I couldn't come off the drug, surely. There was just too much at stake.

MY NEXT ERRAND was to deliver the case of drugs to Faso. I guessed I'd find him in the courtyard, painting over any scratches made to his dragon automaton in the battle against Travast. But hopefully, seeing the contents of the briefcase would finally convince Faso to start spending more time with Taka.

I covered my ears to ward off the grating sound of a mechanical circular saw against metal as I approached. Sparks flew up in every direction from the dragon automaton, and a man in a white shirt, blue dungarees, and a face shield knelt over this, the saw in his hand. I scrunched up my eyes and nose to protect them both from the heat and the sour metallic scent.

"Excuse me," I shouted over the racket.

The man shut off the saw and looked up at me. He lifted his visor, and I saw him to be one of Faso's lab scientists, Casra Opponto. He was a middle-aged man with a thick grey handlebar moustache and a bald pate on his head.

"Dragonseer Wells," the man replied. He tugged on one of the straps of his dungarees. "Fancy seeing you here. We – I thought you'd be resting after the battle."

"We?" I asked.

"Yes. Faso said that you might want quite a bit of sleep."

"And where is Faso now?"

The man looked at the case hanging by my hips. "I…"

"Casra, please. This is important." I didn't mean to be so haughty. But I was pretty tired, admittedly.

"I'm sorry," Casra said. "He went to the stables. He said he had some important modifications to make to Velos' armour."

"Did he now?" I put my hands on my hips. "And do you know what modifications he's making exactly?"

"I suggest you see for yourself. But please, if I could request that you not tell Mr Gordoni I gave you the information? It's already been a long day."

"Very well," I said. "You better be getting back to your oh-so essential work then." I spun on my heels and stormed off towards the stables, fearing the worst.

"Isn't it marvellous, Cipao?" I heard Faso's voice first, just as I reached the open double doors of Velos' stables. "I've surpassed myself this time, more than I ever have before."

Faso stood framed by the doorway standing next to my father, their heads turned to each other. Faso had one hand on his hip, the other on his shoulder, stroking the ferret automaton resting there. My father, while running his fingers through his salt-and-pepper beard, nodded his head in agreement.

In front of them, Velos rested his head on a perch. I looked at him, expecting to see his brilliant yellow eyes and the complex contours of his scales. But Faso had covered his ears and forehead with a monstrous lump of brass, with a convoluted mass of cables making it look like a mechanical brain.

A curved glass panelled plate covered his eyes, tinted black so I couldn't see through it. His snout was covered by what looked like a dog muzzle, a cage split into two parts at the top and bottom of his mouth. It opened out on a hinge, so fortunately he could still open his mouth.

Now, I both wouldn't be able to read his emotions in the collective unconscious because of the cyagora, nor see them on his face because of another of Faso's stupid inventions. Velos had his head lowered to the floor, while Asinal Winda and another of Faso's scientists sat on tiny metal stools tightening some bolts on the helmet.

I carefully placed the briefcase down on the floor by the doorway, before I went right up to Faso and pointed a finger at his chest.

"Faso, what the dragonheats are you doing?" I said. "You said you'd pass it through me before you made any modifications to Velos' armour." I wanted to at least appear angry, but the words came out rather subdued.

Faso turned to me and raised his eyebrows. "Ah, Pontopa. I thought you'd be asleep after the battle. Don't you think it's better to get some rest? I know it's been a long day for you."

"And let you start doing things behind my back again? Faso, you promised... You should be spending some time with your son after everything that happened, don't you think? Doing your fatherly duties."

Faso lowered his head, as if in shame. He and Taka seemed to share a lot of little gestures, despite them being apart from each other for most of their lives. "I planned to do so later. But we need to make this modification now."

"And why," I asked, "didn't you tell me about it? I'm not even sure what this modification is right now. And Papo, why are you here supporting him?"

My father put out his hands in front of him. "It's just a helmet, Pontopa. I don't think it can do any harm."

"A helmet? Every time that stupid inventor has put something on Velos it's always been at a cost." We can't take the armour off without hurting him, and the cannon will prevent him from landing.

"Which is exactly why I designed this to be removable whenever you wish," Faso said. "If you just listen to me a moment, I think you'll agree it's a good idea."

I really didn't have the strength inside me to become too emotional, and I think Faso had latched on to this. But if he thought he would get a free pass because of my current state, he had another thing coming. So, I put my hands on my hips and gave him my hardest glare. From its perch, Ratter responded by opening its mouth and out emanated a drawn-out hiss.

"Go on," I said. "I'm listening."

"Well," Faso tugged on the jacket collar of his pinstriped suit. "What we have here is a remarkable device that augments Velos' abilities even more than the armour. While the armour's primary role is to provide protection and augment Velos, this helmet enhances his hearing and vision. I've designed it to read his brainwaves, and I've provided an interface that Velos already seems adept at using.

"The glass plate at the front of the armour is made from flexible alloyed glass, which adjusts automatically allowing Velos to zoom in on targets he wants to focus on or zoom out to see the world in fisheye vision. It also provides infrared technology, so Velos can see even better in the dark now, much like you do when you augment using secicao, except he can also see heat-signatures through walls. And the sound sensors on his ears work in much the same way, allowing Velos to focus in on sounds and track them for miles, much like a mosquito tracks a stream of carbon dioxide."

Faso took a step back, placed his hands on his hips and looked up at the helmet on Velos, who had now sat up and raised his head high above us.

"See what I mean, Pontopa," Papo said, who was also looking up as if in awe. "Faso really is quite a genius, don't you think?"

I huffed. "Why the dragonheats would Velos need all this?" I asked.

Velos, as if he understood, let out a roar, sending the two scientists in front of him scattering. I sighed with relief, content at least because Velos could still use his voice. Once he'd got my attention, the dragon rose his head to the sky as if looking rather proud. Really, he was looking less like a dragon and more like one of the king's automatons.

"That's where the most useful part of this invention comes in," Faso said. He opened a wooden chest that stood by the far wall and reached inside to produce two human helmets in each of his hands. Faso had worn one of these when he'd arrived on his dragon automaton during the battle against Travast. He selected one and put it on his head.

"This," he said, "allows me to see through my dragon automaton's senses. It's as if I'm watching through its own eyes and hearing through its own ears. Why don't you try it for yourself? This helmet works with Velos."

He held out the second helmet, and he took a step forward clumsily. I clicked my fingers in front of his face silently, and he didn't react. The disadvantage of wearing the helmet is I'd have no way of knowing what was coming at me in the actual world.

I shook my head, then took the helmet from Faso and put it on. He'd added some cushions inside, so it felt snug against my temples and rather warm. I could imagine it getting sweaty after a while. And all I could see was complete darkness.

"It doesn't work," I said. And I tapped the top of the helmet, to try to get a reaction from it. I'd never really been a fan of confined spaces and unlit rooms, and this felt like being in both at the same time.

"Ah," Faso said. "Allow me to…" Something clicked at the side of my helmet. "Yes, that's it."

"I see nothing… Wait?" I squinted against a bright light coming from the strip in front of me. "How did you do that?"

"That, you need not know," Faso said. "I'll make sure everything's configured properly before you take it out in the field. Just wait a minute, it will take a little time to adjust. There… Can you see it?"

The world, all of a sudden, gained a myriad of colours, so stunning that my annoyance at Faso for acting without my permission subsided. In my human sight, the Southlands had always looked flat and drab. But I'd never realised Velos could see it in such brilliance. I could now make out the texture of the brick, the patterns in the clouds, even the creases in Faso's face, all in enhanced detail.

"It's beautiful," I said. "I never knew Velos could see this way." I had seen through his eyes once before, after Colas had shot me in the stomach and I'd transcended the collective unconscious. But I'd been so focused on surviving back then, I hadn't taken the time to appreciate how beautiful it looked.

"Dragons, lizards, and other related families of reptiles have better colour vision than humans, particularly at night," Faso said. "Like all animals their visions have limits, which is why I made further modifications."

I felt another slight tap on the side of the head. Then, my vision gained this fisheye effect, so I could see the whole room around me, with Faso the largest in the centre. It was rather unsettling, really.

"What do you see now?" Faso asked.

"Your big head, all kind of bulbous looking," I said.

"That's working then."

"But what if I need to look at something to protect myself? It's no good if Velos is focusing on flight, when a Hummingbird approaches me from the other side ready to shock me out of the sky."

Velos turned his head to focus on me, and it was strange to see my face with my helmet on up close. I looked like one of those old school divers with those brass tanks over their heads, before they invented oxygen tanks and bits. I saw Faso walk up to me and lift my visor. Then, I was looking back at Faso's smug face, in my own bland vision.

"There's always a simple solution," he said.

I slapped his hand away. "I could have done that myself, you know?"

"I'm sure you could, but I wanted to get to the point quickly. After all, I have modifications to make, and we only have until tomorrow before the briefing."

"You mean you've not told me everything?" I raised an eyebrow.

"No, I saved the best part until last. This switch here –" Faso reached out to flick something else on the helmet. "– turns on the brainwave augmenter."

"The what?"

"I've run many experiments over the last couple of years, on how to read both human and dragon brainwaves. It's hard to decipher what they mean, but I can at least amplify the waves that you and the dragon produce. This will make the connection between you and Velos stronger. Because, rumour has it, that it's been kind of weak lately."

I scowled at Faso. It really was none of his business. "I don't feel any different," I pointed out.

"Ah yes, just one more adjustment." He reached out, and this time I heard something grind at the side of the helmet.

And suddenly, a missing part of me returned to me. I could feel Velos again. I could hear his emotions inside my mind. I felt a sense of rage. Velos was angry. Not because anyone had done something to him. But because my decision to keep taking cyagora had cut him out of my mind for so long. And I knew all this instinctively without having to think about it. After all, I had had a connection with him for an awful long time.

A wave of emotions surged through my heart, and blood rushed to my hands and feet. But the sensation only lasted for a moment, before the drug muted my hormones once again.

I have to do this, Velos, I said in the collective unconscious. He didn't speak my language, but he would at least understand the sentiment behind it. But the dragon turned his head away from me and lowered it to Winda, letting out a deep croon as she stroked his muzzle beneath the cage there.

I took off my helmet and tried to sigh, but nothing came.

"Remarkable, isn't it?" Faso said, but his expression seemed to question why I wasn't impressed.

"I guess."

"I'm sure as you experiment with that amplified connection, you'll find extremely practical uses for it."

"I'll try," I said. And I walked out of the stables. Papo turned to me to watch me go, but I didn't meet his gaze. Before I left, I remembered the briefcase I'd placed by the doorway. I indicated it with an open palm.

"By the way, Faso. You might want to check the contents of the briefcase. Taka gave it to me, and there's more material in here for your testing, once you get around to it."

"What's in it?"

"You'll find out later. I can see you're busy."

"Very well," Faso said, and he turned his attention back to Velos.

My muscles felt weak and my eyes suddenly heavy. So, I decided it was time to leave the room and get some rest. As I walked back through the musty corridors, the only thing I could focus on was the memory of Velos' sense of anger and how I'd not been able to connect to anything lately. I'd spent the last two years devoid of passion, and for what?

Doctor Forsolano might have been right when he'd told me to come off the drugs, but I couldn't imagine being able to cut down to one every few days. I was a bit of an all-or-nothing person, and I'd either take the cyagora or not take it at all.

I opened the door to my bedroom, collapsed on the bed. And just before I slept, I realised that I had to come off the cyagora. Though the thought of it filled me with terror, I absolutely had no other choice.

PART III

WIGGEA

"I was brought into this world to serve and serve is what I did."

— RASTANO WIGGEA

8

I was woken by a heavy banging on the door the next morning. Through my blurry vision, I could see that dawn had broken long ago.

The banging came from the door again.

"What is it?" I asked.

"I'm sorry, Ma'am," Gereve Talato replied. "It was hard to wake you and I don't have the key. The briefing, it's already under way, and General Sako sent me to get you."

"Dragonheats," I said. "Hold on a moment, Lieutenant. I'll be right there."

I took a swig from the glass of water by my bedside table. I'd placed the cyagora right next to it. But I stopped myself from reaching out and taking a tablet, after having resolved to come off the drug the previous night.

I'd slept in my leather jerkin and denim trousers, and so didn't need to change. In the mirror, my hair looked dishevelled and my eyes slightly rheumy from sleeping too long. I gave my hair a quick brush to try to get some tangles out, but I didn't manage to do it for long, before Lieutenant Talato called again.

"Dragonseer Wells, General Sako says it's essential for you to be there."

"Okay, okay, I'm coming."

I put my hairbrush down on the dresser and rushed out the door.

"BLUNDERS AND DRAGONHEATS, DRAGONSEER WELLS," General Sako said as I entered Gerhaun's treasure chamber. "So, you've finally graced us with your presence. What took you so long?"

Gerhaun was now awake and towered high above us. The great golden dragon would stand even taller if her body and tail weren't curled around the huge golden egg that she was guarding. Her massive drooping eyelids made her look just as tired as I felt.

Velos lay at the base of her, wearing both his helmet and his armour, and curled around the other side of the egg. It was amazing how small he was compared to Gerhaun, Velos being three times the size of a man – rather a large dragon compared to the Greys – and Gerhaun Forsi being several times the height of him. Behind Gerhaun lay piles upon piles of coins from different time periods, massive gemstones, and other treasures.

The room had been prepared for a briefing. Ratter had his teeth clasped around the projection device jutting out of its mouth, sitting on a tall table at the back. In front of him, spanned rows upon rows of wooden chairs, with soft cushions. On them sat men and women in olive-coloured uniforms, with yellow chevrons and stars on their shoulders. Meetings in Gerhaun's Treasure Chamber were for officers and higher ranks alone. Larger briefings took place in the courtyard.

General Sako stood at the front by the canvas screen that stretched out across a wooden frame, supported by a pole leading down into a barrel. A beam of light found its way from the projector in Ratter's mouth through the heavy dust, the motes twinkling as they floated through the air. Ratter projected onto the screen an image of a land-scape covered in snow. In the background, a factory puffed out grey smoke from three broad chimneys.

"Well, take a seat, Dragonseer," General Sako said. "You're already late, and we haven't got time to stand around and gawk."

Despite him being a general, I ranked the same as General Sako. Only Gerhaun ranked above me in this place, so I often found it hard to keep quiet when General Sako treated me as an inferior. But I'd hear no end of it if I argued back in front of his troops, and the result wouldn't be pretty.

Faso sat at the back, as he liked to do. He claimed this was to keep an eye on Ratter, but I suspected it was more to stay as far away from General Sako as possible. He and the general rarely saw eye to eye, and it wasn't uncommon for these briefings to turn into a shouting match between them. Faso had an empty space next to him where Winda would usually be. Right now, she wasn't anywhere to be seen.

"Very well, General," I said. "And I apologise sincerely about my lateness. Come on, Lieutenant, let's take a seat." I walked to the front, my head feeling fuzzy as it always had after waking since starting my course of cyagora. Lieutenant Talato followed loyally behind me and sat right next to me.

We took the foremost corner, closest to Gerhaun. Talato on my right, and on my other side sat the well-mannered Admiral Sandao, lithe and short, with a neat grey beard and a bald pate.

I folded one leg over the other and waited for General Sako to speak. He glanced down at his pocket-watch, grumbled something to himself, then turned to the screen.

"This isn't Travast's automaton factory, which we don't yet have any reconnaissance on, but the old shoe factory I used to run in Ginlast, in my home country of Orkc. This was after the dragonheats, and before Sukina and I fled the Northern Continent, so she could become a dragonseer."

The dragonheats were the wars orchestrated by King Cini II, the father of the current king, Cini III. He exterminated most dragons in all continents except the Southlands. This eliminated every coloured dragon except Velos on the Northern Continent, and most coloured dragons in the world at large. Hence, Velos was incredibly valuable to the dragon queens, as only coloured dragons were fertile. The egg that

Gerhaun was protecting was the only egg containing a dragon queen laid in the last fifty years. Which made it incredibly valuable, particularly as Gerhaun was so close to passing on.

"Of course," General Sako continued. "Travast's factory is probably more sophisticated than this. But we suspect he has converted my old factory, situated a good ten kilometres out of town, as it was the largest in the area. It's now winter in Ginlast and the country gets extremely cold this time of year. Everyone will have to pack to stay warm, and we've added an extra blend to the standard draft of military secicao to protect against extreme cold.

"Unfortunately, we don't know exactly what we're going to come up against. But we're expecting Mammoths, war automatons, Rocs and everything else we've seen before. There's no evidence to suggest the king has any unknown technology in his arsenal."

"Well, that's just wonderful," Faso shouted out, standing up at the back. "General Sako, the thin legs of war automatons won't work well on snowy terrain. And if the extreme cold gets to the power cores of standard issue automatons, they won't function at all."

General Sako coughed against the back of his hand and his face turned slightly red. "Did I give you permission to speak out, Gordoni boy?"

"I just thought I'd point out to your men here that your information might be slightly wrong. Dearie me, you've had an afternoon and an evening to get everything together, is this the best you can come up with?"

"Well, as I was about to say, I'm sure the king's inventor might make slight modifications to the automatons based on the conditions. But I doubt he'll build anything new for the occasion."

"I would if I were him," Faso shot back.

"Blunders and dragonheats! Sit down Gordoni boy. You're circumventing everything I say. Both my troops and Sandao's marines have been trained to operate in a broad range of conditions."

"As you say, oh superior one," Faso said, and he gave a lazy salute before sitting down again.

General Sako scowled at Faso, but did nothing else to reprimand him. I guess all of us had realised there was no point chastising the inventor. He'd carry on behaving in his own self-righteous way, regardless.

Instead, General Sako clapped his hands, and the slide changed. The general turned back towards the screen. "Our planned route," he said.

The next image showed a map of the world, with a dotted line leading from the north mouth of the Balmano river, at the northern edge of the Southlands. The line crossed the Costondi sea, which separated the Northern Continent and the Southlands. A long archipelago of islands, known as the Southern Barrier, led around the southernmost perimeter of the Northern Continent. This marked the edge of King Cini III's empire and allowed the king's forces to inspect merchant ships transporting goods between the Northern Continent and other lands. The route would take us towards a huge and sparsely populated island known as East Island, avoiding the Southern Barrier by approaching Ginlast from the northeastern-most point of the world.

"We've already talked to our good trader friend, Candalmo Segora who can supply us icebreakers at Port Szutzko on East Island" General Sako continued. "We can use these to break through the ice and approach the island where King Cini and Travast Indorm will least expect us."

This caused a murmur from the crowd, and I admittedly was surprised too.

"That will take ages, for dragonheats sake," Faso huffed, standing up once again.

"And what do you expect us to do, Faso Gordoni?" General Sako replied. "Have our entire fleet and dragons annihilated at one of the Southern Barrier forts. Ever since East Cadigan Island, King Cini has been fortifying these places right, left and centre."

"Can't we send in a covert force?" I offered.

"Once upon a time, that used to work. But the king has increased security at the Southern Barrier and his arrest policy has become ruthless. Trust me, Admiral Sandao and I have talked at substantial lengths about this, and the planned course seems the best option."

"Besides," Admiral Sandao stood up from his seat. The meekly mannered man stepped up next to General Sako. "I hope you don't mind me butting in like this, General Sako?"

"Not at all, Admiral Sandao, go ahead."

"Thank you. I've talked with Candalmo Segora in person, who I had the honour of being introduced to by Dragonseer Wells' parents. Icebreakers, he tells me, have come a long way in the last five years. Their sharp-edged prows are lined with copper coils, heated using a furnace that cuts through the ice at a decent speed. It might take us a few days to reach Ginlast from East Island, but that's better, admittedly, than being dead at the Southern Barrier."

I nodded, happy that they'd thought this one through. A passive observer might wonder why the dragons couldn't melt the ice. But, although their flames were good for brief spurts in battle, they wouldn't be able to sustain enough energy to melt entire icecaps – even if we took a good thousand of them.

"We don't have a choice," General Sako said, nodding to Admiral Sandao. "This seems the least bad option available to us."

"I agree," Gerhaun offered from high above us. "Sometimes, you need to sacrifice a little time to make the risks less costly. Please carry on, General Sako, I know you and Admiral Sandao have put a lot of time into assessing every possibility."

"Thank you, Gerhaun," General Sako nodded, and then Admiral Sandao returned to his seat. But it wasn't long before General Sako twitched his moustache in irritation and cast his gaze towards the back of the room. "Winda, what the dragonheats are you doing arriving at such a late hour?"

Everyone turned their heads towards Asinal Winda, who had just entered through the double doors at the back of the room. She blushed and gave General Sako a curt bow. "I'm sorry, General," she said. "I had tests to do, under Faso's orders."

"So, what did you discover?" General Sako asked.

"If you don't mind," Winda said, and she walked towards Ratter, took out a small glass ball with the slides inside and replaced it with another one. "I think this might affect everyone here, because we might one day come up against soldiers augmented with this." An image of the vial of the drug came off the screen, with the words, *much more potent than secicao*, written at the top in large letters.

"We tested this on rabbits," Winda continued. "And discovered exactly how addictive this stuff is. Travast added a special compound known as *Tehativin* to it, which is used in some of the most powerful narcotics to keep them coming back for more. That, added to secicao, and what looks like the blood of a dragon queen."

"Exalmpora," I pointed out. "It's what King Cini used on me in the palace."

General Sako looked at me a moment, then blinked heavily. "So, what you're saying, is that Taka might be at Travast's mercy?"

"I think she's saying," Taka said as he entered the room. "That if you don't take me, you can't trust I won't take it again."

"Blunders and dragonheats," General Sako said. "Taka, you're meant to be under lock and key in your room. I thought you were grounded. Lieutenant Candiorno, did you let him get away again?" General Sako looked at the guard sitting at the opposite end of the front row as Lieutenant Talato and me.

"Don't blame him," Taka said and produced a set of keys from his pocket. "I can pickpocket the keys off any of your guards. Anyway, I gave Auntie Pontopa the drugs yesterday, because I want to come off them. But you have to help me."

A momentary silence filled the room, punctuated by sounds of the heavy breathing of a dragon queen.

"*Taka Sako,*" Gerhaun said to the boy in the collective unconscious. "*This is no way to be treating your superiors. Why should you want to go into battle, when you know you'll be safer back home? Blackmail isn't fitting for a leader.*" Gerhaun's voice was kind of faint in my head, so I had to concentrate hard to make out what she was saying.

"*Gerhaun,*" Taka said. "*I told you before, I don't think Dragonseer Wells is strong enough right now to lead the dragons alone. She'll need backup. She'll need my help.*"

My heart skipped in my chest. I had no idea that Gerhaun and Taka had had this conversation.

"*You're far too young to be going into battle, Taka,*" I said. "*Dragonheats, tell him Gerhaun.*"

People around us had now started to murmur, but no one had said anything useful.

"*The boy...*" Gerhaun replied. "*Maybe he's right. Taka may be young. But you can protect him. Isn't that part of your job? And, at the same time, he can protect you.*"

"*But you're talking about taking a boy right onto the battlefield!*" I protested.

"*He'll need to see battle, eventually,*" Gerhaun pointed out. *And his skills have far surpassed any dragonseer known at his age. Even before he started taking Travast's concoction.*" Gerhaun pointed out.

I took a deep breath and tried to close my mind off to the argument that had broken out between General Sako and Faso. It seemed they were both on the same side in thinking Taka shouldn't be allowed to go. But that didn't stop them screaming at each other.

"*Gerhaun,*" I said. "*I'm going to come off the cyagora. I can handle myself.*"

The dragon queen paused for a moment, then asked, "*Is that a decision?*"

"*It is. But I'll need to hand the cyagora to someone reliable, in case Finesia proves stronger than I can handle.*"

"*Then it will be wise to have someone accompanying you also skilled in navigating the collective unconscious, don't you think? A normal person won't be able to tell if Finesia is running rampant inside your mind. You and Taka both need to look out for each other...*"

"*Dragonheats, he's only twelve years old!*" I said.

But Gerhaun had already decided. She boomed out her instructions from high above us, stunning everyone in the room into silence. "You will take the boy into battle, and that's an order."

"Blunders and dragonheats, Gerhaun," General Sako said. "You can't take a child onto a battlefield."

"I behave much older than my age," Taka said.

And now Gerhaun had said it, I realised we didn't have a choice. If we contested her, Taka would just run off and take the dragons out with him, like he'd done before. Then, absolute chaos would ensue.

"Gerhaun's right," I said. "But our reasons are for dragonseers and dragon queens alone and not ones that we can discuss here."

"And what is that meant to mean?" General Sako said. "This is madness, you hear me?"

"Agreed," Faso said. "I forbid you to take my son to Orkc."

"I'm afraid this is Gerhaun's decision," I replied. "Now, if you excuse Talato, Taka and I, I think we've seen enough of the briefing."

I stood up and ordered Lieutenant Talato to accompany me and Taka out of the room.

ONCE I'D LEFT, I took a deep breath outside the treasure chamber, then I turned to Gereve Talato.

"I need you to come with me, Lieutenant. I need to confide something in you." I turned to the guards standing outside with their Pattersoni rifles against their shoulders. "Out of the earshot of anyone here."

"Whatever you need, Ma'am, you can trust me." Lieutenant Talato gave a sharp salute.

"Come then," I said. And I led the lieutenant through the long corridors, past flickering torches set into sconces and towards my room.

I couldn't think of anyone better I could entrust with the job of looking after the cyagora. Taka was only a child. He'd already proven himself susceptible to drugs, and he might start getting the same ideas as me if I gave them to him, given how loudly he'd said Finesia spoke to him. And I don't think any other human in Fortress Gerhaun quite grasped the collective unconscious. We hadn't told them too much about Finesia, admittedly. Taka and I would lose prestige with the troops if they suddenly discovered we heard voices of a mythical empress inside our heads. Most would merely dismiss this as insane.

But for the same reason, I wasn't sure exactly how much to tell Lieutenant Talato. Right now, she was even more loyal than Lieutenant Wiggea had been to me, and that was saying something. But if she didn't consider me in charge of my mental faculties, who knows how she might behave in the heat of the moment.

I stopped her just outside my door, and I put my hand on her shoulder and looked her straight in the eye.

"Lieutenant Talato," I said. "You've been an excellent personal dragonelite to me so far, and I had a good hunch to promote you. But I need to know something."

The older officer furrowed her eyebrows. "Whatever it is, Ma'am, I am yours to command."

"That's good. I need to know if you'll be able to make a judgement call. But first, I want to ask, what do you believe about Finesia?"

She cocked an eyebrow. "What do you mean, Ma'am?"

"I mean, do you believe she's a figure of legend, or do you believe she lives among us today."

If I met the average person on the average street, they'd think I was crazy for suggesting the latter. But here in the Southlands, we didn't even have streets, and Talato didn't seem to me the average person.

"I haven't really thought about it much. I mean, I've never really believed in the tales of old. And if you ask me, the Gods Themselves and all the warriors in the creation myth are just characters in stories. I mean, they never really existed, did they?"

I felt my breath catch in my chest for a moment. It seemed Lieutenant Talato might be a little more difficult to assign the task at hand than I first thought. But then, I didn't really have anyone else I could confide in in this situation, and I had promised Gerhaun I'd come off the drugs.

"Come inside, Talato," I said. I opened the door into my room, letting a little cold light shine into the corridor. I went to sit down on the bed, and I offered Talato the space next to me.

My room was bare bones, as was every room in Fortress Gerhaun. Five years ago, if you asked me if I'd live anywhere smaller than the little cottage that my father had built for me outside his farmhouse, I wouldn't have quite believed it. But King Cini's forces had razed my home in the Five Hamlets to the ground when they'd kidnapped my parents in an attempt to lure me into a trap. Now, I only had this boxy, dusty room with a single bed, a warm woollen blanket, a fireplace, and a small nightstand. The tall narrow window let in a little light, but the Southlands saw no sunlight, due to the thick, brown secicao clouds.

"Talato, I need to ask you something else," I said. "If I told you I'd been hearing the voice of Finesia inside my head, how would you react?"

The lieutenant shrugged. "Well, I'm not sure I'd believe it was really Finesia," she said. "But I know you dragonseers work differently to us, so it isn't really my place to understand."

I smiled broadly. That would do. At least, it seemed, she wouldn't judge me. I reached into the drawer of my nightstand and handed her the jar of cyagora. "I've been taking these recently," I said. "And both Gerhaun and myself agree I need to come off them."

Talato took the jar from me and examined it, turning it around in her stumpy hands. Surprisingly, she didn't comment on how huge the tablets were, or ask questions like how I got them down my throat. Although I didn't doubt, with the questioning look she had on her face, that she was wondering such things.

After a moment, she looked back up to me. "How can I help, Ma'am?"

"As I explained, I've been hearing the voice of Finesia inside my head. I guess the matter isn't really whether or not she exists. But Charth, you didn't see what happened to him because you weren't there. He lost himself to Finesia, Lieutenant. And the reason I've been taking these tablets is I'm at risk of losing myself to her too."

Talato watched me as I spoke with a gentle and concerned gaze, which never seemed to judge. "I understand," she said. "So you want me to keep them from you?"

"Yes," I said. "But that's not all. I need you to promise me you'll be able to make a judgement call if you see me change for the worse. I've become reliant on these, and it's likely I'm going to want them as soon as I start hearing Finesia's voice again. I'm afraid of her, Lieutenant. But if I keep her out with the drugs, I also won't have the ability to sing dragons into battle. And I won't be able to look out for Taka and lead like the dragons and troops expect me to lead."

Lieutenant Talato raised her eyebrows. "But how will I know, Ma'am?"

"Trust me," I said. "You'll know. I can't tell you what I'll become. But you'll see it. You'll see a transformation in me you've never seen happen before."

The lieutenant nodded. A rustling sound came from the window, and we turned to see a plume of secicao gas, ever so faintly pushing through the invisible wall. The lieutenant turned back to me. "I'm not sure how comfortable I feel about this, Ma'am," she said. "I mean, you are my superior, and to circumvent your orders just wouldn't be natural."

"Dragonheats, Lieutenant," I paused for a moment and checked myself. "I'm sorry, I didn't mean to raise my voice. But consider this part of your officer training. Now you're rising up the ranks, you have to learn to decide for yourself. Even if sometimes it means going against the word of a superior, particularly when that superior is relying on you to do so."

The lieutenant lowered her head. "I'm sorry," she said, and she put the jar of cyagora down on the bed between us. I looked at it hungrily, then I realised what I was doing and averted my gaze. "And I'll do my best to keep these from you, unless you absolutely need them."

"Thank you. Can I ask you to also keep them out of my sight? Find a way to store them on your person so I don't know that they're there. And whatever you do, don't tell me where they are."

"At once, Ma'am," she stood up. "Will there be anything else before we set out tomorrow?"

"That's all, thank you," I said. And my gaze followed the jar of cyagora out of the room, before the lieutenant turned to me, nodded and closed the door.

That was that, then. I just hoped that I'd done the right thing, and Talato would actually only give me the drugs if I crossed over the line.

I reached out to Gerhaun in the collective unconscious and told her I had entrusted the cyagora to Lieutenant Talato. Then, I put my head against the pillow for a brief nap.

THE FOLLOWING night I tossed and turned and dreamed vivid dreams, as I drifted in and out of the land of Nod. Thus, as soon as dawn broke, I got up and began to pack my gear. I could already feel the dragons around me, and Velos hadn't yet woken.

"*So, your senses are returning, I see,*" Gerhaun said in the collective unconscious.

"They are," I said. "*But still I worry. What if she takes control?*"

"*Just do as you did before. Close your mind whenever you hear her and pretend she isn't there. Only you can successfully walk the delicate tightrope between your conscious mind and the collective unconscious.*"

I stood up, stepped over to the wardrobe and put on a fresh set of clothes. Being near the top of the pecking order, dragonseers got to choose their own attire, and I didn't want to look like the rest of the troops. So, my regular uniform consisted of a frilly shirt, leather jerkin and black denim trousers that proved comfortable for riding. The uniform also had the advantage of making me look like a civilian whenever I had to go on reconnaissance missions, which admittedly hadn't been for a very long time. I also wore a belt, with a slot for a golden hipflask filled with secicao oil. And I had a bandoleer that ran from one shoulder to the other hip to carry ammunition and other essentials.

I looked at myself in the mirror. I looked much better for wear than I'd done for years. Although I still had those bags under my eyes, the sockets didn't look so sunken. And a little colour had returned to my cheeks.

I took a deep breath. Though the air still tasted eggy, it had a certain freshness to it, augmented by the slight chill of the morning. I walked to the door and reached out for the handle. Just as I touched the cold metal, her voice came.

"*Hello, acolyte.*" She was much louder than I'd expected I'd hear her. "*Did you miss me?*"

A shiver ran down my spine, and then I shook the fear away. I wasn't going to heed Finesia's call.

"*Ah, giving me the silent treatment. Very well, we shall work on that. I've been waiting so long, and destiny has finally determined we shall meet again.*"

No, she wasn't there. I felt an urge to run after Lieutenant Talato and demand the cyagora back off her

"*All you need to do is accept,*" Finesia continued. "*You may have thought you were doing good by blocking me out all this time. But you can't hide forever, Dragonseer Wells. And yes, the Northern Continent is exactly where you should go. Because, I tell you, you are walking right into my plans.*"

The voice went silent in my head, and I waited, expecting more. But I heard only the buzzing of Hummingbird automatons outside and the swooshing of the wind against the secicao branches in the distance.

I decided, for now, that I better put this encounter with Finesia aside. It may have only been part of my imagination after all.

I swallowed hard and then I walked towards Velos' stable. Through my renewed connection to him, I could feel his elation in both his chest and my own. Helmet or no helmet, I hoped I'd never have to sever that bond again.

9

I didn't leave without saying goodbye to my parents. I found them in the teashop. The cyagora hadn't just been numbing my mental faculties, but also the way I reacted to my senses. Thus, when I entered, I inhaled the heady aroma of tea leaves, as if experiencing it for the first time.

Normally, the place would have a few punters. But it was admittedly a little early, and so the room only contained Mamo and Papo, both sat at the table in the far corner. Mamo was tapping her fingers on the table and staring out the window. Papo – of course – was reading the Tow Observer, but the magazine was a few days old as Candalmo Segora was busy getting the icebreakers secured up north, and so hadn't had time to deliver our usual stock.

I hugged Papo first, and he said the same thing he always said when I was going out on a mission – that he wished he could go there in my place, or at least be out there with me. But I think he'd learned by now that his place was here in the fortress. Papo said that Faso would look after me. He'd always seemed to want me to hook up with the arrogant inventor, despite the fact that he and Asinal Winda had a thing going.

Mamo hugged me after that, and she cried on my shoulder for a moment and told me how much she'd miss me. She also took note that a little spirit had returned to me since the previous day. I still hadn't told my parents about the cyagora and I didn't intend to.

My parents closed up the teashop so they could see me off. I walked with them towards the courtyard where Velos and a good fifty other dragons were ready to leave. Because I'd stormed out of the briefing, I'd spent a little time in the morning with Gerhaun, catching up on the rest of the plans. We could only take a limited fleet up north, unfortunately, for three reasons.

First, the larger the fleet, the more likely we'd draw attention to ourselves.

Second, despite having three icebreakers, they'd only be able to cut narrow passages through the ice. So, the fewer ships we had, the faster we'd get to Ginlast.

Third, our fastest route out of the Southlands was through the north leg of the Balmano river. The Phasni which ran from East to West had a much wider riverbed, but would have also increased our estimated journey time from three to five days, as we'd then have to worm our way around the perimeter of the Southlands. Lieutenant Talato and Taka had already mounted Velos when we got to the courtyard. Taka waved down to my parents from on top of the dragon. He had his gas mask pulled up over his hair and a broad grin on his face. In front of him, Velos kept his head craned high, looking rather proud in his helmet.

"You sure you want to take the boy with you?" Mamo said. "It seems kind of dangerous. I heard the troops talking about it at the tea shop last night, and it seems no one agrees with your and Gerhaun's decision."

"Mamo, there's many layers to this, which we can't explain. But Gerhaun told me all the dragons believe Taka is safest with us." I didn't want to tell them he was also there to keep me in check, to calm me if Finesia started running rampant inside my mind. My parents had enough to worry about.

Faso walked over to join us. He looked up at Velos with an assessing glance, as if to check everything was in working order.

"Faso, you will look after them, won't you?" Papo asked.

"With our new technology, I'm sure we won't run into any problems at all," Faso said. "We'll go straight in there, my dragon automaton will unleash unexpected chaos on the factory, and we'll be right back out in a jiffy. There's absolutely nothing to be concerned about."

I shook my head. Surely, the inventor didn't believe it would be that easy. Mind, this *was* Faso we were talking about.

I gave my parents one last hug, and then I climbed the armour via the ladder on the side. I sat down in my place just behind Velos' steering fin.

"Is everything in working order?" I called back to Lieutenant Talato.

"Affirmative, Ma'am," she replied. "By the way, Faso told me to tell you he put the helmet in the crate underneath the seat should you need it."

"Hopefully, I won't have to use it for quite a while," I said. I really wasn't a fan of automatons. I didn't like it when Faso had wrapped one around Velos in the form of the armour, and I certainly didn't like the idea of wearing an automaton on my head. "Are you ready, Taka? You can sing the dragons into position. We'll need fifty on the dragon carrier. Take no more, because they won't have anywhere else to go."

"Affirmative, Ma'am," Taka said. I smiled. It sounded quite cute to have him imitating the way the other troops spoke.

"And how about you, Velos," I said more quietly. "Are you ready?"

Velos crooned underneath my feet, sending a soft trill through the armour.

"Then we can get going. Gas masks on." I secured my clip onto my nose, put the breathing-bit between my teeth, then I pulled back on Velos' steering fin to launch him into the air. A green glow pulsed in the armour underneath as the tanks on either side pumped secicao into it.

This gave Velos an increased launch speed that pushed me back in the seat and sent a tremendous gust of wind over the troops, Faso, and my parents, causing them to stumble backwards in surprise. Not long after, we hit the clouds, which stung at my skin like acid rain.

"Woo hoo!" Taka screamed.

"It works, Ma'am," Talato shouted from the back. "Now I know how to use the armour better, which should help if we ever get into a fix."

"Lieutenant Gereve Talato," a voice came from the speaker at Velos' side. I looked down to see Faso speaking into a talkie below. "That was a waste of precious secicao resources. You're to cut off the supply immediately. Do you hear?"

I laughed as I turned around to see Talato silently mouthing Faso's words out of her own mouth mockingly as the inventor spoke. "Ignore him, Lieutenant," I said. "It's good to know that it works."

As the green glow subsided a little in the armour, Velos let out a loud roar into the sky. Soon enough, Taka sang a dragon song through his mask and a good four-dozen dragons also joined us in a three-layered V formation. The dragon automaton soon caught up with us, with Faso and Winda on board. Together, we sped towards the small flotilla that had already sailed ahead.

WE MET up with the Saye Explorer at the northernmost mouth of the Balmano River, before it opened up into the Costondi sea. The ageing frigate had recently had an extra command room installed at the top of it, that wrapped around the two massive funnels. The ship had with it a few thin cruisers, a heavily armed destroyer, and one of Gerhaun's smaller dragon carriers with room enough for carrying fifty dragons. We had forty-eight greys, which together with Velos and the dragon automaton filled the capacity.

When I thought about it, I couldn't believe how long it had been since we'd last taken the dragons on a sea journey. It had been over two years since our fleet had almost got destroyed by a superstorm on the way to East Cadigan Island, and then was virtually destroyed by King Cini's forces during our retreat. We'd lost many dragons that day, and only the Saye Explorer had survived the onslaught. This time, we were taking a much smaller number of boats and dragons with us, and I hoped things would go a lot more smoothly.

A thick fog had settled at the Balmano northern estuary, bringing an unnatural chill to the Costondi sea. Also, the visibility was terrible. Although we could see the outline of the ships, we couldn't quite see from our height who exactly was on deck.

We flew at the front of the dragon flock with Faso and Winda next to us on the dragon automaton. Yet, though they were only ten or so yards away, we found it hard to see even them.

The conditions are getting worse on these seas," Faso said over the speaker system. "I still don't agree with a lot of what Gerhaun wrote in Dragons and Ecology. But one thing's for sure, cold weather like this is becoming more and more commonplace."

I shook my head. I didn't need to be reminded about it. Once, my father had owned quite a prosperous vineyard in our hometown of the Five Hamlets in Tow. But as I grew older, it became too cold to grow grapes there, which is why I started flying Velos on runs to the Southlands to harvest secicao for the king. But then Sukina Sako came to visit and informed me of how my efforts were actually harming the planet. On that day, everything changed.

I pushed down on Velos' steering fin and took him closer towards the Saye Explorer. Taka could command the dragons into the hatches on the dragon carrier, but I thought we'd be better placed on the flagship.

"And where are we supposed to land?" Faso complained over the speaker system. "There's only room enough for one dragon on the Explorer's quarterdeck."

"Can't you make yourself useful on the dragon carrier?"

"Dragonheats, Pontopa. I need to make sure I also have a say in the decisions. Winda and I are the only ones on board who understand technology."

I sighed. Faso could have tried being nice for once when asking for a favour. "I'll send Velos over to the dragon carrier once we land." And that caused a deep growl from Velos. Perhaps because of all the time he spent around Gerhaun, he seemed to be starting to understand our language more and more. And he hated being stuck in confined quarters.

"Good," Faso said. "I'll wait for you to complete the operation."

I could now see General Sako and Admiral Sandao sitting at the trestle table waving us in. I landed Velos at our place on the quarter-deck, and I removed my harness, as Faso wheeled the dragon automaton overhead.

"Hurry up," Faso said over the speaker system. "We shouldn't be wasting fuel."

I turned around and gave Lieutenant Talato and Taka a sly grin. I scurried down the armour's ladder, and Lieutenant Talato came behind me, while Taka slid down Velos' tail, landing with a thud against the iron deck.

I sang a dragonsong to instruct Velos to fly over to the dragon carrier. He turned to look at me, and although I couldn't see the expression through his helmet, I felt his reluctance in my heart. So, I sent out a song with harsher notes to remind him to follow my instructions. Velos whacked his tail against the floor, causing the deck to rock and the teacups on the table to spill some liquid.

"Blunders and dragonheats!" General Sako stood up and turned around to see Velos lifting up into the air. I didn't even bother to watch the dragon automaton land and instead went over to join the general and the admiral for tea.

DURING THE EARLY hours of the next morning, I woke up in a cold sweat. We'd been sailing for around half a day now, and I checked the luminous dial on my bedside clock on the metal compartment besides my bunk. Unlike my bed in Fortress Gerhaun, the cabin bunks on the Saye Explorer were as solid as planks of wood. Though, admittedly, the room was well heated.

"Wiggea," I said out loud. Had I dreamed him? No, he was close. I could sense him. Flying somewhere nearby.

"What is it, my acolyte?" Finesia's voice came again in my head. *"Now, you've stopped blocking me out, I see no reasons why my minions shouldn't be allowed to accompany you."*

Wiggea, my former dragonelite guard and the last man I'd kissed had fallen into the volcano in East Cadigan Island. Admittedly, I'd heard his voice in my mind, when the black dragons had arisen from the erupting lava. But that had to have been a figment of my imagination, surely.

Beneath me, I could feel the gentle rocking of the ship and other than the clock dials, I could only see darkness straight ahead.

"Why do you insist on trying to escape your fate?" Finesia continued. *"Do you not understand that you're the chosen one? Chosen by prophecy not to save the world but to destroy it. And despite your efforts, you unwittingly sail closer and closer to your ultimate destiny. You might as well submit, because there's no way you can stop the inevitable."*

As my sleepiness subsided a little, I realised that I didn't have to listen to this. I could bang on the wall, wake up Gereve Talato sleeping in the cabin next to me, order her to give me a tablet of the cyagora. But no, I could keep Finesia out, and besides I'd instructed Talato only to give me the cyagora when absolutely necessary.

I relaxed my mind and focused on ignoring Finesia's nattering inside my head. After a while, I drifted back off to sleep.

THE NEXT MORNING, I woke up, realising I'd overslept my alarm. I cursed, since I had wanted to be getting up at a decent hour and setting an example to the rest of the men. I emerged from my cabin into the foggy murk. Lieutenant Talato was standing outside the metal door, her hands against the railing, looking out to sea.

"Good morning, Ma'am," she said, turning to me. "I hope you don't mind, but I did keep checking on you. It seemed like you were having quite a fitful sleep."

I nodded. "I didn't sleep very well."

Talato turned back towards the sea. "We're almost at Port

Szutzko," she said. "We sent some men ahead on dragonback to scout the city, and Mr Segora is approaching to meet us now."

"Glad to hear it," I said. It would be good to see old Candalmo again.

The lieutenant pointed out at a colossal form ghosting through the murk. A trawler, three-times the size of the Saye Explorer. "Say, is that him now?"

Indeed, it was Candalmo Segora's ship. I'd sailed on it many times when I was a child, so I knew it well. Its funnels were lower than usual though, which probably meant it was already stacked full of cargo – a good thing.

From the distance, Candalmo sounded his ship's foghorn. We responded in kind, and then Velos let out an immense roar from the dragon carrier. Every single Grey on board his ship joined in Velos' chorus, sending out a sound so loud that it whipped up waves around the ships.

Not wanting to alarm Candalmo or any of his crew, I sang a dragonsong to calm the dragons. Once things were a little quieter, I turned to Talato.

"Come on, let's get to the quarterdeck," I said.

I bumped into Faso coming out of his cabin on the way, Winda followed sheepishly behind him, her hair mussed and her glasses askew.

"Faso, I need you to get the dragon automaton out of the way, so I can call Velos over and greet Candalmo on board."

"Wonderful," Faso said. "It looks like Segora's ship is big enough for two dragons... Much better than this piece of junk."

I put my hands on my hips. "Since when are you Candalmo's friend?"

Faso scowled at me. "I'll have you know that I often met the good man sipping tea in your parents' teashop and he expressed significant interest in the progress of the dragon automaton."

I furrowed my eyebrows. "Faso, we're on an important mission here, and I remind you we're going over to secure the icebreakers, not to boast about your latest technologies."

"Affirmative, Ma'am," Faso gave an annoying half salute. "But I'm coming anyway."

"Suit yourself, just don't get in the way," I snapped.

And the inventor nodded to Winda and skipped ahead. Winda shook her head and looked down at the floor.

How she put up with the man, I had no idea.

CANDALMO SEGORA WAS A TALL, lithe man with a full beard and neat moustache, who I'd always thought looked more a city type than a sailor. He waved us in on deck as we approached.

Velos landed just behind him, and the dragon automaton touched down next to us. I scurried down the ladder quickly, and Talato followed in my wake. We'd left Taka behind on the Saye Explorer, since we realised we might need to ferry Candalmo across for negotiations. Candalmo didn't believe in chairs and was already sitting on the floor by a low table that only came up to ankle height and had a cafetière of secicao laid out on it.

I looked down at the floor. The temperature had really dropped since we set sail, exacerbated by the fog that had followed us through the journey.

"Don't worry, I put some coals underneath to heat it," Candalmo said.

I nodded, placed myself down on the floor, and beckoned Lieutenant Talato to do the same. Faso and Winda soon joined us.

"Secicao?" Candalmo offered, and he lifted the cafetière over the delicate and tiny china cup in front of me.

I shook my head. "No, thanks. I'm abstaining."

Candalmo scratched at his beard. "Nothing changed there then. Really, I don't know how you can live without it. How about you, Mr Gordoni, and Ms Winda, is it? I believe this is the first time we've met."

Winda nodded, her hands folded over her crossed legs. At the same time, Faso grinned.

"How could I refuse?" he said. "I've certainly missed this stuff. I've not had a cup for months. And Winda will have some too, won't you, darling?"

"Yes, please," she said, but I couldn't miss the expression of annoyance that momentarily washed over her face.

Candalmo poured out the secicao and then called down to one of his crew to bring up a pot of tea. I waited for the navy-suited sailor to emerge carrying a small dainty teapot, blue wispy dragons painted on the sides. From it, Candalmo poured into my cup a stream of light green, delicate tea. I raised the cup to my mouth, inhaling the fumes before taking a sip.

"Thank you, Candalmo," I said. "Not just for the tea but coming out here to meet us at such short notice. I don't know what we would have done if you hadn't offered to secure some icebreakers. We're really not equipped for these kinds of operations."

"Oh, think nothing of it," Candalmo replied. "You know I'm always willing to help. Although I don't know how much longer I'll be able to risk my neck and crew, before King Cini cottons on that I'm not always on his side."

"You do what you do for the good of the people, right?"

Candalmo laughed. "I'm a merchant trader, meaning there's always a little cash at the end of it. Money buys me happiness, or at least a home in the Towese countryside where I can hide away from the wrongdoings of our monarch."

I smiled and took another sip from my teacup. Faso finished his cup and reached out for the cafetière and poured Winda and himself another cup without even asking. Instinctively, I wanted to slap his hand out of the way and tell him he shouldn't be drinking it. But then, how could I admonish Faso for taking advantage of this rare opportunity when General Sako smoked secicao every day?

"I've sent out a couple of tugboats to escort the icebreakers," Candalmo said. "They should be bringing them back from Port Szutzko as we speak. But shortly after, I have a run to South Saye to acquire supplies for the king's pharmacy. Hopefully, I'll also be able to get you some good tea."

That reminded me. South Saye was where Doctor Forsolano got the cyagora from. I considered asking him for some. Perhaps I couldn't use it, but Doctor Forsolano might need to prescribe it to other patients.

"Surely, you don't want to become reliant," Finesia said in my mind. *"You need to keep the drug away, remember? You don't want to become addicted."*

And even though I didn't want to listen to Finesia, on this occasion I felt she was right.

"Captain Segora…" The same crew member who had brought us the tea emerged at the top of the ladder to the quarterdeck, looking rather alarmed.

"Yes?" Candalmo turned to look at him.

"The tugboats have just returned from their mission," he said.

Candalmo stood up quickly and walked towards him. "What? They weren't meant to come back without the icebreakers."

"It's not their fault, Captain," the man said. "King Cini has sent his forces in and Port Szutzko is under lockdown. They're lucky they didn't dock as no boats are now allowed to leave the harbour."

"Dragonheats," I said and stood up. "King Cini knows we're there. Candalmo, I need to get back to the ship. Perhaps you'd like to accompany us?"

Candalmo nodded and headed towards Velos.

"Oh, don't worry," Finesia said in my mind. *"I'm sure I'll find a way to help you. The king's soldiers cannot get in your way."*

But I wasn't listening. Instead, I was rushing towards Velos, helping Candalmo up the ladder, mounting, checking everyone had strapped themselves in, and then pulling down on Velos's steering fin to lift him up into the sky.

"It never goes smoothly," General Sako said. "There are always complications."

We were now on the upper bridge of the Saye Explorer, and

General Sako sat at the head of a long oval meeting table. This was in the centre of the long room built around the two ship's funnels. I sat on the side of the table facing the windows that looked east. The fog had lifted a little, and I could vaguely make out the cliffs of East Island in the distance.

"This is the way of the military," Admiral Sandao replied. "Nothing is ever certain."

"I know, I know," General Sako said. "Lieutenant Candiorno, have you sent out the Hummingbirds?"

"Yes, sir," the ruddy-faced lieutenant said sitting opposite me. "No word as of yet."

"But I've already scouted the perimeter with my dragon automaton, General," Faso said. "There's no sign of boats anywhere outside the port."

"I just want to be certain," General Sako replied. "The question is, why would they blockade Port Szutzko?"

"Because King Cini must know we're here?" I said. "I can't think of any other possible reason."

A private came over with a tray full of glasses of water and sweetened wheat biscuits, and I gladly accepted one of each.

"Unless Alsie Fioreletta has also stationed her dragons somewhere nearby," Faso pointed out, standing up and leaning against the desk. "I wouldn't be surprised if there's another force at play in this. They've probably been watching us closely and now they've decided to take advantage of our movement."

"And how would they do that?" General Sako said.

"I don't know," Faso replied. "Until recently, I hadn't believed Alsie could turn into a dragon. But we've all seen these things happening with our own eyes."

"Blunders and dragonheats," General Sako bawled. "Sit down, Gordoni boy. You aren't the most important person in the room, and we all need to rationally work out what to do next."

"Well, isn't that obvious?" I said. "We can't go in by boat with the port under lockdown, so we need to take the dragons out and scout out the surrounding terrain."

"But that will increase our visibility," Admiral Sandao replied.

"Actually," Faso said. "I've installed radar blocking technology on the dragon automaton, although not on Velos, as I fear it will stop Pontopa's ability to communicate with her dragon."

"But that won't stop the flock being seen by human eyes," General Sako said.

"Which is why we should send out my dragon automaton," Faso said. "And I'll go on board too, although I'll want some extra fire-power if anything goes wrong."

"I'll also go," I offered, and I scuffed my feet against the carpeted floor. "With Velos and my dragonelite," I nodded to Talato, "and Taka."

"Blunders and dragonheats, why would you take the boy out there? It was bad enough bringing him out on this mission, but now you want to send him into the most dangerous places."

But Finesia was definitely in my head, and if anything went wrong, Taka could be the only hope of bringing me back to reality. Particularly, as General Sako suggested, if Alsie Fioreletta – the apparent right hand of Finesia – also turned out to be there.

"General Sako," I said. "Taka is a dragonseer and so he's my responsibility. It is my decision where I take him, not yours."

General Sako twitched his moustache. "I guess I can't stop you. But make sure nothing happens to the boy, otherwise you'll have to deal with me."

"I will," I said. Because it wasn't really Taka we needed to worry about, but me.

I STOOD beneath Velos on the quarterdeck. Lieutenant Talato had mounted and Faso and Winda were circling in the sky on the dragon automaton above us. I didn't see any point wasting time trying to find Taka – telepathy was definitely the fastest way.

"Taka," I called out in the collective unconscious. *"It's time for us to go out for a while."* I could talk to him this way since I was a drag-

onwoman, which also meant I was a source of the collective unconscious. Clearly, the cyagora had worn off a little.

"Auntie Pontopa," Taka replied. *"Didn't you say we shouldn't use any of
Finesia's gifts?"*

*"I think talking like this is okay. As long as we don't turn into dragons, or
anything."* I answered Taka.

"I'm not sure I know how to turn into a dragon." Admittedly, that was
reassuring to hear. It meant that Finesia might not have carried Taka
as far over to her side as she had me.

"Good," I said. *"How quickly can you be on the quarterdeck? We're going
out to see East Island."*

"OH GOODIE," Taka said. *"Give me a minute."*

And he got there much quicker than that, skipping on his two little
legs, clearly excited he was going on a fresh adventure. He scrambled
up onto Velos' middle seat and I followed him up. Then, I pulled back
on Velos' steering fin, singing at the same time to make sure Velos
didn't roar and alert anyone to our presence.

We lifted into the sky, and the icy wind buffeted against my face as
Velos sped towards Port Szutzko, Faso's dragon automaton trailing in
our wake.

10

The Szutzko Mires, the name for the land surrounding Port Szutzko, were boggy and damp. Before the fog, the skies must have unleashed quite a bit of rain, for it was difficult to find a dry patch suitable for both Velos and the dragon automaton. Certainly, I don't think Velos would have appreciated landing in swampy water.

"Ah, an old friend is here to greet you," Finesia said in my mind. And I would have ignored her if, at the same moment, a black form hadn't shot through the murk straight ahead of us. At first, I thought it must have been a cormorant or a goose. But the thing turned around, and streaked across the sky above the horizon, and then I saw it to be a dragon.

Faso's dragon automaton let out a kind of silent hiss. I sang a dragonsong to stop Velos also opening his mouth and roaring. The last thing we needed was the guards in the town on red alert because they knew there were dragons nearby. Ratter scurried up on Faso's shoulder, its back arched and its red glaring eyes tracking the black dragon.

The dragon arced down towards the ground and landed on a grassy tuft around fifty yards away. As soon as it touched down, a plume of black dust rose around it, that shortly settled to reveal a full head of dark hair, and a hard-edged, handsome face. He wore a redguard uniform – the same attire as the king's loyal soldiers. There he stood, his hands behind his back, stretching them as he looked up at us in the sky.

"Impossible," Lieutenant Talato said.

"What's he doing here?" Taka said from behind me. "I thought he was dead."

And I swallowed hard.

"*Why, hello darling,*" Wiggea said in the collective unconscious. "*I missed you.*"

"What the dragonheats does he want?" Faso said over the speaker system. "Winda, be careful."

But, in all honesty, I didn't want to know. "*Wiggea, you were thrown into the lava lake by Colas. I saw you burn.*"

"*And you sensed me rise again, my darling. Finesia has told me she's been waiting patiently for you to return to us. And now, here you are.*"

"*No, Wiggea,*" I said. "*This isn't you. Finesia has taken control of your mind, and you're a different creature now. We lost you to the void.*"

"*Why don't we talk in person on the ground? I'm sure your comrades will be quite eager to hear what I have to say. After all, it's been so long.*"

"*And how do we know you're safe? You might have others waiting to ambush us as soon as we touch down.*"

"*Because, if I wanted to attack you, I would have done so already. So, stop being so ridiculous and find somewhere to land.*"

I sighed, and then again sang to Velos to stifle his sudden urge to roar out into the sky. I didn't have a clue what Wiggea was doing here yet, or who he had brought with him, but we certainly didn't want to add King Cini's air fleet to the mix.

"What are we going to do, Pontopa?" Faso's voice came over the loudspeaker. "Can we trust him?"

"That outcrop there." I pointed over to a larger island that jutted out of the bog, covered in grass and mud, but looking stable otherwise. "We'll land and find out what he wants."

"Can't you talk to him using your telepathy thing?" Faso said. "I'd rather know what we're going in for first."

"I've already talked to him," I replied. "And this is what I've decided to do."

I pushed down on Velos' steering fin and took him towards the land. The dragon automaton fell behind a little, so I checked over my shoulder to ensure that Faso was following suit. Velos' claws soon scuffed against the ground, and he groaned as he landed a little harder than usual.

Faso brought his automaton in much more smoothly, and we looked over to see Wiggea swimming through the bog towards us, rather fast for a human.

But then, he wasn't human anymore...

"Isn't it a bit cold in there?" I asked. "Why don't you fly?"

"There's absolutely no need. And I've not had a swim for a while. These kinds of things make me appreciate life."

"You're not alive," I pointed out. "And if you continue to serve Finesia, you'll destroy everything."

"That's where you're wrong. Finesia isn't here to destroy, but to create. To remodel this world into something better. Isn't that what King Cini and scientists like Faso Gordoni have been trying to do all along?"

I dismounted via the ladder on the armour and instructed Taka and Lieutenant Talato to stay where they were. Talato read my meaning perfectly and took her rifle off her back and tracked Wiggea through the sights as he approached us through the water. If he was just like Alsie and Charth, then in human form he would be vulnerable. In dragon form, he'd be almost impervious, save for the weak point at his throat.

Faso had already sent Ratter down to accompany me. The thing climbed up my back and perched on my shoulder as I walked towards the bank. Even though it sent a shudder down my spine, at the same time, I appreciated it being there. But I wasn't sure the automaton would do much good against a dragonman.

Wiggea reached the shoreline of the island and pulled himself out using a thick clump of grass. He shook the water off like a dog, and then approached and looked right into my eyes, still absolutely dripping wet.

Wiggea – once my loyal guard dog, and the man I'd kissed while we stared out at the fiery rocks dancing out of the lava lake inside the Pinnatu Crater. Now, he should be dead. And I felt repulsed to see him looking at me with such admiration.

"What do you want, Wiggea?" I asked.

"There was once a time that you'd called me Lieutenant. And after, as I recall, we managed to reach first-name terms."

"You've long since left Gerhaun's military ranks and joined our enemy."

"But is Finesia your enemy, really? She speaks to both of us and she wants what's best for you." He ran a finger against my jaw. "And yet, you've shut her out for so long."

I knocked his hand away. "Is that how you found me?"

"Don't be so thick. You may have been invisible, but the boy wasn't. He will also one day make a loyal subject. But you are by far Finesia's favourite, much to Alsie Fioreletta's chagrin."

"He speaks the truth," Finesia said in my mind. No matter how hard I tried to keep her away, she would always come back with these little remarks. *"In the ultimate battle between you and Alsie, it is you who shall win. You know that, don't you, my dear?"* I pushed her away and turned back to the matter at hand.

"Wiggea," I said. "You didn't answer my question. Why are you here?"

"Because I love you, Pontopa."

He stepped forward and took hold of my chin. But I shoved him back by the shoulders. It wasn't like Wiggea to be so forward. This wasn't like the man I'd had feelings for.

"Don't give me that crap," I said. As I took a step back and glared daggers at him. I worried that I might end up backing into the bog. But I didn't want to turn around and check what was behind me, in case he tried anything.

"It pains my heart for you to treat me this way," he said.

"You don't have a heart," I said. "Not anymore."

Wiggea fell silent for a moment and looked me straight in the eyes. He seemed sad about what I said, but I knew it was all an act.

"Haven't you thought why I might be in the king's uniform, Pontopa?" he asked after a moment.

I raised an eyebrow. "Because you want to infiltrate his ranks?"

Wiggea nodded. "You know full well that the port is under lock-down. And my sources tell me you need to get those icebreakers to get over to Ginlast. You could waste your own lives trying to get what you need, but that would be contrary to Finesia's plans. And she doesn't trust you to use your gifts to remove the guards and automatons there, even though it's clearly the safest option for everyone involved."

"It's never safe to take anything from Finesia," I replied.

"Oh, and one day you'll learn," Finesia said. *"You can't keep pushing me away forever."*

I swallowed hard and tried to still my heavily beating heart. Wiggea watched me silently, his eyes constantly fixed on me. But I kept my distance from him, and Ratter stayed on his perch atop my shoulder, continually scanning the dragonman, in case he made any sudden moves.

"Why bother with the uniform?" I asked. "Do you think they won't recognise you once you get close?"

"It won't matter once they're dead," Wiggea said. And a crow cawed overhead.

Would they really deserve to die? We'd come over to perform a covert operation, not a complete massacre. Not everyone in the king's military was bad. I'd known many honourable men and women in his ranks when I was growing up, and a couple had even been friends of the family. Now, Finesia would kill them without remorse.

"Where's Alsie?" I asked Wiggea. She'd announced, when the dragonmen and dragonwomen had emerged at East Cadigan Island, that they couldn't go far from her before they were reduced to delirium.

"She's otherwise engaged."

"And you don't mind that I must kill her."

Wiggea remained silent.

"Of course, he doesn't mind," Finesia said in my head. *"For that is my will."*

"And how do I know you're not lying? How do I know you're not saying exactly the same thing to Alsie?" I replied.

"So, you've finally decided to acknowledge me. We're making progress, my dear acolyte. Things are going according to plan."

I cursed and shut her out again. I shouldn't even be responding to her. She was that dangerous.

A flock of crows had now gathered where the single one had flown overhead. They cackled out into the sky as they circled around us, as if they could taste death on the air. Meanwhile, the fog was thickening, and the air was getting colder.

"Do what you want," I said to Wiggea. "But regardless, we'll fly into the port and get the icebreakers our own way."

"But I don't think you'll want to do that. Not when your friends and my old comrades are in peril."

My heart skipped a beat. "What do you know, Wiggea?"

"Simply that the king's automatons are on the way to ambush your little fleet. And if you don't do something about it, they'll wipe them out in one fell swoop."

"No, that's nonsense," I said. "We scouted the area and saw nothing in the air or on the sea for miles."

Wiggea's stern expression became a cocky grin. I didn't like this new Wiggea one bit.

"That's because they're not coming from on land or on the sea."

"Dragonheats, what do you mean?"

He took a step to the side, and a plume of black dust rose around him. I stepped backwards even more so I didn't inhale any of that magic, and Ratter hissed loudly at him from my shoulder and bared his razor-sharp teeth.

"I'll handle the icebreakers, Pontopa," Wiggea said. *"You go back and help our friends."*

"Wiggea..."

"Didn't you say you'd call me Rastano before I died? I would much rather be on first-name terms."

"Wait... Wiggea..."

"I'll always love you, Pontopa. And I'll protect you for eternity."

And those words left me feeling both empty and disgusted at the same time.

Wiggea rocketed into the air in dragon form and sped off towards Port Szutzko. I watched him go a moment, kind of sad that we'd lost a good man... Or more, that I'd lost a good man. Then I turned back towards Velos and rushed back up the ladder. Ratter leapt off my shoulder as I did and scurried back towards the dragon automaton.

"I heard everything through Ratter," Faso called over to me. "So, we're going after him, I take it? We can't trust him, surely?"

But deep inside I knew that he wasn't lying. He had no reason to. "We're going back to help General Sako and Admiral Sandao," I said. And I mounted Velos and strapped myself back in.

"I knew you'd do the right thing," Finesia said as we lifted into the sky. I tried my best to ignore her presence as I turned Velos back in the direction from whence we'd come.

O nce we got out of the Szutzko Mires, the fog had lifted quite
substantially. But still the sky remained grey, and it retained a
cold humidity. It was late afternoon, and the light had dimmed.
Beneath us, the sea was calm and the soft lapping sounds of the waves
susurrated from below.

Soon enough, we came in view of the Saye Explorer. General Sako
was out alone on the quarterdeck, looking out towards Port Szutzko,
probably wondering if his grandson would return safely.

I pushed up on Velos' steering fin and had him land on the deck.
Lieutenant Talato and Taka dismounted fast on my command, and I
removed the helmet that Faso had placed in the compartment beneath
my seat before I dismounted too. General Sako now stood at the
bottom of the ladder, pungent fumes rising from his secicao pipe. He
turned his head between Lieutenant Talato and me and regarded us
underneath furrowed eyebrows.

I sang a dragonsong, to instruct Velos this time not to head to
the dragon carrier, but to keep aloft. He seemed to prefer this and
didn't show any signs of resentment as he cleared space for Faso
and Winda to land. The dragon automaton touched down, then
lowered its neck, creating a ramp for Faso to slide down while

Winda scurried down the segmented tail at the back. Faso lifted himself off his haunches, then dusted down his suit, then approached.

I looked down at Taka, who looked awfully pale. "Go to the bridge to get warm," I said. "We'll meet you there soon."

He nodded, and I watched him climb down the ladder to the lower deck, until he disappeared out of view. I turned to General Sako, who had remained silent up to this point, waiting patiently for my attention.

"What the dragonheats is all this urgency about?" General Sako said once I met his gaze. "And why haven't you returned on the icebreakers?"

"There's no time," I replied. "We're about to be ambushed."

"What? No, you're misinformed. The Hummingbirds have been monitoring our surroundings constantly, reporting back every ten minutes. There's nothing visible for leagues."

"With all due respect, General, do the Hummingbirds operate underwater?"

"No, but neither do other automatons. So, we have nothing to worry about in that respect."

"That's untrue," Faso butted in, and Winda put a hand on his shoulder as if to stop him raging. "I've tested my dragon automaton underwater and made sure Velos' armour and helmet work too, though not his cannon. I'm sure Travast is also capable of developing such technology."

General Sako raised an eyebrow. "Have you tested it in salt water?"

"No, but it will work," Faso said. "There's no reason why it shouldn't."

"Then I guess there's no harm in sending them scouting beneath the waves."

Faso turned to me and smiled. "Oh, now I get it, all this was an act to give you a chance to finally try out the helmet. If I was in your position, I might have done the same."

"Faso, be serious," I said. "We don't know what King Cini has sent out and when it might attack."

"You don't know if there's anything there at all," Faso said. "How do we know he wasn't trying to stir up trouble?"

General Sako shook his head hard and then held up his hand to stop Faso. "Hang on, hang on. Backtrack. What happened out there, and what made you think we would suddenly be ambushed by technology we've never even heard of?" He took another draw from his pipe.

"We saw one of Alsie's agents out there," I said.

Faso nodded. "Lieutenant Wiggea."

General Sako coughed out plumes upon plumes of smoke, almost choking on it. "What? Impossible, Wiggea's dead."

"He's a dragonman now," I said. "I never told you, because I knew it would be hard to believe. But during the eruption of the Pinnatu Crater, Wiggea was one of the dragons who arose."

General Sako regarded me a moment, his eyes wide open and his cheeks puffed out. Then he laughed. "No, you're pulling my leg. Come on, where are the icebreakers? You retrieved them, didn't you? And everything's fine."

"It's true, sir," Lieutenant Talato said. "I saw Wiggea with my own eyes."

General Sako assessed her for a moment then nodded. Faso and I might jest with him, but there was no way a lady who had spent thirty years of her life as a subordinate officer would dare test General Sako's temper. "Blunders and dragonheats! If this is true, then we need to get moving at once..."

While he spoke, Lieutenant Talato's gaze had drifted out into the distance. "Ma'am, there's something approaching," she said.

I only needed a moment to see what she was looking at. A blurry form gaining definition as it approached through the grey clouds. It wasn't on the horizon but hovering above it slightly. From this distance, it looked kind of like an inverted rock with the top flattened out. But, on closer inspection, I noticed it also had two flat wings jutting out from its sides.

General Sako noticed what we were staring at. "What is that?"

"It's the same platform we saw Travast Indorm floating on in the

Southlands," Faso replied. And I turned to see that he already had a field glass to his eye.

"Give me that," General Sako snatched the field glass out of Faso's hands and looked through the eyepiece. He grunted and then handed me the device. "I've never seen anything like it. What's that thing on top?"

I looked through the field glass. It was just about close enough that I could make out the felt crown and long, extravagant fur coat. "It's King Cini. What's he playing at?"

"Well I never." General Sako's nostrils had flared out and his face had gone bright red. "Lieutenant Talato, hand me your rifle."

The lieutenant glanced at me. "Ma'am?" she asked. She was, after all, under my authority, not the general's. I gave her a nod of approval, then I looked through the eyepiece again, astonished that the king would come this close, and without escorts.

"General Sako, Dragonseer Wells," Admiral Sandao came rushing down the stairs from above the quarterdeck. "Have you seen? I've been watching the thing approaching from the bridge."

"Yes," General Sako said. "And because the fool responsible for my daughter's death has dared come out here, I will kill him."

"Remember, General," I said, "that his secicao makes him impervious. You need to get a point where there's not much skin to punch through. Like the neck."

"Blunders and dragonheats! Why always the neck?" He twitched his moustache. "Well, I'm a good enough shot."

I unstrapped the rifle from my back. I handed it to Talato. "Take this, just in case, Lieutenant. But let the general take the first shot. After all this time, he deserves it."

"Affirmative, Ma'am," she saluted with her right hand as she took the rifle in her left. Then she ran into position on the opposite side of the deck and crouched down.

The sun broke through the clouds for a moment and then hid away again. All the while, the king was getting ever closer. Close enough that General Sako could take a shot.

"Now..." General Sako said. And I watched the scene unfold

through the field glass. King Cini looked every bit as resplendent and pompous as always with his white powdered face and that heavy, luxurious fur collar. The bang came from General Sako's rifle, followed milliseconds later by the crack of a report from Lieutenant Talato's.

But the king didn't flinch.

"Did you see that?" General Sako said. "I hit him, and it went right through him."

"Me too, sir," Talato said. "A definite shot to the throat."

And then a loud raucous laughter resounded from the floating platform. "I knew you'd try. And I thought I'd demonstrate how far our technology has come since I last saw you, General Sako. This is what we call a hologram. Travast Indorm invented it, and now I can get close and talk to you in person, without having to get shot."

"A holo-what?" General Sako asked.

"A hologram," Faso said, his head held high. "It was me, actually, who published a paper about the possibilities of such technology in the scientific journals."

"Blunders and dragonheats. Why didn't you say anything?"

"I didn't think King Cini would gain the resources and finesse to create such a thing. It's quite a delicate operation, you know?"

I noticed some kind of a bulbous device on the front of the platform, probably a camera lens. And, just like with Travast's platform, what looked like hundreds of little guns stuck out of the front. Pointing straight at us. The platform jerked to a stop around ten yards or so from the ship, let out a great screeching sound, and then its wings quickly folded in on its body as the propellers faced downwards and whirred.

A good two dozen of Sandao's marines filed out of the superstructure and took positions on either side of the deck. "Aim for the platform," Admiral Sandao said. He held a talkie in one hand and another telescope in his other, placed against his right eye. "We need to take this down before it takes any of our men."

Beside me, both General Sako and Lieutenant Talato reloaded.

Although, much to my satisfaction, the dragonelite was much faster doing so than the general.

"Well, I thought I'd warn you of an unexpected attack before it actually happens," the king continued. "Really, this is so entertaining, I've not had this much fun since that time with Miss Wells and Miss Sako in the palace. I noticed you scouting the skies, but you didn't even think to check underwater." Dragonheats, this king liked the sound of his own voice far too much.

Admiral Sandao had his hand raised up in the air, and he watched the platform astutely as it started to edge slightly around the ship. To our left and right, the other ships of the flotilla had lined up in a defensive arc, forming a wall around Candalmo's trawler and the dragon carrier. On deck, every marine and sailor had their guns trained on this one device. Velos also hovered nearby, with the dragon automaton now next to him, its claws poised ready to attack. Faso stood next to me, wearing the helmet with which he controlled the mechanical beast.

"Aim," Admiral Sandao said. A whirring sound emerged from the automaton platform, and I watched in horror through my telescope as one gun turned upwards towards Velos.

The lines tightened around Admiral Sandao's wizened face. "Fire," he shouted.

And every single marine out on deck fired their rifles. The shots hit their target true. The platform erupted in sparks. A shot also came out from a gun on the platform, but it hit nothing. The floating machine let off a droning sound, tilted over to the side a little, and then tumbled into the water.

For a moment, the skies were clear, other than a single nearby seagull diving for fish. Then, there came a massive crashing sound from below, and a huge squall erupted from the water, rocking the Saye Explorer, and almost sending me reeling towards the edge of the deck.

"Blunders and dragonheats!" General Sako said. "We've been hit."

"You can say that again," Admiral Sandao said. Then he spoke into his talkie. "Lieutenant Commander Farage. Check the hull. I need a full scan on the bulkheads, and I need a damage report quickly."

Faso lifted his visor and turned to me. He opened his mouth to speak, but was interrupted by another crash from below. Velos roared out to the sky as an enormous splash erupted from the water. The momentum hit the ship and sent me stumbling to the other side of the deck.

"Dragonheats, get that helmet on, Pontopa," Faso shouted. "We need to take the dragons underwater."

"I think you should get to the bridge first," Admiral Sandao said. "Get yourself sitting, otherwise a direct hit might send you flying overboard."

I realised he was right, and so without even conferring with Faso, I climbed down the quarterdeck ladder, and I headed towards the aft steam tower and climbed the spiral staircase around it. The clanking of footsteps resounded on the steel behind as Faso followed me up the stairs. At the top, someone opened the door onto the bridge for me, and I was happy to see Taka on the other side.

"Auntie Pontopa, what's happening?" he asked.

"Take a seat, Taka," I replied. I didn't want him stumbling into any sharp objects. "We're being attacked."

"But by who? I've been watching from here, and there's no one on the water. I only saw that platform with King Cini on it, and we shot him down."

"It wasn't King Cini. And the attacks aren't coming from above the water."

Taka's eyes went wide. "Underwater automatons?"

"Yes," I said.

Faso pushed onto the bridge behind me. "Come on, what are you milling around for? We need to get to the front of the ship."

A klaxon sounded. Red lights pulsed around the room, and even more sailors and soldiers ran out the door and down the stairs. Faso sprinted towards the front of the bridge, and I took hold of Taka's hand and led him around the two funnels, to the arched, glass-windowed section of the bridge at the front. Several comfortable looking leather armchairs had been arranged around the outer funnel wall behind us. By the windows, Sandao's officers had taken their places in front of their control stations, with a complex array of charts and diagrams laid out, none of which I understood.

Faso sat down. "Get your helmet on, Pontopa, and stop gawking."

Dragonheats, he was right. I checked Taka was secure first, then placed myself down on another seat. Velos hovered right in front of the windows ahead of us, staring into a thick grey layer of clouds.

"Taka," I said. "Call the dragons out and scout for any airborne automatons that might have joined the perimeter. I'm going to take Velos underwater."

"You can do that?" Taka said.

"Yes, Taka," Faso said, sounding slightly annoyed. "Velos' helmet also contains a breathing device, connected to a layer of compressed oxygen I've built into the secicao tanks. Now hush, I need to focus."

And there was another modification he'd neglected to tell me about. I sighed, then put on the helmet. I flicked the switch I remembered Faso playing with on the side when he'd introduced me to the armour.

Now, I could see through Velos' eyes. The vision was fisheye and showed the sea stretching out in a splendid spectrum of greens and blues. Beside me, Taka sang a dragonsong, and Velos turned his head to see the Greys swarm out of the dragon carrier that had positioned itself behind the protective wall of destroyers and cruisers.

I sang to Velos to remind him to focus. The dragons weren't important now, the underwater automatons were. The ship rocked again, and I heard a muffled shouting from outside. I ignored it.

Instead, I recalled the dragonsongs I'd known all my life, I'd chanted them in my dreams since birth and recently in the actual world. It was strange not piloting Velos using his steering fin. But, at the same time, it felt completely natural, seeing the grey churning sea shoot up towards Velos as he dived towards it. Breaking the water and feeling the crash of it against Velos' skin as if it were my own.

"It's remarkable what you and your scientist can do, Acolyte Wells. But

you know, all you'd need is to claim my gift. Become a dragonwoman and tear your attackers apart with your own claws."

Finesia was the last person I needed in my head right now. I pushed her away and turned my attention back to the display in the helmet.

Underneath the water, their brass metal exterior glowing green, our attackers looked similar to sharks: razor teeth that flecked the upper and lower edges of their long mouths; streamlined bodies designed for speeding through the water; dozens of spear-like missiles attached to the undersides of both of their fins, with tips so pointed they looked as if they could puncture an ironclad. The automatons accelerated towards their targets, sending whole shoals of minnows scattering in their paths.

Under command of my song, Velos turned his head to see the dragon automaton swimming right next to him. And the dragon automaton turned his head back as if acknowledging Velos' gaze.

"You can't breathe fire under there," Faso said to me. "But I modified the Gatling guns, so they'd work automatically."

Thank goodness for that, I thought. But I didn't say it out loud to Faso. Even with my abilities as a dragonseer, there was no way I could sing and speak at the same time.

"Dragonheats, watch out, Pontopa!" Faso shouted from beside me. And I turned Velos' head to see the menacing tip of one of the missiles heading straight for us. I veered Velos downwards, towards the body of another shark coming straight towards us. But this one hadn't yet fired any of its missiles, and Velos' Gatling guns took the automaton down, causing it to crumple and then sink towards the sea floor.

From my right, a stream of bubbles rose out of another shark that had stopped dead in the water. "Got one," Faso said. "That's one each. Taka, you should try this sometime. It's great fun."

I turned Velos towards the Saye Explorer's hull and went after a shark heading towards it. Velos' body bucked from both sides as the Gatling guns unleashed their load. But the shark swerved upwards out of the way, leaving four missiles heading towards the hull. A propeller on the missiles' backs edged them forwards, and each one was rotating fast.

And any one of them, I was sure, could create a massive hole in the Saye Explorer, sinking the ship. We'd left the tap on before he lifted into the air. So, now augmented, he sped up towards the missiles and gnashed three out of the way. But the last hit its target, just as Velos' massive body crashed against the ship's hull.

Distantly, I felt my body rock in my seat. But I was so focused on what was going on underwater, I didn't let myself get distracted by the sensation.

"Blunders and dragonheats," I heard General Sako say nearby. "Dragonseer Wells, what's going on down there?"

"Let Pontopa sing her songs, General," Faso replied. "She needs to stay in control."

"Very well, Gordoni, boy. So, you tell me. What are they, and how many do we have to deal with?"

"I've counted exactly twenty," the inventor replied. "And we've taken down four. That's three to one, by the way, Pontopa. You have some catching up to do."

But he probably wasn't counting the missiles I'd stopped from hitting our ship's hull. I turned Velos around and commanded him to wrap his jaws around the missile that was trying to sever the rusting steel outer walls of the Saye Explorer. Probably, there were men behind the bulkhead trying to plug up the gap. But I guessed, like an arrow in a wound, it would be much easier for them once the missile was removed.

It took exceptional strength in Velos' neck, but eventually he snapped the missile in half, so it was no longer a threat. The front barb rotated as it sank, and I noticed the spiral outer thread snaking around the head, exactly like a drill bit.

"Incoming," Faso said.

I turned around to see another shark coming straight on, this time with missiles shooting out in front of it, spaced out far enough that one would surely hit Velos if he tried to swim out of the way, no matter which direction he went. If they could pierce the Saye Explorer's hull, I didn't want to find out what they could do to Velos' armour. He turned to face them head on and his Gatling guns went into overdrive. They shot six missiles down, leaving just two. Velos turned so he could catch one of them in his teeth while he thumped the other downwards with his tail, redirecting it towards the sea bottom.

Behind, the shark got caught in the crossfire from the Gatling guns, curled into a ball, and sank towards the seabed.

"That's two you've got now, Pontopa," Faso said. "While I've got fifteen. But I wouldn't take it personally. After all, I have the superior technology."

"Dragonheats, this is not a game," General Sako said, and I had to agree with his sentiment.

"Well, there's three left," Faso said. "Meanwhile, anything happening up above?"

"No, there's been nothing else up here for miles. They must have been so confident that they'd take us out from underwater, that they didn't even bother to send reinforcements."

Under the surface, I caught sight of another three sharks. They were swimming in formation and heading right for the Saye Explorer's hull. They let off every single missile on their fins, as they propelled themselves forwards with their massive flippers, gaining on the Saye Explorer. We had to give chase.

But I turned to see Faso's dragon automaton heading away from the boat, and I realised I would have to handle them myself. I willed Velos in my song to swing his tail and push him forward, as he kicked with his front feet. But he wouldn't get there fast enough.

Unless…

Velos could now control the guns on his armour through his helmet, and I willed him to pivot them around, so they faced behind him. Then, I let them fire an entire controlled volley all at once. This projected Velos forwards, swimming as fast as a sailfish. The Gatling guns swung around to face forwards, and they unleashed their load into the sharks. Two of them crumpled up in the water, leaving that single shark on his tail, pursuing fast.

Velos was now decelerating, but he still had a lot of speed, gaining on a good fifty or so missiles that were heading straight towards the hull of the Saye Explorer. Enough, I guessed, to take down the entire boat.

The Gatling guns laid into their targets, shooting the missiles off their trajectories. They were so thin they were hard to hit. But we still reduced the number of on-target missiles by half.

Meanwhile, the shark on Velos' tail was getting ever closer. We could turn and face it, but that would mean abandoning the missiles. I added some special reassuring notes to the song to will Velos to carry on, even though his instinct wanted him to turn around and face his pursuer head on. He caught up with the missiles and he shifted his body in an elaborate dance to knock many away from the hull.

The shark had caught up now and started gnashing at Velos' tail. With one swing, Velos batted it away, but it came in for another pass. Meanwhile, he caught a missile in his mouth, and spat it out, so it spun down towards the seabed.

There were only two missiles left now.

"Dragonheats, there's one on your tail," Faso said. "You should have said something. Hold on, I'll be right there."

Both missiles drilled into the hull. In my own body, I felt the Saye Explorer rock underneath me. Velos wrenched one missile out of the ship with his jaw. But when he turned towards the other one, it was too deep inside for Velos to pull it out with his own strength. He clenched on to it with his teeth, while the shark circled around and approached Velos from his side. It was going straight for Velos' neck. If Velos didn't let go of the missile, he'd have his head torn off by that thing's razor teeth.

But still he had to hold on. He couldn't let go.

He thrashed at the water with his tail, and his leftmost Gatling gun targeted the shark. But it sputtered out one bullet and then stopped firing, depleted. I willed Velos to pump more secicao into the armour. And not to let go of the missile.

But as I watched the shark close in on. I knew that we'd have no choice. I commanded Velos to let go. But he wouldn't. I added notes to my song to spur him into action. But his will was resolute.

Dragonheats, he'd sacrifice himself for us. He wanted to be a hero.

"See how weak you humans and dragons are," Finesia said in my mind.

"Shut up!" I snapped.

And I readied myself to use one of her gifts.

The shark was secicao powered. So, one of Finesia's screams would disrupt the collective unconscious and disorient the automaton.

But I didn't have to, because something big barrelled forwards from the side, knocking the shark off kilter. And just as that happened, Velos found some strength to tear the missile out of the hole. He dropped it out of his mouth towards the sea floor.

Velos turned his head to see the dragon automaton looking right back at him.

"We did it," Faso said.

"Are there any more?" I asked.

"We should scout around," Faso replied.

And so, we took Velos and the dragon automaton twice around the perimeter of the flotilla, before we decided the coast was now clear.

I raised the visor and noticed Faso had done the same.

"That's Faso Gordoni sixteen, Pontopa four," Faso said.

I really wanted to knock that smug look off his pretty face. "Shouldn't you also count how many missiles we shot down? I mean, they were equally dangerous."

"No," Faso said. "The count only goes to automatons. Ammunition doesn't count."

I sighed, glad that we'd subverted the attack. But one officer in front of us pointed to something out of the window, and we saw another platform come into view in the distance. The cloud cover had abated quite significantly now, and so we could see it pretty clearly, even though it must have been a hundred or so yards away. The Greys were circling the ship above us.

"Taka, don't let the dragons near," I said. "I don't want them shot down."

But the platform didn't seem to want to get near them either.

General Sako looked through Faso's field glass at it, then he handed it to me. It wasn't a projection of King Cini standing on top anymore, but Travast Indorm with his purple bandana over his face.

His voice boomed out of a loudspeaker system from the distance. "You may have thought you've won this battle," he said. "But you've only angered the king. We'll send reinforcements, and you shall not win this war."

Faso chortled. "I think we will," he said. "Our technology is definitely superior." And his dragon automaton shot out of the water, sending up a tremendous splash over the deck of the Saye Explorer. Velos emerged shortly after and let out a roar, then joined his brothers in flight.

I wasn't sure whether our technology was superior. But I had a feeling that King Cini would overwhelm us with numbers. Particularly if that factory was operational, since we'd only brought a small fleet.

I put the thought aside, because I knew we had to focus on getting those icebreakers. We had to take things one step at a time.

PART IV

PONTOPA

"The worst thing you can lose is yourself."

— PONTOPA WELLS

We were graced with a beautiful vista on our journey back to Port Szutzko. I was in flight on Velos' back, with Taka and Lieutenant Talato behind me. Faso and General Sako flew alongside us on the dragon automaton. The general had insisted on coming along so he could be part of the negotiations. I'd half expected both men to spend the journey arguing with each other, and I'd even considered having General Sako on Velos' back and Talato on the dragon automaton's. But General Sako didn't know how to operate the armour, and both he and Faso were pretty quiet anyway, presumably exhausted after all the commotion.

The clouds had now lifted much higher in the sky. The sun was setting underneath them, casting an amber cover overhead. It all looked like a burning fire, reminding me of the lava lake that I'd stared at beneath the Pinnatu Crater two years ago, with Wiggea's hand in mine.

And now, he'd become a different man. I dreaded learning of the destruction he might have caused at Port Szutzko. But, if we hadn't left him to his own devices, then our fleet would have had no chance of fending off the automaton sharks.

I could feel Velos was tired, and so I didn't want to push him too hard. Faso had refuelled his armour, but I had asked Lieutenant Talato not to use the secicao unless absolutely necessary.

"How are you doing, Auntie?" Taka said in my head. At that instance, it surprised me Taka could talk to me like this. But then I remembered I was a dragonwoman now. Even if I refused to transform, I still had the capabilities Finesia had given me. And one of them was the ability to serve as a medium for telepathy.

"It's been a long day," I said. *"But thank you for asking, Taka. How are you feeling?"*

"Great," Taka said. Typical kid – acting as if he hadn't a worry in the world. *"It looked so cool what you were doing with that helmet, Auntie. Do you think I could have a go someday?"*

"Someday," I said. *"If your father lets you."*

"Oh, he will," Taka replied. *"He will."*

I shook my head. Knowing Faso, he'd say his inventions weren't toys for Taka to play with.

"Say, Auntie," Taka said. *"Do you miss Wiggea?"*

I sighed. It seemed the boy was just as insightful as his mother had been. *"He was a good soldier and a good man,"* I replied.

"But he's still out there." I mean, *"we saw him. And he didn't seem so bad".*

"That's exactly what Finesia wants you to see, Taka," I replied. *"Never trust her. She only aims to deceive."*

I turned around and Taka nodded at me. *"But Wiggea was more to you than just a soldier, wasn't he? I saw the way you looked at him sometimes."*

"There was something," I said. *"But it wasn't meant to be."*

"But maybe we could bring him back Auntie. Maybe someone can talk to him and help him get Finesia out of his head. Doctor Forsolano tells me that sometimes people's minds just get sick for a while, and they often only need to be talked to in a certain way. Sometimes, he says, he may also give them pills. Is that why you took the tablets, Auntie? Did you need to get better too?"

I shook my head. It seemed Taka might have asked Doctor Forsolano about me and maybe the doctor let on more than he should have. *"It doesn't matter now. I won't need to take them again."*

"But maybe we can get Wiggea to take them. And maybe we can get

Charth to take them, and Alsie. Do you think we can save them that way, Auntie? Can we make them good again?"

"I don't know," I said. Somehow, I didn't believe there was any turning back for these creatures. I don't believe Gerhaun did either. But while I didn't want to lie to the kid, I didn't also want him to lose hope.

The sun had almost sunk beneath the horizon, and now the brilliant amber ball behind us seemed to limn the cliffs of East Island in red fire. As we progressed, an icy wind picked up from behind, evidently heading inland as the sea cooled.

"The thing the boy doesn't realise," Finesia said in my head, *"is there is no turning back. But it doesn't matter, because when my acolytes discover what they can gain through me, they never want to let go. Accept it, Acolyte Wells, my world is a better one. Why do you fight for a life which will always be a constant battle to the grave?"*

But even if her question was valid, I couldn't open myself up to her. If I answered her question, she'd just try to reason with me that we, as humans, had no better choice. Yet, humans didn't work that way. We lived for our emotions, and what Finesia seemed to offer was an empty, emotionless world. But then, cyagora had also killed my emotions. And I couldn't help but wonder if one option was really better than the other.

"You will become greater than any creature that's ever lived on this planet," Finesia continued. *You will surpass even me, when I had form in this world. You cannot control your fate, my acolyte, but you can embrace it."*

I shook her away once I realised I'd let her enter my head again. It seemed that Doctor Forsolano was right and Finesia would get stronger. But I had to keep in control.

Suddenly, a sparkle came off the sea, then another, and then a third. I noticed them to belong to the coils at the front of the icebreakers. And Wiggea was down there somewhere and he had retrieved them.

"Darling," this wasn't Finesia inside my head now but Wiggea. *"Aren't you going to at least say thank you?"*

"What did you do to get these, Wiggea?" I asked.

"Oh, how it hurts not to have your appreciation. You used to give me so much more."

"Answer my question, Wiggea."

"Rastano, please... It's Rastano, remember."

"Wiggea..." Calling him by his first name would bridge the distance between us, which I was trying to avoid.

And he said no more in response.

I caught a faint whiff of smoke in the air, and I thought I could see burning in the distance, ever so faintly. What destruction had Wiggea caused? A whole town ransacked, perhaps. How many innocent civilians had he killed?

But we had no time to find out. We needed to get moving before King Cini or Travast Indorm sent those automatons they'd promised.

"There are the icebreakers," General Sako's voice came over the speaker system installed on Velos' flank. "Blunders and dragonheats, we've got them."

I shook my head. "But I don't know at what cost."

And as they came clearer into view, I gazed down upon the silhouette of a man standing on the narrow prow of the leading icebreaker. He wore the king's redguard uniform, and he looked out at the red light spilling out from beneath the horizon.

I took Velos down towards the ship so I could face my former dragonelite and find out exactly what he wanted from us.

THE LIGHTS CAME on on the icebreakers as Velos and the dragon automaton descended. They shone out from the side of the ships, casting long reflections on the calm, cold water. Others lit up the narrow, flat roofs of the ships' superstructures that spanned almost the entire length of each one, making them look like massive barges. Only at the back did each one have a second cabin with a flat raised roof, with barely enough space for either Velos or Faso's automaton to land on. So, I took Velos down on the roof section of the lower superstructure. The floor was slippery, and Velos slid across the deck, men in bright fluorescent orange life jackets scurrying out of his path, before coming to a halt several yards away. Faso brought his dragon automaton down for a much smoother landing on the upper deck.

Wiggea stood on the foredeck looking out to sea, not seeming to have paid much attention to our landing, or at least cared too much about it. I instructed Talato to stay on Velos, with her rifle cocked, but not yet aimed. I scrambled down the ladder, the rungs cold against my delicate fingers.

A man with a wizened face and a thick scar running from his left temple to his right cheek came over to greet me as General Sako descended the ladder from behind. "Miss Wells, I presume," he said. "I've heard a lot about you. I'm Captain Pitash. Explorer of the coldest parts of this world, wildlife enthusiast, trained zoologist, and owner of these three vessels."

I took his gloved hand, relishing the slight warmth against the chill that was numbing my hand. I made a mental note to, when I got back to the Saye Explorer, ask Admiral Sandao for some gloves. Even in the coldest conditions, I only covered my hands when I absolutely needed to. But I was quickly reaching that point of necessity.

"Thank you for offering to lend us your vessels at such brief notice," I said. "I'll make sure you're well compensated."

"Oh, don't worry," the captain replied. "One of Candalmo's clerks has already handed over the funds. All you need to worry about is making sure we don't run into any danger as agreed, otherwise the price will triple."

I nodded. It had been good of Candalmo to offer to fund this, he'd said he wanted to do his part to help a noble cause. But I didn't want him to end up overpaying because of our oversights. And somehow, Captain Pitash didn't look the most trustworthy type. But then I really shouldn't judge someone based on the size of their scar.

I turned to General Sako.

He coughed against the back of his hand, then lifted his secicao pipe from his pocket and lit it with a match. "You are under our protection now, Captain Pitash," he said. "And Gerhaun Forsi will cover whatever extra costs occur – within reason, of course."

"And I hear that she's never been one to break an agreement," Pitash said. "I respect that."

I looked over to Wiggea, a little surprised he hadn't even budged from his position to greet us yet. "I see you couldn't shake him," I said.

"Aye," Pitash said, looking at Wiggea out of the corner of his eye. "He's been standing there since he landed. No one's even dared approach him. We've never seen anything like him."

I nodded. "It's probably for the best to keep your distance. What happened, anyway?"

Pitash looked out to sea. "It was terrible," he said. "I didn't realise what he was at first, and I thought I was hallucinating. But the rest of the crew also saw him. There was this massive roar from the sky, then the dragon landed on our icebreaker. It was black as oil, with this dark rainbow sheen over it – quite unnatural." Pitash glanced at Velos, then turned back to me. "We had a redguard on deck, making sure that we didn't try fleeing the port. But as soon as he raised his rifle at the dragon, it just swooped down out of the sky and took him up in his claws. Then it dropped the body, and the last we saw was the redguard crashing into the water, defenceless.

"The other guards on other ships tried firing too." He turned in the direction of the town. "But one by one, the dragon picked them off in the same way. Bullets wouldn't hurt it. Then, the thing flew out to town, and doused Port Szutzko in flames. Fortunately, none of our crew have family in the city, but some of my sailors have had, well, other connections…

"As we fled, we caught sight of the shantytown next to the port. The whole neighbourhood was made of wood, and so became this raging inferno. We saw people throwing themselves out of the high windows into the sea. We wanted to help them. But we feared if we turned back, the dragon would take our ships too.

"So, we fired up our propellers and fled as fast as we could. Next thing we know, the dragon has landed again on our deck. And there was this great black cloud rising from it. Then that man was standing there. And he's been there, like a sacred statue, ever since… Do you know what he is, Miss Wells? Do you know how to get rid of him?"

"I intend to find out," I said. Wiggea had certainly lost himself to Finesia. But was Taka right? Would there be any chance of bringing him back?

"Thank you, Miss," the captain said. "And maybe if you get rid of him, we can give you a slight discount."

"That won't be necessary," I said. "But maybe you'll consider waiving any *exceptions* that might occur."

"I understand, Ma'am," the captain said, and he turned to look towards the port.

All this time, Faso had been sitting on his dragon automaton, watching our exchange from a distance. But he chose this moment to descend and walk over to us. Winda stayed on board, fiddling with something at the back of the dragon armour with a screwdriver. Faso knelt down and rapped the floor of the deck with his knuckles. "I've often wondered about how well the fabled icebreakers are constructed. Say, have you ever considered an upgrade? I'd be happy to supply you with some superior technology – for the right price."

Captain Pitash turned to Faso and raised an eyebrow. "And you are?"

"Faso Gordoni, inventor extraordinaire, at your service." He held out his hand.

Pitash shook it. "Well, Mr Gordoni, maybe we'll see if we can do business, but you have to understand it will have to be in both of our best interests."

And I left Faso to present his business pitch to the captain, wondering what the wellies he needed money for. I approached Wiggea at the front. He turned to me slowly as I stepped cautiously forward. The deck became quite narrow towards the front of the ship, necessary I guess for cutting through the ice. Soon, I had to step with one foot in front of the other, my hands stretched out at my sides to keep balance. Yet Wiggea had placed himself on the raised edges of the deck, not teetering one bit as the boat rocked.

"I delivered what I promised," he said in the collective unconscious. *"That's how much I love you."*

I ignored his false expressions of love, *"And the means you went to do so, Wiggea. The captain of these vessels told me what happened. Why did so many have to die?"*

"I merely did what was necessary to get the ships you needed."

"And how does this fit into Finesia's plans? Why does she want to help us?"

The pale-faced man looked mortally offended, but I knew it was all a ruse. *"I came to offer my help. And now, are you saying you don't want it? I love you, Pontopa, and I will do what I can to make your life easier."*

I shook my head. *"You know, the real Wiggea always worried about his emotions getting in the way of his duty. And now you say you're being dutiful because you love me. The real Wiggea is dead."* My heart sank in my chest as I said these words. I was denying his existence, yet I was still looking at the handsome lines of Wiggea's face, just as I remembered him.

"He isn't dead," Finesia said in my head. *"He's merely become the man you wanted him to be. You tried to tell him yourself that he needed to let go of his sense of duty to become complete. And I merely showed him the way to a better life."*

As Finesia spoke, Wiggea watched me with patient eyes and a lopsided smile. A cold gust of wind came off the sea, blowing my hair into my face, and causing me to shiver.

"Wiggea, you should stop this nonsense, and leave immediately," I said out loud. "You've proven through your actions you're not trustworthy. And the only thing you're bringing to this ship is fear into the men who are trying to run it."

"As you wish," he said. And a plume of blackened dust rose around him. He was so close, that the energy from it sent me stumbling backwards as if hit by a shock wave. I might have tumbled off into the water if General Sako hadn't been standing behind to catch me.

"Dragonheats, he's getting away," General Sako said. His breath reeked of stale secicao.

"And good riddance," I replied. As I watched him go, I couldn't help but worry about what might lie in wait for us. I had no idea what Finesia wanted.

You'll understand everything soon enough, Finesia said in my head.

Once I know that I have your complete allegiance then, I promise you, I'll reveal every single one of my plans.

Finesia. Wiggea had lost his mind to her. Charth had lost his mind to her. And nothing terrified me more than also losing my mind to her. Such a fate seemed even worse than death.

It took us a few hours to navigate the icebreakers to the rest of the fleet. After that, we sailed the small flotilla around the top of the Southern Barrier without incident.

The first sign of the icecaps appeared mid-afternoon the next day. The sun was fast descending from its low apex in the sky. It brought with it a pleasant warmth that allayed the harsh chill coming off the ice, on which some seals lay bathing lazily in the sun, seemingly unaffected by the cold.

I watched the scene from the conference section of the bridge, while a few sailors placed pads of paper and cups of hot tea on the table behind me. Lieutenant Talato was already sitting in her place, examining her nails. A large overhead fan heater blew warm air at me, and I now wore a thick woollen jumper and a stuffed gilet to help keep this in. But, I really wasn't one for stuffiness, so I stood by the open window relishing the fresh draft against my face, as the rest of my body remained warm. I'd also got hold of some gloves, but I didn't need to wear them indoors, and so these hung from my sleeves on cords.

I soon heard General Sako and Admiral Sandao coming up the stairs around the aft funnel to the bridge.

"Blunders and dragonheats, Dragonseer Wells," General Sako said as he came through the hatch. "I thought you were warm-blooded. Close the window, will you? It's bloody freezing."

"Freezing? Don't you think it's a little airless in here? We have a heater to add some warmth." I glanced at Sandao, who lowered his head sheepishly.

"It's okay when you don't have to wear a proper uniform," General Sako said. "But our suits weren't designed for intense cold."

"Didn't you bring thermals with you?" I asked, with a sly smile.

But he didn't seem to want to jest. "I'll put on my long johns when I finally need to. For now, please keep the window closed."

I shrugged and reached out to swing the window shut, only turning its clasp halfway so we at least got a sliver of fresh air. General Sako nodded, then took a place at the head of the table, while Sandao took his place at the other.

I sat down next to Lieutenant Talato. The ruddy-faced Lieutenant Candiorno, a couple more of General Sako's lieutenants and three of Admiral Sandao's officers had been waiting in the control section of the bridge in front of the foremost funnel. But as if in response to General Sako's bawling voice, they marched over, saluted then took their place at the table.

"And guess what? The inventor's late again," General Sako said, looking at his pocket watch.

And just a moment later, we heard Faso Gordoni's heavy boots clambering up the stairs. He nodded and took a seat next to me. Ratter emerged from the inventor's flared suit sleeve and lay down in front of him on the table.

"No Winda today, Faso?" I asked.

"She's repairing the dragon automaton. Those sharks left quite a few scratches and we want to ensure everything is in working order."

"And what about Velos' armour?" I asked. "Shouldn't you check that for repairs too?"

Faso scowled at me. "I thought you didn't want us touching the armour without your express permission?"

"Repairs are okay. Just ask next time you make a modification, okay?"

Faso snorted and then took hold of a pad of paper and squared it out on the table in front of him.

"Right then," Admiral Sandao said and stood up. "Shall we start?"

"Absolutely," General Sako said. "I'll let you take the lead, admiral."

"Very well. The purpose of this meeting is to discuss our next steps. General Sako and I are both worried about our present course of action, particularly given Travast Indorm's warning that he'll send more automatons –"

"Absolute baloney," Faso cut in. And Admiral Sandao turned to look at the inventor, his eyes wide in surprise. "Travast is just making empty threats."

"Blunders and dragonheats, Gordoni," General Sako said. "Do not interrupt a senior admiral like that. Don't you know your place?"

"As a civilian, you mean," Faso said twiddling his steepled fingers. "I'm the only non-military type at this table, it seems."

"On a military vessel, meaning you're under military jurisdiction," General Sako pointed out. "So, start showing some respect for the rules."

"Aye aye, sir," Faso gave a lazy salute.

I took a sip from my cup of tea, relishing the warmth that coursed down my body. Opposite, Lieutenant Candiorno was clicking the top of his pen repeatedly, rather annoyingly. I stared at him, and he returned an abashed look, then stopped.

"Thank you, General," Admiral Sandao said. "Now, intel has suggested that the factory can produce automatons at an astonishing rate. As we draw closer, we're likely to see increased resistance. My concern specifically is that if we try pushing through a solid mass such as ice, the king's war automatons can waltz right over and board our ships before we can even fight back."

"But the automatons' narrow legs won't work on ice," Faso said. "The king has never had to do battle in this region. I explained all this before." This time, he ignored the hard glare from General Sako.

"It doesn't mean Travast hasn't made the necessary modifications," Admiral Sandao said in response.

"There's no way he'd do it in time," Faso said.

"And with all due respect, Mr Gordoni," the admiral said. "Have you enough knowledge on the factory to know that Mr Indorm lacks the capabilities?"

"No," said Faso. "But wouldn't it be rational to send out scouts to find out, so we're not planning our next course of action on mere speculations?"

"Candiorno, make a note of that," General Sako said. "Possibility one, send out scouts to factory. Also add as a footnote: 'if we can spare the resources'."

Candiorno nodded, clicked his pen once more. Then he scratched some notes quickly on his notepad. I couldn't quite see his handwriting, but with the manner in which he wrote, I assumed it to be terrible.

"Have we got any alternative?" I offered. "I mean, we could be sitting ducks here, if as Sandao suggests the king's automatons are equipped with the technology to navigate the ice."

"And the dragons might be necessary to defend the fleet," General Sako said. "If we send them all out, what defence will we have if there's an attack?"

"But surely getting through would take forever?" I said, and I glanced out at the windows at the three icebreakers that were now approaching the icecaps. The copper coils at the front of their hulls were now red hot, and steam floated up from the front of the ships.

"Actually," General Sako said. "With all this modern technology, Captain Pitash has advised it might only take three days to get to the mouth of the Ginfro River. Depending on the thickness of the ice, of course, which he can't ascertain at this stage."

"Which gives us an opportunity to take the dragons out," I said. "A couple of scouts – the dragon automaton and Velos would be ideal." The smug look on Faso's face showed me that he also agreed.

"That's a suicide mission," General Sako said. "You're far too young to be throwing your life away like that, Dragonseer Wells. And no doubt you'll want to take my grandson with you too."

"What other choice do we have?" Clearly, the dragons were needed here to protect the boats in the event of an attack.

Outside, the icebreakers had widened a thick passage in the ice. It ran a yard or two into the icecap now. But I could see even with their heated coils on the front, our journey through would be slow.

"We could patiently sit this one out," General Sako said. "Hold off any attacks sent against us."

"Or," Admiral Sandao raised an eyebrow. "We could split our forces."

"What do you mean?" General Sako asked.

"We could ferry your commandos and my marines out to land, with a small force of dragons accompanying them. That way, they can march forwards as the icebreakers weave their way towards Ginlast proper."

"And what about the other dragons?" I asked.

"They can stay on the carrier, ready to be called out by Pontopa and Taka, if and when you need them. You can follow us for a while, make camp on the land, and send scouts out to the factory when you think it's appropriate."

"That could actually work," General Sako said. There came footsteps from the steel staircase and Candalmo entered via the door.

"I'm sorry, am I disturbing an important meeting here?"

"What is it, Mr Segora?" General Sako asked.

"You asked me to report on the status of the icebreakers, General. Unfortunately, the ice is a lot thicker than we first thought. Progress through is going to be incredibly slow and could last up to ten days."

I nodded. "General Sako, how long would it take to march from the closest land point to Ginlast?"

"As little as three days."

"Then I think our course of action is decided," I said. "If we're all agreed, it looks like the best solution here is to march inland."

"I think we have no choice in this scenario," Admiral Sandao said. "I'll supervise the situation here where I can best serve and try to get the fleet as close as possible to you if you need to retreat. We'll use Hummingbirds to maintain communication."

And there was a murmur of agreement around the table.

As Admiral Sandao and General Sako continued to discuss plans, with the occasional snarky interjection from Faso, I turned to look out the window. The coils on the icebreakers were touching the ice, and some steam was coming up from the contact point, but the passage hadn't moved much further. Indeed, it looked like melting our way through the icecaps would take an awful long time.

I HAD HOPED, after dealing with so much grey weather on the journey up, that we'd at least have some sunshine on our march to Ginlast. Unfortunately, we weren't to be so lucky. Although the fog didn't return, the sky again had got rather grey and bleak. This made it feel even colder as we marched, though it probably also decreased visibility, making it less likely for patrols to see us coming. A blessing in disguise, I guess.

We had brought out eight Greys in the end, as well as Velos and Faso's dragon automaton. Between them, the dragons had ferried across thirty-three of General Sako's Commandos, eleven of Sandao's marines, Winda, Faso, General Sako, Lieutenant Talato, Lieutenant Candiorno, Taka, and myself. General Sako hadn't been too happy about bringing his grandson. But I'd pointed out that we'd have no idea where he'd be safer – on the ship or on land. At least this way he could keep an eye on him.

It had taken a good couple of hours to complete the operation, and it was mid-morning. Now, we had to march across a tundra landscape blanketed by six inches of snow. Fortunately, we had thick boots, but the dragons didn't enjoy marching too well. We couldn't let them up into the air as that would increase the chances of being spotted. So, even Faso's dragon automaton had to progress on foot.

Each dragon and the automaton wore snowshoes around four times the size of a tennis racket on their feet. They looked ridiculous, and the dragons seemed to know it. Velos, in particular, growled and grumbled about it constantly as he walked.

We made a good pace over the terrain, six commandos in a snow-white camouflage uniform taking the lead and scouting the territory ahead as we pushed forward, and then small mixed squads of marines and commandos supporting two dragons each. Velos and the dragon automaton marched together, and Faso, Winda, General Sako, Taka and I marched with them. Velos had his helmet on, and both Faso and I had our helmets on with the visors raised, just in case we needed to use them in a hurry.

"All your advances on technology, and still you end up having to walk miles on foot. Why is that, when you have the benefit of wings?" Finesia was there inside my head again. Nattering away. And maybe the boredom of the march caused me to be a little more receptive to her. She might have been scary, but that didn't mean she wasn't entertaining.

Despite the bleakness of the landscape, occasionally we came across a snow fox, or a white rabbit, or a dove. But sometimes, all I needed to do was blink, and they weren't animals at all, but war automatons and hornets ready to close in on us.

The first time this phenomenon occurred was with a small colony of white rabbits that I saw as four war automatons. I blinked again, and these automatons became dark shade-like creatures that I'd only before seen in my nightmares, with white glowing eyes. After another blink, I saw again the wildlife, as innocent as it had always been.

I shook my head and moved over to check on Taka, instructing Talato to accompany me. If I was going to start hallucinating, I figured it was best to keep both of them nearby.

Taka was talking to Faso, or rather should I say, listening to Faso boast about how advanced the dragon automaton was compared to anything anyone had seen before. As I approached, Taka yawned and turned to me.

His eyebrows knotted. "What is it, Auntie Pontopa?" he asked in the collective unconscious.

I shook my head hard. "It's nothing," I said. "Nothing at all," I then said out loud. And one of the marines marching just ahead of us turned to me and looked at me in surprise.

"Get on with your duty, soldier," I snapped. "There's nothing to see here."

He appraised me with a concerned look for a moment and then turned back to focus on putting one foot in front of the other.

"Are you sure you're okay?" Taka said. *"I remember you told Gerhaun that you needed me here if anything went wrong. What's happening, Auntie?"*

"Really, it's nothing... It's going to be okay."

The wind howled across the barren land and whipped against my cheek, numbing it slightly. It brought with it a cold powdered drift of fresh snow. I lifted my scarf to block it off, and Finesia chose that as an apt opportunity to enter my head.

"I can speak to the boy too, you know?" she said. *"There's nothing you can hide from him."*

No, I didn't want this. "Get out of my mind!" I screamed out loud. And Taka jumped back, startled.

This time, several troopers turned to me and put their hands on their rifles. General Sako stepped up from behind and walked up to me. "Dragonseer Wells... What is the meaning of this? You're scaring the boy and unnerving the troops."

"See what I mean about life being one constant struggle?" Finesia said. *"Why don't you just quit now?"*

I pushed her away, then I turned to the general. "Sorry. It won't happen again."

"It better not. Look, I know this is a hard march, and if you need to take a rest at any point, let me know."

"I'll be fine," I said again, and I could hear the irritation in my own voice.

"Good." General Sako nodded and fell back behind the dragons.

"Auntie," Taka said. *"You told me yourself. Don't listen to Finesia. She's talking in my head as well, but I'm not listening to a word she's saying."*

"I know," I said. *"I know."*

And I realised suddenly that I wasn't looking at a little boy's face, but the snout of a black dragon. I recoiled in shock and reached out for my rifle. I felt a hand on my shoulder, and I turned around to see Lieutenant Talato's wide eyes.

"Ma'am?" she asked.

I glanced back at Taka, who was still there. "It's nothing," I said. "Let's continue with the march."

We were all silent for the next several minutes. My muscles were sore from never having walked this far. And I appreciated the pain, because it gave me something to focus on besides my own thoughts.

Ahead of us, the snow lifted off the ground and blew across the horizon in impressive spirals. It danced over the slightly hilly terrain, while sparkles glistened off it from the sunlight. The wind boxed against my right ear and I wished I'd procured some earmuffs.

"Use my gifts," Finesia said. "And you'll never have to worry about pain again. Why fight the weather when you can dance in its shadow?"

"No," I said back to her. "I'll never succumb."

"But it's not a case of succumbing. It's simply you accepting your most natural state. This is what every one of your species ever wanted. To live forever. To propagate and become the most dominant in the whole world. That's why you have doctors, isn't it? To defy death."

"We have them so we can live another day, but we know that death is always on our doorstep."

"Oh, how misguided you are, young acolyte. Soon, you shall realise the truth of your existence."

All of a sudden, I saw the air shimmy in the distance. Behind the eddies of snow dancing in the background, something blossomed. A rising explosion, then another next to it, then a third. Next came the booms, like thunder.

I crouched down, drew the rifle from my back. "Take cover," I shouted. "Defensive positions!"

Several of the marines and commandos ducked down on my command and glanced around, looking for something they could hide behind. But Lieutenant Talato and Taka didn't do anything. Nor did the dragons, for that matter.

"This is no bloody jest," General Sako bawled out from behind me.

He stood behind me, but I didn't turn to him as he spoke. Instead, my gaze was locked on waves upon waves of green shimmering Hummingbirds rising into the sky.

"Can't you see it? We're under attack."

And I had the sensation of something crawling under my skin. Dragon scales, ready to emerge. Ready to complete my transformation.

"This is what you want, my acolyte. Accept who you are."

"Dragonseer Wells," Lieutenant Talato said, and she reached to take something out of her pocket.

General Sako stormed forward, and he turned to me, his face purple. He had a pistol in his hand, though he didn't point it at me, yet. "What's the meaning of this? Explain yourself, or I will have to ask my troops to restrain you."

I blinked, and then I noticed on the horizon nothing was there. Only the silent drift of snow, resplendent and innocent. I put my hands to my temples, and the skin there felt rather dry.

"I'm sorry," I said. "I thought I saw something…"

General Sako's moustache twitched, then he holstered his pistol on his belt. "Lieutenant Talato, make sure you keep a close eye on her and alert me if there's any danger."

"I intend to, sir," she said. And she surveyed me, worry evident in her eyes.

Finesia was no longer in my head, but my heart was pounding heavily in my chest, and my own worries surged within me.

I couldn't do this. There was no way I could keep control. Finesia had a greater dominion over me now. And what if she could also speak to me using my own voice? What if the thoughts I were thinking right now weren't my own? How then could I trust anything at all?

I took a deep breath and centred myself, just as both Sukina and Gerhaun had trained me to do. And, although it wasn't easy, for the rest of the day, I didn't let myself think anything at all.

14

I kept myself calm for the rest of the march. Because I'd blocked off any thoughts that tried to surface in my mind, Finesia had no chance of entering it. We encountered no opposition, and so I only needed to put one foot in front of the other and focus on my breathing. The troops kept eyeing me warily, as well as Faso. But my behaviour had made no one want to talk to me, allowing me to enjoy a period of respite.

Soon enough, the sun sank below the horizon and we entered from day into night. Though it was still pretty early – only early evening – we decided it best to make camp. At this point we were only a few hours' march away from the factory.

We'd seen movement in the distance, thus we knew where we were heading. It turned out that our objective wasn't General Sako's shoe factory, but a remote location in the countryside – a craggy rock face a good fifty or so miles from Ginlast city and out of sight of Ginlast's surrounding villages.

We approached from the north, with the Ginfro river swishing gently in the distance. Lieutenant Candiorno had gone over to the river with a couple of commandos to catch some fish for breakfast. The rest of the soldiers worked, setting up the tents under the flickering light of oil-lanterns attached to stakes driven into the ground. Soon they had the roll mats and sleeping bags laid out, and with the low orange light revealing the interiors through the open flaps, the tents looked much cosier than I'd expected.

To keep warm, I'd already acquired and crawled into my sleeping bag. I'd perched myself upright on a low log as I watched the men work. They had now started setting up a large and tall communal tent in the centre of the camp.

It was early, and I wanted to sit awhile and enjoy the silence of the night, the occasional call of a fox in the distance, and the fresh, cold air. This was the first time in a couple of years I'd been able to leave the Southlands. When you lived in a place for that long, you forgot how good fresh air tasted, despite the slight flavour of camphor coming off the lanterns.

Talato sat next to me – one perk of being my dragonelite, was that she didn't have to muck in on the work, as she needed to stay close to me at all times.

"I hope you don't mind, Ma'am," she said to me once she'd sat herself down. "But General Sako suggested I should sleep in the same tent as you tonight."

Usually, as one of Gerhaun's most senior military, I'd have my own tent. But despite that, I'd already agreed with General Sako and Admiral Sandao that I'd share the tent with Taka to guard over him – and secretly for him to be able to watch over me. But the circumstances, it seemed, had changed this decision.

"I understand entirely," I said. "And it's probably a good idea."

"Very good, Ma'am," Lieutenant Talato said. "Those drugs you gave me. I almost thought I should drop a tablet down your throat. You looked as if you were going to lose control."

I nodded. "I thought so too. Though, this is probably just an effect of me coming off the cyagora. I need to learn to control Finesia inside my own mind."

"Does she really talk to you, Ma'am? I mean, the reason I don't believe in the Gods Themselves and stuff is I like to believe..." She blushed and tugged on her collar. "I like to believe that we're agents of our own free will."

"So did Charth," I said, and I gazed off into the darkness, wondering if any wildlife was watching us from the void.

General Sako and Taka sat on a log a few yards away from Talato and I. The older man stayed close to the boy, warily looking up at me every so often. And Taka looked completely bored, without even a book to read. But every time he shifted even an inch, General Sako would place his hand on Taka's knee as if to keep him in place.

Meanwhile, the troops had almost finished setting up the central communal tent – where we could soon sit to get some extra warmth. I watched them scurry around, producing long metal poles from the rucksacks and slotting them together to form a scaffolding.

Suddenly, there came a commotion from behind me, and one marine leapt to his feet, drew his rifle, and pointed it into the distance.

"What is it, Private?" General Sako said, leaping off his perch.

"There's a man coming in our direction. Halt right there!"

But the man didn't stop, and soon enough I saw him in the light. He had a gaunt face, a bald head dotted with blood clots, an emaciated body, and was wrapped in rags that didn't quite look like they'd protect him from the cold. I could see how pale his skin was, and it had a very light green glow to it – a sign of secicao addiction.

"What should I do, sir?" the marine asked.

"Challenge him," General Sako said.

And the sentry stepped in front of the intruder aiming, his rifle at him "Halt! Who goes there?" he shouted. Only then did the visitor seem to realise he was in danger. He stopped, looked at the man, and raised his hands as he tottered from side to side.

"I come in peace," he replied, though his words sounded slurred. "I mean you no harm…"

"State your intention, man," General Sako said. "Why did you come here?"

"I came from the factory…" he said. "Please… I needed it."

"You needed what?"

"I needed to escape. They don't let us out, I tell you. But *I* got out."

I shrugged the sleeping bag off my shoulders, stepped out of it, and walked over to the man. No one moved to stop me, although Lieutenant Talato tagged along closely on my heels.

"What did they do to you?" I asked. "And how could you come from a factory that is run by automatons?"

That's what the article that Papo had shown me last week had said. The factory didn't need a single person on site.

"That's what they say? But –" His eyes glazed over. "– the rabbits, they watch over us. And beware of the Gods Themselves, because they have deserted us and left bears and wolves in their place. The squirrels and the rabbits, they talk to me in the night. They climb trees and they fly in the sky. And the shades will descend from above, and the sky will turn dark. Then it shall start."

"He's stark raving mad," General Sako said. And the old general glared at me, as if suggesting I might be the same.

"He shouldn't be here," Finesia said in my mind. *"You must destroy him."*

I felt an urge to reach for one of the knives in my boots, but I restrained myself. Beneath the man's rags, I could see how much he was shivering. After all, he was barely wearing any clothes.

"He needs medical attention," I said.

General Sako nodded and turned to the communal tent. It now had the canvas over it and emitted a soft warm glow from the fire burning inside and the oil lamps hanging from the supporting poles.

"Set up a bed. And make sure he's kept warm. Bostok, you're the medic here." General Sako turned to one of his own commandos – a man with a thin moustache and pockmarked chin. "Congratulations you have your first patient."

"Affirmative, sir." The medic saluted.

A marine stepped forward and then restrained the gaunt man with an arm-lock behind his back. He jostled the man towards the communal tent. Bostok retrieved a medical kit from the backpack in his tent, and then followed after the marine.

General Sako looked at me, turned to Lieutenant Talato, and then cast his gaze back at me again. "Dragonseer Wells. I must ask, are you now in charge of your mental faculties?"

I lowered my head, feeling a little ashamed about what had happened before. I could try telling him I'd never really lost it, but that would cause the general and the troops to lose confidence in me even more.

"I am," I said.

"Good. You need to keep yourself in check. We can't afford to have any incidents out here."

I nodded. "Don't worry, I have given Lieutenant Talato express orders about what to do in such extreme circumstances."

General Sako twitched his moustache. "Very well. Candiorno, look after Taka a while, will you?"

The ruddy-faced lieutenant saluted sharply and walked up to the boy who didn't look too happy.

"Can't I come into the tent too?" Taka asked.

"Not until we've assessed the danger of the situation," General Sako said. And decided, I knew he was implying, if we'd need to interrogate the prisoner using extreme measures.

Taka huffed, some steam arising from his mouth into the air. "Fine, I'll just stand out here in the cold."

I shrugged and gave Taka a sympathetic smile. *We'll get this out of the way quickly,* I promised him in the collective unconscious. *Meanwhile, keep Velos company.*

Taka nodded, then turned to Candiorno. "Come on, Lieutenant," he said. "We're going to pay the dragons a visit."

Surprise registered on Candiorno's face, obviously not expecting to receive an order from the boy. But he shrank under General Sako's glare and hastily followed Taka around the side of the tent.

I'D NEVER APPRECIATED warmth so much in my life. The fire had just lit up in full, and as soon as I entered the tent, it already made the place feel like a sauna, as it melted the snow off the ground.

"Hot and cold... why do you need them?" Finesia said in my mind. *"To an immortal, they serve no purpose. You'll never have to worry about freezing in the snow or burning your hand in the fire."*

I let the voice run wild in my head, not doing anything about it. Then, I walked up to the man lying on the bed. His eyes had distinctive purple bags under them, now half-closed, evidently about to drift off. But still he turned towards me as I approached.

"The bears... the wolves. Automatons come to murder us in the night, and if we don't comply. The man. He's not a man, but one of the Gods Themselves. The lady, she's in my head, and calls herself... No, no, the automatons. They will murder me. I must say no more..."

"This man doesn't belong here," Finesia continued. *"It's your duty to put him out of his misery."*

Meanwhile, General Sako reached out and felt the man's forehead with the back of his hand. He was sweating buckets underneath the blanket, but then that wasn't surprising with the amount of heat roaring out from the central fire.

"It burns, yet it's so cold," the man said. "The claw of an automaton and the hand of an empress. Silence, no. My thoughts are my own, but they are not my own. What can the wolves and the bears tell me that the Gods Themselves can't?"

General Sako turned to Bostok who was sitting at a small table at the head of the bed, transferring some blood from a syringe into a petri dish. "Can you give him something to calm him down?"

The medic shook his head. "Unfortunately, Doctor Forsolano told me we were out of our supply of suppressive drugs when I asked for a restock."

Out of the corner of my eye, I noticed Talato wanted to say something. But I glared daggers at her to stop her from doing so. To reveal we had the cyagora might also mean – after my brief 'incident' – General Sako would demand I was put on it without realising the consequences.

"I'm a slave," the man continued. "A slave to the automatons. A slave to humanity. A slave to those that live outside the void. Bring the whole place down and melt the automatons into liquid metal. But I can't… She won't let me. She's not ready yet. She watches me every step of the way…"

I'd had just about enough of all this. We didn't know how much time we had. I stepped forward and took hold of the man's chin. He didn't seem to resist and looked at me with glazed over eyes.

"That's it, my acolyte. You're learning fast." Dragonheats, I couldn't get her out of my head.

"Tell me what this is about?" I said. "What are these automatons, and who is it that's watching you?"

The man's pupils dilated as he looked at me, and he paused a moment, before coughing slightly. I turned my head away from him and removed my hand from his chin.

"The void," he said. "The demons, they'll come for you, lady. She'll come, and you will become like her. In the land where the demons roam. You mustn't trust her. She wants to destroy everything."

And, suddenly, I wasn't looking into a man's eyes, but two white stones set into a pitch dark form that seemed to suck in the surrounding light. The darkness swirled, and out of it grew obsidian-coloured tendrils towards everyone present in the room.

They would lash out and sap our life force. They would kill without remorse.

I jumped back, startled.

"He's not of this world," Finesia said inside my head. *"And he will destroy you if you don't take his life first. You must embrace your destiny, my Acolyte."*

"Ma'am?" Lieutenant Talato had stepped in between me and the patient. "Is everything okay?"

I looked past her to see that the gaunt, pale-faced man had now fallen asleep.

"I'm fine," I said. "I'm going to get some rest, I think. It's been a long day."

"I'll stand guard outside your tent, Ma'am," Talato said.

And we both walked out into the bitter night.

IN A WAY, I regretted leaving the warmth of the tent so early. I mean, the sleeping bag was pretty warm, and the sheepskin mat protected me from the hoary floor. But still the cold air stung at my cheeks. All the while, I lay on my back with the darkness whirling above me and Finesia running rampant inside my head.

I reached that point between dreams and reality, where I didn't know whether I was awake, and as far as I was concerned, it didn't matter. Finesia's nattering voice abated in my head and the dreams came.

A majestic alabaster light replaced the void, and dark creatures whirled above me, not the shades I'd seen in my hallucinations earlier that day, but brilliant black dragons.

I woke up, and I realised the danger in such dreams. I needed the cyagora to push them away, but I didn't have the strength to lift myself. Lieutenant Talato was outside. Yet I couldn't force my mouth open wide enough to call her, and I couldn't force my eyes open to will my body into action.

I was asleep, or was I? Beside me, I saw Talato's backpack. Maybe she kept the cyagora in there. Unlikely, but there was a chance, wasn't there? After all, the jar was far too big to fit in her pocket. She would likely, therefore, keep only some tablets on her, and a larger amount somewhere else.

I pulled myself up in the sleeping bag, and I rummaged around in her bag, feeling no guilt for rifling through her belongings. In it, I found clothes, and a selection of daggers meant for murder. Each one was a unique colour, and they looked exactly like red and white striped candy canes. Yet I found no cyagora.

But I wasn't in the real world anyway but an imaginary one in my dreams.

And I couldn't awaken. My eyelids were too heavy, my muscles too numb.

So, within this dream, I put my head against the trench coat I'd laid out as a pillow, and I drifted off into another world.

I WOKE up with a sour tang on my tongue.

I wasn't at camp, and it was light outside.

There was no tent covering me. There were no troops around me. I had no sleeping bag. I was naked, alone, and shivering.

Above, the brown clouds roiled. Secicao, marvellous secicao, spraying the world with its aroma. Branches of it twisting out into a gloriously sodden sky. Its roots plunging into the soil, sapping out the chances of any life to grow here.

secicao... I can breathe here without a mask.

And I'm alone.

Except I'm not.

For there's another.

"Wench," she says. Not Finesia, but Alsie Fioreletta inside my head. *"You've been refusing to accept your destiny, and now I have been sent to destroy you. You will not take my place as Finesia's right hand, I will make sure of that."*

I jump up off the ground, and find myself looking straight into Alsie Fioreletta's brilliant green eyes. The cool secicao wind whips her raven hair against her face. It spills down her bare shoulders and over her naked back and breasts.

Yet, when I blink, I notice she's not naked but tightly clad in a suit of black armour. She has a claymore strapped to her back, which she draws with surprising deftness and grace. She points the tip of the tremendous weapon at me, wielding it like it's as light as a piece of hollow wood.

Fortunately, I'm not naked either but also resplendent in a hardy coat of leather armour, mine more brown. It's flexible and I stretch out my legs. I have on my boots and garters, and I reach down to retrieve my knives.

"This will be our ultimate battle," I say to Alsie out loud. "And I shall win, as I always do."

"Not yet, you won't," she replies. "For you do not quite understand your true destiny. How can you assume what will happen when you have paid no heed to Finesia's plans?"

I grit my teeth. "No! I shall never succumb to her will."

"And that is why we must battle."

I don't need to listen to any more of her nonsense. I scream out in rage and I lunge forwards with a flurry of knife strokes. But Alsie's sword transforms into a whip which she lashes around me, restraining me for a moment. She retracts the weapon, and transfers it to another hand, where it becomes a burning short sword. Then she vanishes, in a plume of black smoke.

I search around for the dragon, but find nothing. Impossible, she has to be here somewhere.

"What's the matter?" she says from behind.

I spin around again, but there's no sign of her.

"Have you already forgotten the nature of my abilities? I can make it so you can't see what's there. And I can also make you see what's not there." It's as if I have an invisible monkey perched on my shoulder, nattering in my ear. I can't see her anywhere, but she's so close.

"Reveal yourself, Alsie Fioreletta. This is cowardice."

"Said the barbarian to the master tactician... And this is why you'll never truly win, because deep inside you cannot understand."

And there she is, lying on a marble sacrificial altar in front of me. She wears a long royal red dress that shows off her slender shoulders. A brilliant light shines out from her alabaster skin. Her eyes are closed and she looks placid, as if sleeping. She has her hands folded on her lap, and one calf is crossed over the other.

"Give Finesia what she wants and end this now, she says. It is, as you said, our ultimate battle."

My hands start to tingle as sparks dance around the metal of the knives.

"This is what you've always wanted, my dear," Finesia says in my mind. "It shall complete you."

I approach hungrily, and raise my right hand above my head, feeling the power coursing through the hilt of the weapon. I take a deep, satisfactory breath, and then I plunge the knife down into Alsie's chest. She opens her eyes in shock and gasps.

Then, out of her wound emerges another plume of black smoke. I stand, panting, watching the patterns dance in the smoke, that soon conceals the body completely. After it subsides, both Alsie and the altar have vanished.

Next thing I know, I'm being grasped by firm hands from behind. Alsie's voice rasps in my ear, an acrid unpleasantness to her flowery breath. "Do you really think it's that simple, Dragonseer Wells? Our destinies are not meant yet to intertwine and still you insist on destroying me. One day, we will fight and only fate itself will determine who wins. And it won't be until the day you finally learn to embrace what's meant to be."

I smell a whiff of something metallic and enticing. Exalmpora. And I want it.

"Do it," Finesia's says. "Claim your destiny."

"No!" I say, wrestling within Alsie's grasp.

"Do it, acolyte. This will complete you... Or choose not to and accept your death."

I try to bite at Alsie's hand, but the grip is too strong. I slash at her leg with one of my knives, but she already has my wrist in a hold that I cannot escape from. She twists this, causing pain to sear into my tendons. I let go of the knife and it falls to the ground..

But I still have the second one in my left hand. I squirm and draw strength from the rage inside me. I use this to plunge the knife into Alsie's thigh.

She roars out from behind. But before she can transform into a dragon, I duck and throw her over my shoulder. She lies flat on her back on the ground, again clad in a suit of leather armour. I launch myself upon her, straddling her chest with my thighs as I go for her throat with my knife.

Vile creatures surround me, closing in. Once again, it's the shades. From their bodies, dark, wispy tentacles lash out into the air. They suck in all the light around them as they close in even further.

Soon, they'll lunge, and if I don't take Alsie's life they will destroy me.

I ready myself to cut at the skin on Alsie's throat.

But the shades open their mouths collectively and let out this terrible scream. It washes over the secicao jungle, plunging the sky into momentary darkness. The scream comes again and I drop my knife to the floor.

Alsie knocks it away with her hand, and it spins through the seci-cao, cutting through branches with its lightning infused blade as it goes.

"*Auntie Pontopa,*" a voice says, like a child's. "*Push her away.*"

"*Taka?*" No, he mustn't be here. This battle is between me and Alsie.

"*Shut the voice out,*" Finesia says. "*Don't let anyone claim your destiny as their own.*"

I nod, and I grasp Alsie's throat with my hands. Power surges through me. My arms grow, my fingers become claws, scales crawl underneath my skin, my body writhes, and I roar up to the sky, ecstatic in pain.

One shade, a tiny ratty creature, comes up to me and looks upon me with those evil, white eyes. "*Auntie, please. You don't want to kill her.*"

"*Taka? Are you here?*"

I lift myself slightly, giving Alsie enough room to slide away from me. Dragonheats, I'm letting her get away. She produces something from her pocket and something hits my head hard. But I recover my power quickly, dark secicao coursing through my veins.

I'll defeat Alsie in dragon form if that's what it takes. I'll rip out her throat, removing her from the immortal coil.

But the terrible scream comes again, so strong it forces me to the ground. I clutch at my head in pain. Next thing I know, Alsie is upon me with a vial of green poison in her hand. I try to push back, but I lack strength.

Alsie pours the poison into my mouth, closes it, holds my nose, and yanks my head back by my hair. I have no choice but to swallow. The liquid travels down my throat – feeling like a massive solid lump.

Pain, intense pain. A throbbing in my head. Forces trying to take over my body. And something within me, fighting back. My body shaking as if wracked by a terrible disease. Sweat flooding to my brow. Stinging tears welling at the corners of my eyes…

Whiteness embracing the void. Everything white... No clarity for miles...

The wide scared eyes of my dragonelite guard, Lieutenant Talato, waving her hand in front of me. Over her right thigh, a gashing open wound.

"Ma'am? Are you back with us?"

"Lieutenant..."

She had me pinned against the side of the tent by my arms, her strength astounding. But once she realised I was safe, she ripped off a piece of her shirt and wrapped it around the wound on her leg.

I turned my head to see the jar of cyagora broken on the floor; the tablets scattered around it. At one end of the tent, I saw the malnourished man from the factory, lying dead on his bed, one of my knives buried deep into his chest. At another end, Taka was crouched down, crying into his hands.

He looked at me with red-rimmed eyes, and a tear dropped from his cheek. Then, he ran over to me and hugged me around the neck. "Please Auntie Pontopa, whatever you do, never do that again? Promise me?"

But without knowing what had just happened, I didn't know what to say.

I felt remarkably tired all of a sudden. And so, I fell onto the hard, icy floor, and I drifted into a deep, silent sleep.

PART V

TRAVAST

"Why is it that the imbeciles get all the fame, while scientists' names can only be found in journals and textbooks?"

— TRAVAST INDORM

15

I woke up just before dawn on the same bed that the man from the factory had been resting on. I shifted my body, expecting to see myself lying in a pool of blood. But I was stopped by restraints clamped around my wrists and ankles. I jangled the chains in an attempt to get free, then I turned my head towards clean sheets. If they'd had blood on them, someone had wiped it away.

I took a deep breath, and then I lay back, and let the warmth from the embers of the fire pit wash over my cheek. The lanterns were still on, suffusing the inner walls with a soft, amber light.

Lieutenant Talato was sitting behind my head, in a chair. She stood up and walked over to me. "I'm sorry, Ma'am. But I needed to take precautions."

"I understand," I said. "And I cannot express the guilt I feel. I'm sorry, Talato."

Talato's eyes opened wide. "You mean you know you did it? You looked like you were sleepwalking or something, Ma'am?"

I nodded. "I was. Kind of. Look, it doesn't take a genius to piece together what happened. How much cyagora did you give me?"

The lieutenant shook her head. "About three tablets in the end. I wasn't sure how many it would take."

"That should last a while. And presumably Taka used his scream... That's what weakened me? Where is he now?"

"I don't know what he did, Ma'am. He went back to General Sako's tent and promised to remain silent about this. I don't know about any scream. I saw Taka put his hand to his temples. I had no idea what he was doing, but he looked very focused."

That made sense. The scream only worked in the collective unconscious and would have only hurt those that had a connection. The dragons would have felt it. But not the men in their tents, although they would have been awoken once the dragons started roaring.

Taka... I'd forced him to use Finesia's gift, drawing him even closer to her. That part hurt the most.

"Did anyone else see what happened?" I asked.

"Negative, Ma'am. The lights weren't on in here, and then the dragons started making a commotion, so I heard the men running off to check on them. I doubted they even thought to look in this tent."

"Probably for the best." I wondered if the dragons had created a diversion to protect me. "Has anyone woken up yet?"

"No, Ma'am."

I let off a sigh of relief. I had less explaining to do than I'd feared. I turned towards the crackling firepit to see a piece of charcoal break off and crumble into red-hot embers on the floor.

"You can release the restraints now," I said. "I'm safe..."

Talato raised an eyebrow. "But can I trust you? What I saw, it looked like magic... The skin on your face started twisting, and you looked in so much pain, and then I could swear I saw scales. Did this Wiggea creature do this? Did he cast some kind of curse on you or something? Because I can't find a rational explanation."

I looked her straight in the eye. If she was going to be my bodyguard, she needed to learn how to safeguard me from every possible danger. "Is there a rational explanation to Wiggea, Talato?"

Talato looked down at her hands. "No, Ma'am. Try as I might, I can't seem to think of what could have happened to him."

"Then, it's about time you started to accept that the world isn't quite as you think. Faso's science can't explain this stuff. What you saw was the work of Finesia. This is what I've been so afraid of all this time."

Talato's face blanched. "It's impossible. I've seen some strange things in life. But something taking over your mind like that and altering your physical substance without permission? No, that's something I can't believe… I'm sorry, Ma'am."

"We may see things a little differently, Lieutenant, and it's up to you what you believe. But please, right now, I can assure you. The threat has passed."

Talato looked me straight in the eye a moment. Then, she moved a little closer and perched herself on the side of the bed. She started unbuckling the leather straps around my wrists.

Soon, my legs were also freed, and I shifted the blanket away from me. Again, I wondered if I'd see bloodstains on my clothing but, remarkably, I couldn't find a trace.

"What happened to the rest of the cyagora?" I asked. I remembered seeing the shattered jar last night, but there wasn't a single shard of glass on the floor.

"I've retrieved them all and put them somewhere safe. Ma'am, with all due respect, I really think you should continue your course. What did Doctor Forsolano recommend? I don't want to have to fight you again."

I looked down at the makeshift bandage that staunched her wound – an olive-coloured piece of cloth, a patch of dried blood in the centre.

"I understand your concern, Lieutenant. But when I'm on cyagora, I can't command the dragons. And without knowing exactly what we're up against, we might need an organised force. What about the man, by the way?" A sour taste developed in my mouth. "Is he dead?"

"Yes, Ma'am. And I disposed of the body as soon as the coast was clear."

"Do you know if anyone got something out of him, before…"

"No. But the medic didn't feel his condition was because of his mental state alone."

"What do you mean?"

"He found traces of a drug in his blood samples that might have caused his delirium. We called Mr Gordoni and Miss Winda in to confirm, and they said something about the drug being much like that one you caught Taka taking."

My heart skipped a beat in my chest. "What is Travast Indorm up to?"

"I wish I knew, Ma'am. But there's a lot more going on here, I think, than meets the eye."

I stopped to gaze at the walls of the tent for a moment. The embers kept crackling in front of us, and a fox yipping in the distance punctuated the swishing of the wind. The sound of the tent door unzipping interrupted the relative silence. I turned to it, startled. The flaps gave way, to reveal General Sako's stout figure, framed by darkness.

"Blunders and dragonheats! What are you both doing here yapping away at this time?" He turned to me, sitting on the bed. "What the hell happened to our prisoner, dammit?"

"He got away, sir," Lieutenant Talato lied. "Slashed me with a knife and ran out the door."

General Sako's eyes opened wide. "Then we must raise a search party. If he alerts the enemy to our position, we're toast."

"That won't be necessary," I said.

"Why not?"

"Because I've already killed him. I threw a knife in his back shortly after he ran out the doors."

He eyed me warily. "You don't seem to me like a cold-blooded assassin."

"I understand the risks of the situation, General, and I did what was necessary."

"And how the dragonheats did he get hold of the knife in the first place?"

"He stole it out of my garters as I was seeing to the fire. Somehow, he seemed to know exactly where it was. I guess it was unlucky for him he didn't take both of them."

"And so, what happened to the body?"

I turned to Talato. "We've already buried him. We figured that having his body around would just lower the morale of the troops."

The general's gaze drifted off towards the fire pit as if deep in thought. He took his secicao pipe from his breast pocket and lit it up. Then he took a huff on it. But he said nothing more, and turned on his heel towards the door, the pipe clenched between his lips. "I guess now that we're up, we might as well call an early march."

He stormed outside and started clapping his hand against the sides of the tents. "Rise and shine, soldiers. It's time to make up some breakfast." And with the volume at which he bawled out his orders, one would have thought there was no danger of being detected at all.

16

By the time the stew was ready, dawn was breaking. The aroma of fish, tomatoes, oregano, and pepper wafted into the air filling the tent. The fire burned bright again, and the troops had gathered to warm their hands in the heat from it. Meanwhile, the cooking pot continued to cast its spell, making us hungrier and hungrier.

Lieutenant Candiorno, the chef, huddled over the pot, stirring the bubbling red stew with a wooden spoon. He'd added two large fish and twenty cans of tomatoes, alongside generous doses of herbs and spices. With such generosity, one wouldn't think we were marching on rations at all. Another pot of rice bubbled underneath the stew, containing a good kilogram of grain.

I walked over to peer out of the tent flap for a moment to see the sky had got even greyer. Faso, while sampling the stew, had told us a blizzard was en route. I cast my thoughts over to the Saye Explorer and the rest of the flotilla and wondered how they fared. I hoped they hadn't had to deal with automatons, as they were much more sitting ducks than we.

I had sensed no distress from the dragons on ships. But then, I remembered, I'd just taken three tablets of cyagora. That's why I didn't feel so well and also why I couldn't feel the pull of the dragon's souls. I'd never taken three tablets before in one dose. So I had no idea how soon its effects would wear off.

But at least Finesia had stopped raging inside my head. I truly couldn't understand the extent of her powers. Which meant, without the cyagora, I'd never know if I was safe.

"Okay, plate up," Lieutenant Candiorno said, banging his wooden spoon against the pot. "Breakfast is served."

Everyone but Lieutenant Talato, who watched me with her characteristic caution, pushed their plates forward, eagerly eyeing the ladle. Ratter found his way through the tangle of forearms and perched himself on the rim of the pot. A metal bowl hung from his snout on a piece of wire. He lowered this into the stew and scurried back to Faso, Winda, and Taka, who had seated themselves by the canvas on three folding chairs.

As if on its own accord, the bowl rose towards Ratter's mouth. Soon after, the automaton clasped its brass lips around the edge, and tipped the stew into Winda's, Taka's, and Faso's bowls on the floor.

General Sako looked at them disdainfully, but his attention was quickly diverted by Lieutenant Candiorno pouring two ladles of stew over a serving of rice on his plate. I took two more plates – one for me, one for Talato – from the stool by the pot. I pushed them forwards, and Candiorno, gentlemen that he was, served me before everyone else.

It was the best thing I'd tasted in a long time, not just because of the cooking but also it really helped heat the body up from the inside. This kind of weather got you cold underneath the clothing, no matter how many layers you had on. But the meal gave me the energy I would need to march another day.

Unfortunately, the cyagora also pushed away any pleasure I might gain from the taste. Where I expected the tanginess of tomatoes and slight bitterness of oregano, instead there was only emptiness.

"You know," Faso said between mouthfuls. "We should tamp down this fire immediately. It was bad enough when some moron turned the lights on in the tent last night. But now, the heat signatures will attract attention, for sure."

"Don't be a fool, Gordoni," General Sako said. "Who's going to see anything behind these grey clouds?"

"People might not, but automatons will."

"I thought you said they didn't operate well in cold conditions."

"I said that they're not equipped for marching over ice. That doesn't mean their sensors will fail. A blizzard won't freeze them out of operation."

"Very well," General Sako said. "Everyone put out the fire before you eat another spoonful." The troops let out a groan but jumped to their feet. They took hold of some buckets of melted snow that rested beside the tent wall and threw the contents over the fire.

I noticed how quickly they'd got the job done. Clearly, everyone here was pretty hungry. And so, we all continued to tuck into our food – Ratter even edging over the pot to get another portion for Faso, Winda, and Taka.

Just as I was down to my last few spoonfuls, a whirring sound erupted from outside. The marines and commandos jerked their rifles off of their backs and filed out the door. Outside, they crouched in a defensive formation.

"Don't shoot, don't shoot," Faso shouted, and he ran out and started scurrying around, pushing the soldiers' rifles down. I followed him out, trailed by Talato and General Sako.

"Gordoni, boy…" General Sako said. "What's the meaning of this?"

"Those are my Hummingbirds that you hear approaching. I sent several out last night on a recon."

General Sako's moustache twitched. "Lower your weapons, soldiers. Next time, you should tell me before you send anything out into the field. What if they alerted the enemy to our location, or that same enemy extracted information about our origins from their recordings?"

"That is exactly why I programmed them using advanced techniques so they wouldn't be spotted," Faso replied, his hands on his hips. "As for the data, I've made sure none of my new-generation Hummingbirds start recording until they get to their destination. Technology is evolving, you know, General Sako."

"And how can you be so sure these are our automatons, and not some decoys sent by Travast Indorm?"

"Because this device tells me so." Faso took a small flat disk from his pocket. It consisted of two glass plates, sandwiching a layer of water and what looked like a glob of liquid metal. The silver part pushed towards the edge of the disc in the direction from which we could hear the Hummingbirds approaching.

I watched in anticipation as they appeared from behind the ever-thickening cloud cover. They wavered in the strong wind currents, and settled just in front of Ratter, who was supervising their approach from the ground.

"I'll set up in the tent," Faso said. "We need to examine their findings." He rushed back inside.

ONLY HALF of the commandos and marines were in the tent once the pot had been put away and Faso had set up his devices. The rest stood outside, either standing guard or washing the cooking equipment using the remaining buckets of melted snow. Meanwhile, the more senior of us – the sergeants and corporals and lieutenants – had chairs set up in front of a section of the tent wall to serve as the screen. Meanwhile Faso fiddled with Ratter at the back of the tent.

Soon enough, he screwed the projection lens into the socket inside Ratter's mouth, and the first image came up on the screen. The night before had been a little clearer than I'd realised, and a streaky Aurora Borealis stretched across the sky. The initial Hummingbird we'd sent out as a scout hadn't got close enough to the factory to see how it was constructed. But now, Faso's automatons had captured it in its full glory.

The complex was impressively melded into the rock face, with a few chimneys spewing out green smoke. A heavy brass door sealed off the entrances to the factory, operable by an intricate network of cogs on one side. Hummingbird and war automatons guarded the surrounding terrain, but they weren't the only forms to grace the night.

Many men and women were also scattered around the grounds, hammering at the rock with pickaxes. They all looked malnourished and barely wore any clothing, much like the man that I'd killed in this very tent. At first, I wondered how they could survive the extreme chill. But the green tint to their skin told all – they were augmented on secicao.

One Hummingbird had got right up close to the face of one male to create a magazine-worthy portrait photograph of him. His skin was pockmarked and his eyes looked glazed, as if he didn't know the automaton was there.

"Hah," Faso laughed out from the back of the room. "It seems that Travast Indorm's autonomously producing automaton factory is not so autonomous after all."

I ignored his snarky comment. Faso's internal ego match with Travast Indorm didn't seem so important right now.

"I guess the first question we need to address is," I said, "where did these men come from?" Then I remembered the articles that Papo had talked about in the Tow Observer, and I suddenly put two and two together… "The convicts."

General Sako nodded. "I read about them. Wellies, you aren't saying that–"

"Cini increased the number of arrests in the northern continent, so he could send them to the factory to work as slaves."

"See what I mean," Faso said, sounding rather amused at the back. "This factory isn't even complete yet. And who knows when they'll even finish it."

"And if the king completes it, then we will have a whole lot of trouble down south." General Sako said. "We have to take it down now, before they finish whatever it is they're building."

"I think it might take a while," Faso said.

"Blunders and dragonheats! Have you seen the size of this thing?"

"No, all I see is a wall of rock, with a few cogs arranged around it, some chimneys, and some big, heavy doors."

"And a lot of automatons," I said. "Where do you think they came from? Don't you think there might be a lot more beneath that rock?"

Behind me, Faso shrugged. "There's just no way Cini could have built so many automatons in such a small timescale. He just doesn't have the resources."

"I think you're wrong, Gordoni," General Sako said. "And I also suspect there's more to this factory than meets the eye."

Taka now leaned against the wall next to the entrance to the tent, one leg crossed over the other and his arms folded over his chest. Seeing him there reminded me.

"What's the purpose of this drug that Travast is feeding them, I wonder. They all look like they're augmented…"

"To make them loyal, of course," Faso said from the back. "And from what we saw yesterday, it would seem this drug causes some kind of insanity."

"But then why would Travast also give the drug to Taka?"

The boy straightened up his posture when he realised we were talking about him. But when everyone present turned to look at him he shrunk back towards the doorway. One by one, we returned our eyes to the screen.

"Maybe," Faso said. "Travast Indorm wanted Taka to be obedient. So, he would do exactly what he was told to do. Much like, I hear, Exalmpora did to you in the palace."

"No, it's more than that." I stood up and clenched my fists. "This is the work of Finesia."

Beside me, Lieutenant Talato turned to me with an expression of shock. She reached into her inner pocket. A murmuring came from everyone seated, and General Sako was again watching me cautiously.

I walked over to General Sako and turned to face the room. "It's about time, you all learned what we're up against. Because it's come to my attention that many of you don't understand the true nature of the threat." The fact that Lieutenant Talato couldn't quite believe it, told me that others might also be in the same boat.

"You may think our enemy is King Cini, but he's only part of the threat. You may think our enemy is Alsie Fioreletta, but in fact she's just acting under orders of another. Our true enemy is the Empress Finesia. Much as dragonseer minds can transcend the collective unconscious, the empress you know from myth is trying to take control of our psyche. She lives inside the head of every single dragonman and dragonwoman. She'll take control of mine and Taka's minds if we're not vigilant. She recently took control of Charth's. And, from what we saw at East Cadigan island, it looks like she may one day control the minds of normal humans too."

I kept scanning the faces of the marines and commandos as I talked to them, but I only saw astonished, incredulous faces. At the back, Faso was also scratching his chin, Winda standing beside him looking at me with a concerned expression.

"Sit down, Pontopa," General Sako said. "And please, stop it with your fantasies."

I sighed. "I think I'd rather get a breath of fresh air. Please continue with the briefing. I'll be back shortly."

And I walked towards the exit. Lieutenant Talato and Taka followed me outside.

WE WALKED out into a nascent blizzard. The wind stifled my breath, making the air not seem as fresh as I'd hoped.

I wasn't even angry as such, the cyagora wouldn't let me be. I just didn't like the way everyone here had started passing judgement on me. They didn't understand what we dragonseers had to deal with. If Gerhaun was here, she'd quickly set them straight.

I stared out at the men who patrolled through the growing wall of snow. Others were working at packing up the tents, which couldn't have been the easiest job in such strong winds. Lieutenant Talato lit a cigarette and she stood between Taka and I, as if worried I'd damage the boy.

"I didn't know you smoked," I said.

"Not usually, Ma'am. But sometimes I need to, you know, introduce a little comfort."

"I understand," I said. Not everyone in this world had to be so austere.

Taka had edged around Talato a little and was looking up at me, his hands on his temples. He seemed to be concentrating hard on something, and it didn't take me long to work out he was trying to speak to me in the collective unconscious.

"It won't work while I have the cyagora in me," I said.

Taka smacked himself on the head. "Of course. That's why I've not been able to reach you. I've been trying to, after –"

"I know," I said. "And, yes, I guess we need to talk."

"But with the cyagora, you can't communicate with the dragons, right?"

"That's right," I said, feeling empty all of a sudden.

"They're doing well, by the way," Taka said. "They're a bit unnerved by the blizzard because none of them have ever gone through one before, but otherwise okay."

"That's good," I said. Then I crouched down to him. "Taka, I'm sorry."

"It's okay, Auntie Pontopa. Now I understand why you needed the cyagora. I'm just worried. After what happened to Charth... And what's happening to you... Will it happen to me too?"

"Not if we find a way to keep Finesia out. We've got to keep trying. We can never give up. If we focus only on the fear, she will take dominion."

"Does that mean you won't take any more tablets?" Taka asked.

I turned to Lieutenant Talato, who nodded. "I'll only take them if I absolutely need to," I said. "My connection to the collective unconscious is important for all of us. And Lieutenant Talato has agreed to keep an eye on me."

"I just hope you don't hurt anyone again."

I raised my eyebrows, surprised that Taka trusted me after what I'd done. I really thought he'd be more afraid of me. But maybe what he'd experienced when taking Travast's concoctions helped him understand. I guess he'd seen things that terrified him too.

Taka walked around Lieutenant Talato and took hold of my hand.

He tugged me back towards the tent. "Come on. You know what you have to do, Auntie Pontopa."

I looked down at him, surprised. "What's that?"

"If you can't prove to them that they can trust you now, they're never going to. But you're still in charge of the dragons, and in this weather it's a perfect time to spy on the factory, don't you think?"

"But our troops will march there in a day."

"The blizzard will be gone by then. Auntie, you know this makes sense. You need to get there fast."

"Taka, the drug won't have worn off by then."

"And nothing will see you coming. No one would expect you to fly in this weather. But with dragonsongs, you can handle it. And I can come and help as well."

"No... It's too dangerous."

"Auntie, remember what Gerhaun said. Besides, I'm sure Talato will look after me."

I sighed. How had we been roped into taking a child on such a dangerous mission, anyway? What would Sukina have said? "Let's see what your grandfather thinks about that," I said. And before Taka could get in another word, I turned to Talato. "Come on, Lieutenant. I have some convincing to do."

And I marched back into the tent, my vigour renewed.

"WE MUST CHARGE while we have the element of surprise," General Sako said to the room just as I entered the tent. "We know where the factory is, and now we can take it in force."

"No," Faso replied from his place standing at the back, waving his arms animatedly as he spoke. "There are civilians there. Charging in guns blazing during a blizzard is just going to get innocent people killed."

"Innocent? These people have been committed for crimes, many of them heinous."

"And can you rely on King Cini's judicial system to be just?"

"Blunders and dragonheats! We have no choice. They still work for the enemy, and that's enough reason in my book to consider them collateral."

It seemed, in my absence, the meeting hadn't progressed. And really, given the only person who dared answer back to General Sako was Faso, I wasn't sure there'd been any point calling a meeting at all. It was incredibly warm in here. The heat from the dying fireplace plucked at my thawing cheeks.

"If we have no idea what's inside the factory," I said, as I walked over to my seat but remained standing. "Then we should find out, surely, before we make any further decisions."

"One or two scouts are just going to get shot down." General Sako said. "There could be a host of war automatons ready to ambush whoever we send out there. We need numbers, not scouts."

"The very fact that the factory is being run by convicts and not automatons, suggests that they don't have as many there as we first thought."

"And," Faso said. "One thing I didn't tell you about the dragon automaton and Velos' helmet, is both can also see heat signatures through walls."

"Wellies, Gordoni," General Sako said. "Once we get out of there, I want a document written up on all the schematics of your inventions. You can't be revealing things like this at crucial times. What happens if you neglect to tell us something, and it costs us lives?"

Faso rolled his eyes. "I won't let that happen I assure you."

"And if you fall sick, what then?"

"Then my dear beloved, Asinal Winda, has all the information you'll need."

General Sako's face was turning red by this point. "Winda, you will write up the schematics for me at the earliest opportunity, is that understood?"

"Yes, sir," she replied from her seat. She glared daggers at Faso, as if to say that there was no way she would do his job for him. It felt good to see her sticking up for herself, even a bit, and so I hoped with all my heart she'd win that battle.

"So," I said. "We can take Velos and Faso's dragon automaton in. They'll scan things from the air. And come back with a report. And we'll do this before the blizzard passes, so we know what we're up against."

Velos would hate me for forcing him to fly in such conditions, but really, I felt we had no choice.

"No," General Sako said. "As the only fertile male dragon known alive, we can't risk Velos. The dragon automaton will go in alone and unmanned."

"Actually," Faso said. "I think we'll need both dragons, with troops on them. We'll need to investigate the inside of the factory, as there may be automatons inside that haven't yet powered on. Such automatons won't register heat signatures. So, the men will have to dismount and reconnoiter inside for themselves."

I nodded, and I glanced at Taka, who stood by the tent wall.

"So, it's settled," I said. "We need the two dragons to deposit us on the ground. Faso and Winda can take the dragon automaton. Me and Talato will take Velos. Oh, and Taka wants to come too." And I said that, knowing exactly what the general's response would be.

"Taka?" General Sako's eyes opened wide. "Oh no. There's no way I'm putting him right in the enemy's sights, no matter what Gerhaun said. He's a child, for wellies' sake. Taka stays here under my protection."

I turned to Taka and met an angry glare. It had been a cheap trick to pass it off as General Sako's decision, and he hadn't fallen for it.

"I'll be okay," I said to him. He nodded, and didn't interject, although the scowl didn't leave his face. I just hoped this wouldn't mean he'd jump on a Grey and rush ahead of us.

But, this time, I was sure General Sako would keep him under a much tighter guard.

"Also," General Sako said. "Now we have the helmet, Faso and Winda don't need to pilot the dragon automaton. I'm not sure you even need to go, Dragonseer Wells, but I understand you want to be close to Velos. So, here's my plan. We'll send out two of my commandos – actually make it three – on the dragon automaton.

Another commando will accompany you and Lieutenant Talato on Velos. Meanwhile, we'll continue our march ahead to the factory, and if there are any complications, we'll take the factory by brute force."

"Three?" Faso said. "I only designed my automaton for two passengers."

"My commandos can hold on," General Sako replied.

"And how am I meant to march with you when I've got my helmet on my head?" Faso asked.

"You're inventive, Faso," I said. "You'll find a way."

My little joke was rewarded by a collective chortle from the commandos and marines in the room. And I might have been seeing things, but I could swear Winda smiled too.

17

We set off into a raging blizzard, which carried a horrible sleet on its heavy winds. The icy blasts stung the skin on my cheeks and around my neck, and the frozen residue melted and slithered underneath my scarf. The conditions were tiring Velos, who found it tough to fly in a straight line.

But the weather also kept us from being spotted, and for that I was grateful. A commando named Private Yorin sat in the central seat between me and Talato. I refrained from augmenting as I feared the night vision from my secicao blend would interfere with the helmet's sensors.

Once we got closer to the factory, the winds subsided a little. Private Yorin then signalled we were close, and I put my helmet on. Once again, I saw the colourful world through Velos' eyes, and my connection to him got even stronger. Faso had already shown me the switch I needed to toggle to see the heat signatures. So, I flipped it, and the display through the helmet's visor transformed.

I didn't see speckled green, as I usually would from augmenting, but shades of red, yellow and blue. The reddest areas were the hottest around the chimneys of the factory and where the slaves worked away at the ground. Another cluster of slaves had grouped up in lines of three, with huge metal girders propped on their shoulders, which they carried towards the door.

Faso had explained that all active automatons would emit these signatures. They would be hottest at their power cores, and cooler near the metal on the surface. Now, through the dissipating grey clouds, I could make out the outlines of Hummingbird automatons – glowing red at their centres. They buzzed around close to the slaves. There was also a little heat coming from the doors themselves, which I guessed were also powered by automaton technology. All that, added to a thermal bloom from the manufacturing processes and a temperature gradient that diffused from red inside, to yellow through the rock, to blue in the frigid outdoors.

A good two-score war automatons also patrolled along the edge of the rock face that concealed the factory. As I turned my head, I also saw the signatures from Faso's dragon automaton flying level with us. Three muscular commandos straddled its back – a female on the front and two male ones perched behind her on the back seat, their names: Solice, Myargh, and Forkand respectively.

I diverted my attention back to the rock face. Behind its cold blue surface, I could only see the heat signatures of a few guards. No sign of any automatons.

"See what I mean?" Faso's voice came over the speaker system on Velos' armour. "No threat at all."

"We still need to check it out," I said. "For all I know they could be using some kind of technology that doesn't emit heat."

"That's impossible," Faso said. "But I have to admit, I'm curious to see what's behind it all too. Have you got your shoulder-cam?"

I checked the bulky cube-shaped object that Faso had clipped on to my left shoulder, on the opposite side of my body as my hipflask.

"Everything's ready."

"I do," Faso replied. "Be careful, won't you?"

I snorted, although I felt a little grateful at the same time. It wasn't like Faso to care about my well-being. "Faso, land the dragon automaton on that knoll to the north of the factory, the one higher than the rest around three hundred metres from here. You see it?."

"Of course," Faso said. "And if there's any danger, I'll make sure you get optimal support."

"Good. Now, open up a channel to the other soldiers. Unfortunately, I can't relay commands to your automaton using dragonsongs."

"Affirmative. But I'll stay on channel."

I waited for the telltale click of the speaker system connecting to the dragon automaton before I gave my orders. "We're going in. We'll land on that knoll over there, be ready to cover the rest of the distance on foot."

I pushed up on Velos' steering fin and glanced over my shoulder to check that Faso was also bringing down the dragon automaton. We landed as silently as possible. The wind still screamed over the barren land, and the murk had started to thicken once again.

I kept my helmet on for a while, so I could study the automatons' patrol routes. After I felt I had a decent plan together, I raised the visor on the helmet, then I scrambled down the ladder on Velos' flank and indicated for Lieutenant Talato and Private Yorin to do the same. The other three commandos from the dragon automaton joined us, and I signalled everyone forward to give Velos and the automaton enough room to lift into the air.

The camera on my shoulder also had a talkie built inside. Faso had installed a special headset for each of us, housed underneath a hatch at the top of the camera. I took hold of this and pulled it towards me, stretching the extendible cord. I clipped the device onto my ear.

"Faso, are you reading?" I asked, and I put up my hand to signal for everyone to hold their position.

"Loud and clear. I'm glad you've finally had a chance to try this invention. You have to admit, it works much better than talkies."

"We've not got time for bragging. Just make sure the dragon automaton keeps its distance."

"Fine."

I sang out to Velos to instruct him not to get too close. The cyagora was slowly wearing off, and so my connection to him had strengthened a little – not as crystal as it once was, but cohesive enough to at least give him some basic commands.

We were soon within range of the factory. A few war automatons milled around the entrances. But they, oddly, seemed unperturbed by our presence. Perhaps they hadn't yet noticed we were there, or perhaps they simply didn't care.

We reached a patch of snow that had grown thick between the two smooth sandstone boulders jutting out of it. I signalled the commandos to stop, and I took a swig from my hip flask to augment so I'd be able to see through the darkening clouds. The world ghosted into speckled green, and I kept scanning the horizon, looking for an opening. I could see no way around it. We would have to split up.

I planned for us to keep moving forward in a wide formation so as to draw less attention than we would if we were clustered together. Such tactics could confuse war automatons, as it took them longer to work out who to target first. This would give us more time to take advantage of the terrain.

"Myargh, get in position on that patch behind that bush," I said. "And stay low."

"Yes, Ma'am," the commando whispered. He got down on his hands and knees and slithered over the snow into position. "Forkand, take that patch of grass over there." I pointed at a raised tuft not yet covered by snow.

"On your orders," he said. And crawled forward.

"Solice, climb the boulder, and take position at the top of it."

"Affirmative, Ma'am," she said with a salute. She ran towards the rock, leapt at it, and clung to its face like a monkey. Then, she scrambled on top of it and lay down on her tummy.

Between the two male commandos, Forkand got into position first, and he stayed low. He rested the barrel of his Pattersoni rifle on the raised patch of grass and pointed it at the entrance to the factory.

But then, there came a gunshot, and blood splashed out from the commando's head, and landed on the snow. "Dragonheats! Myargh, fall back."

Myargh lifted himself up slightly. But I hadn't given the order quickly enough. Another shot cracked out, and I watched in horror as a dark stain pooled on the back of his camo, just behind where his heart would be. The man fell backwards onto the frozen ground.

Before I could even work out how to protect Solice, she got shot too. She fell off the boulder and sank into the snow. She lay there, a stream of blood flowing out of the hole in the centre of her forehead.

"Dragonseer Wells," General Sako said, through the headset where I'd expected to hear Faso. "What's happening out there?"

"We have a sniper," I said. "Yorin, Talato, scatter." And I thought about calling in Velos, but without knowing where the sniper was shooting from, I'd only be endangering his life.

And before we could even move, there came another shot. Blood spurted out in front of me, some sticky warmth clinging to my cheek. Yorin gurgled as he clutched at the side of his neck. The sniper had shot him right in the artery, and I knew he had no chance.

"Run, Talato," I shouted. And I sprinted away from the factory, hoping the wellies that the sniper didn't shoot her down next.

Her soft footsteps padded behind me as I made my way up a gently sloping barrow. I rushed forwards in zigzags to help avoid any more sniper bullets, but none came.

In front of me, all of a sudden, a tall lump of snow erupted out of the ground. I tried to swerve around it, but another emerging lump blocked my path. Shortly after, two more cut off our retreat to the left and right.

Lieutenant Talato already had her rifle raised, and she spun around, pointing it from target to target, as if trying to work out which enemy would reveal itself first. The snow in front of me crumbled away, to reveal a war automaton, a massive drill whirring on its head. Others popped out of the nearby terrain until we became completely surrounded.

"Impossible," Faso said in the headset. "I didn't see their heat signatures."

I clenched my teeth. "Not now, Faso."

The dragon automaton flew by overhead, and I sensed Velos approaching to rescue us. But I sang a sharp song to push him back again. There were just too many of them, and I couldn't risk Velos getting shot down – armour or not.

That familiar hovering platform emerged in the distance, in my green-laced vision. I saw Travast standing on top of it, and I wanted to draw my rifle and shoot him. But then, common sense took over. This wasn't Travast, but only one of those fancy holograms of him. His hoarse voice resounded from the platform.

"Well, well, well. Look what our automatons brought in," Travast said. "And now, I have two pretty hostages for the king."

I clenched my teeth. "You took out four of our men, Travast. For that, you must pay."

"And what are you going to do? I've already tracked the wavelengths and frequencies of your communications and triangulated the data, so I know exactly where your friends are. Now, I would advise you to come peacefully, as no one else needs to get hurt."

"You're a bastard, Travast Indorm…"

"That may be. I never actually learned who my mother was, but my father was quite the womaniser, and I don't think he ever married. Now, drop your weapons."

And, as one, Talato and I both lifted our rifles off of our backs, unholstered our pistols, and placed the weapons on the ground.

A FEW HOURS LATER, Lieutenant Talato and I sat on two hard wooden chairs in a holding area beneath the factory. We had our feet in fetters and our hands cuffed behind our backs. Our chairs weren't secured by anything and so, if I wriggled too much, I worried I might knock my chair away. There were no windows and the large room contained four barred cells, two on each side.

It was surprisingly warm in here because of a massive coal furnace at the far end of the corridor. The furnace hatch was slightly ajar, and a fire crackled behind this. At the other end of the room, stairs contorted up a spiral staircase. A couple of torches in sconces at the opening to this added a little light into the room.

Two war automatons had led us down here, and pushed us inside the cell, after which some guards had given Talato and I a moment to change into the same kind of rags we saw the slaves wearing. After that, they had trussed us and locked us into the cell.

The cell doors had automatic mechanical locks – rectangular devices glowing green with a complex arrangement of cogs and pendulums visible underneath thick glass. I could only just turn my head to make out the walls behind me out of the corner of my eye. They were made of stone blocks and covered in a thick layer of moss. There wasn't much else in our cell other than the chairs, only a long-drop and a metal basin that wasn't even connected to a tap. Of course, both were useless in our current predicament.

The cell opposite us housed a male factory worker. He sat with his arms folded, staring in my direction but not quite at me. I tried to gaze into his eyes to find some sense of humanity, but he didn't even blink. The only movements that came were the swirling green glowing patterns playing underneath his skin.

We had no food, no access to water, and other than this strange, oblivious man and the moss on the back wall, there was no sign of any life. I couldn't help but wonder if they were planning to leave us down here to die.

And yet still, my mind felt vacant. No sign of Finesia at all. Nor could I sense any dragons, including Velos. Thus, I had no idea what had happened to him outside.

"What do you think they're going to do with us?" I asked Talato.

"I wish I knew, Ma'am," she said. "But I'd die before letting them put you in danger."

I shook my head, remembering how I'd almost killed her the previous night. If Taka hadn't let off his scream, I might have. I didn't deserve to be saved. "I'd rather you lived than I…"

"But I don't have the abilities you have. I can't control the dragons. I know you had a rough patch the other night, but your life is more valuable than any other human's on this world."

"Even Taka's?"

"You and he are both valuable, Ma'am. I just hope he's safe."

"Me too," I said.

There came a clanking sound from the staircase which sounded like chisels hitting stone. I turned my head to see two standard-issue war automatons descend. A man in a redguard uniform, with a deep scar across his left cheek, followed down after them. He carried a syringe in his hand with a green liquid inside.

He walked past us and turned to the slave's cell. He took hold of a device from his hip, touched it to the door, and there came the sound of cogs grinding together before the lock clicked open.

"Is that it?" I asked. "Not even a hello?"

But the guard completely blanked me. He unlocked the man's fetters, took the syringe, and plunged it into the prisoner's arm. The slave remained stock still, without even flinching. The guard released the cuffs at his back and locked them again at the front. He grabbed these and dragged the slave back towards the staircase without offering us a parting glance.

"Friendly, aren't they?" I said to Talato.

Her bottom lip was quivering. I never thought I'd see her so afraid.

When she was working for Admiral Sandao on board his dragon carrier, she'd probably never imagined she'd encounter this kind of danger. Things on ships were much more black and white – you either survived or went down with the rest of the crew. But now, as a bodyguard to a dragonseer, she had one of the most dangerous jobs in the world. And I'd promoted her into it.

The war automatons continued to stand vigil at the bottom of the stairs. They had their guns pointed right at us. This time, it was our turn to sit stock still. Even a slight flinch could trigger the automatons' Gatling cannons.

Another redguard came down the stairs. This one had a full-growth russet beard and carried a leather briefcase. He unlocked the door to our cell with his device and placed this back in his belt.

He walked up to me first, and opened the briefcase, to reveal a line of empty syringes. He took one of these and held it up to the light. "Orders are that every human in this factory must have their blood samples taken for DNA monitoring purposes. Prisoners are no exception."

He stepped behind me, pulled up my sleeve, and I felt the sting of a needle entering my forearm. I glanced over my shoulder to see the guard also take a blood sample from Talato, before returning both full syringes to the briefcase.

"Are you at least going to give us some food?" I asked. "We're pretty hungry after our march."

The guard nodded. This one seemed at least to have an ounce of humanity to him. "We were ordered not to feed you until we'd taken the samples. But now that's done, I can put forward your request."

"Just make sure it's not drugged or anything," I called after him as he closed the door behind him. Although, at this point I was so thirsty, I would rather have drugged water than nothing at all.

The war automatons followed the guard up the staircase, leaving us alone.

Lieutenant Talato and I waited in silence for what must have been a good ten minutes. The anger and frustration inside me was rising. Meanwhile, I could do nothing but wait, wondering all the time what they had planned for us. I was worried about Velos, and Taka, and General Sako, and the fates of everyone else we'd left behind, including Faso.

I don't know how much time passed before our next visitor arrived. This time, Travast Indorm emerged from the bottom of the staircase, wearing his purple bandana and ambling with a peculiar limp. Indeed, this was the first time I'd seen him in physical and not holographic form.

He surveyed us from outside the cell without opening the door, as though afraid we might somehow break our cuffs and fetters and strangle him to death. With the right blend of secicao I could. If only some magical fairy would fly right up and pour some down my throat. I could also have just claimed Finesia's gift and transformed into a dragon, but I really didn't want to do that.

"So, we finally meet you in the flesh," I said to him. "Only when we're completely incapacitated do you have the courage to show yourself from behind your technological walls."

The scientist narrowed his eyes. "I'm wise to take precautions when facing dragons and a remarkable breed of human they call a dragonseer. Too many charge blindly into battle. But I'm no such fool…"

"So, what do you want of us exactly? Given the trouble I caused at his palace, I would have thought the king would have ordered me killed."

I couldn't see the shape of his mouth under his bandana, but his eyes lit up as if amused. "Oh, King Cini doesn't want that, believe me."

Static sounded from the talkie at his hip. He raised it to his ear and listened. Unfortunately, I couldn't quite hear what the man at the other end said. But his voice sounded regimented, and his sentences short.

"Wonderful," Travast replied. "Bring the boy in first and keep hold of the general until I give the orders."

I clenched my fists behind my back, digging my nails hard into my palms. Dragonheats, he had Taka. They must have ambushed the camp shortly after we'd got caught. A short while later, a redguard appeared with Taka at the bottom of the stairs, with his hair all mussed up.

He shot an angry glance at Travast. "Traitor," he said. "I thought I could trust you." His voice was almost breaking.

But Travast didn't even look back at him in response.

The guard threw Taka in the cell opposite us where the slave had been. He didn't cuff him or put him in fetters, clearly unaware of how elusive the boy could be. Taka slumped against the far wall and turned his head away from me when I tried to meet his gaze.

"You can't keep a boy down here in conditions like this," I said. "Particularly the same child the king considers as his nephew."

"Oh, King Cini would be quite happy with me selecting a suitable punishment for such an itinerant child. And, when he arrives, he can decide what to do with him."

He took a step back towards the entrance. But I wasn't going to let him get away so fast.

"What do you want, Travast?" I asked again.

He responded by wheezing out a laugh so sharp it reverberated off the walls. "Always to the point, young dragonseer. I like that. I want to do my duty by holding you here until King Cini arrives. But then the question you probably want answering is what does he want of you? He was rather excited to hear that you'd arrived. So much, in fact, that he left his luxurious suite in Ginlast to come and meet you."

I clenched my teeth. I had no idea how Taka could have trusted Travast. But now, the boy was glaring at the back of Travast's head, with a look that said he wanted to kill him. I calmed myself and focused on my surroundings. From the distance came a drip, drip, dripping of water – maybe snow melting off a roof. An open entrance, perhaps.

"Very well," I said. "I'll rephrase my question. What exactly does Cini want?"

"Isn't it obvious? If he'd have wanted you dead by now, he would have killed you. You and the boy are the only people in this entire world who can control the Greys. Our loyal king would pay a thousand golden airships to have your allegiance in his war effort. If only you could convince him you'd joined his side..." He steepled his fingers together and lowered his head as if deep in thought. "And if you could do it without my coercion, imagine the potential. Imagine the riches. Imagine the life you could create for your family and your future children. All it would take is a little shift in worldview."

"You'd sooner see me roll in pig muck than support King Cini."

Travast scratched at his chin underneath his bandana. Though he didn't move it far enough for me to see underneath, it was clear he wore that thing for more purpose than fashion, perhaps concealing a scar or terrible breath. "I thought as much. The king had warned I'd probably have to resort to drugs." He reached into his breast pocket and produced a vial of silver liquid.

Examlpora.

My mouth filled with saliva, and I jerked towards it, knocking my chair on the floor.

"Dragonseer Wells," Talato said.

But I wasn't listening. Instead, I felt the hunger. Travast turned around in a full circle and displayed the vial to Taka, who stood up with wide eyes and moved towards the front of the cell. We were like ghouls after flesh – dead to our senses.

Yet, still something was missing. Finesia would usually be screaming out in my head at this point, telling me to get hold of that vial through any means possible. But she wasn't there.

Travast gave a curt nod and pocketed the vial. "Most fascinating. Exalmpora – the blood of a dragon queen. If only they had informed me of its benefits sooner, I could have moulded Taka to the king's perfection. But Alsie Fioreletta kept it hidden from me, as she always had her own agenda. Anyway, I hear you've also found ways to overcome it, so I thought I'd try more conventional means."

He lifted the talkie to his mouth. "Bring him down," he said.

"Travast what are you –"

But I stopped myself as he raised a finger to his lips and stared at me with his dangerous grey eyes. "Shh."

Heavy metallic footsteps came from the top of the staircase. They belonged to two massive automatons, much more heavily armoured than the war automatons that had visited us before. Thick brass plates shifted around their joints, with something hissing underneath as their bodies moved. Between them, in their thick hands, they carried a wooden plank that reached down to the floor, but I couldn't quite tell what it was until they turned it around.

A rack, and on it lay General Sako, gagged by electrical tape.

My heart skipped a beat, and I gasped.

Travast walked up to the general and ripped off the gag. General Sako grimaced but remained stoically silent. He lifted his head and glared angrily at his captor.

"Blunders and dragonheats, Indorm. You will pay for this. My troops will soon come in and rescue us and torch this place. You underestimate the size of our operation."

Travast chuckled. "I believe the truth is quite the contrary. It's you that underestimates the power contained within this factory."

He walked over to the rack and turned a crank handle by 180-degrees. General Sako grimaced, though he did not cry out.

"You see," Travast said. "I thoroughly researched you, Dragonseer Wells. The king has a detailed dossier on you, and we know that you're much more likely to save friends in need than yourself."

He turned the handle again, and this time General Sako cried out in pain. His face went red and his breathing heavy, as sweat pooled on his wizened brow.

"Dragonheats, Travast," I shouted. "Stop it. He's defenceless."

Travast turned to me and gave me a knowing look. "Isn't that the whole point of torture? To demonstrate where the balance of power lies until your subject gives you what you want."

I jerked towards him and yelped out in pain from the fetters pulling back on my ankles.

"Don't tell him anything, Dragonseer Wells," General Sako called out.

Travast turned back to the general and slapped him with a back-hand to the face.

"Just tell me what you want," I said. "I need to know your terms before you harm anyone else. Let's at least be civil here."

"See, I told you I didn't need Exalmpora. And I don't ask for much. Only a little good behaviour. Simply be civil when the king arrives and convince him you'd make an excellent ally to his cause. It's not too hard, is it?"

Blood rushed to my cheeks, and I bit my tongue to stop me saying anything I regretted. Travast nodded and turned back to the rack. The features on the general's face were wound tight – the old man was a tough nut who was usually great at hiding his fears.

Travast put his hand on the handle. But before he could turn it one more time, a guard came running down the stairs. He turned to Travast and saluted. "Commander Indorm, sir." Commander? So Travast was military...

"What is it, soldier? Spit it out."

"The dragon automaton's back and is unleashing havoc. We've tried firing on it, but nothing's connecting. It's impervious. Requesting your advice, sir."

Travast sighed. "So, my peer, Faso Gordoni, is strutting his stuff. It can be taken down, and I'll show you how."

The guard saluted again and ran back up the stairs. Before Travast left, he gave the handle another quick turn, causing a wince from General Sako. "We'll start dislocating joints when I return." He gave me a cursory glance before running up the stairs.

Roars came from outside and I could sense Velos was nearby too. Machine guns sputtered in the distance. I sang a dragonsong to keep Velos calm and to thank him for being brave, and Taka soon joined in. The skittering of tiny automaton feet soon joined the loud chorus, and Ratter emerged at the bottom of the stairs, glowing green with secicao power.

The automatons turned their massive cannons towards him. But Ratter hissed and scurried up the wall and along the ceiling. The massive automatons tried to track Ratter with their guns, but they moved far too slow. Ratter dropped onto the head of the first automaton and then edged down its back, and bit into something. The automaton collapsed to the floor. Meanwhile, the second had a massive fist raised over Ratter, bringing it down fast.

But the tiny automaton darted between the legs of its gigantic cousin. There were two cables loose on the back, connected to a green glowing power core. Ratter wrapped his teeth around one of these cables and pulled it out. The automaton dropped its arm first, then it fell sideways, letting out a tremendous crash.

I remained silent a moment, half expecting a guard to come down the stairs with his rifle drawn.

"Blunders and dragonheats, Ratter, is that you?" General Sako said. "I never thought I'd be so pleased to see you here."

Ratter was already at the top of the rack, chewing at the ropes tied around General Sako's wrists. It freed them and then scurried to the bottom and worked on the ties at the general's legs. Once free, the older man sat up, stretched, and threw his arms around in windmills a few times. Meanwhile, Ratter scrambled over to us and clambered up the bars of the cell door, towards the automatic lock. It opened its mouth, and a spark shot out from the back of its throat. The lock whirred, and the door clicked open.

Ratter blowtorched the cuffs off our wrists and fetters off our feet. He rushed over to Taka's cell to free him too, and while he worked, I walked over to General Sako.

"What's going on?" I asked. "How did you get captured and how the dragonheats did Ratter get here?"

The general's face went white, and he shook his head. "They ambushed us while we were marching forward. One moment, the terrain looked barren. Then all around us, war automatons jumped out of the ground. Thousands of them. They shot down all our troops and the Greys. We didn't stand a chance. Then that hologram of Indorm rucked up on his floating platform and he shot me with some sedative dart that knocked me out cold."

I clenched my teeth. "They planned this. Travast Indorm lured us into a trap."

"Yes, well. It's lucky Faso and Winda went out foraging for some herbs they said they needed. I left them with Lieutenant Candiorno as an escort. It looks like they're orchestrating this entire escape plan, bless them. What happened to the other men?"

"Also killed."

The features on General Sako's face fell. "So, it's just us then."

I nodded. "Once we get out of here, we must either retreat or call for reinforcements."

"I vote for the latter. I saw some of the factory as they brought me through. And... Well, there are a lot of automatons in here like these two," he pointed to the massive disabled machines.

"Then we must escape."

"Agreed," General Sako said, and he indicated the staircase.

I turned to the lieutenant. "Come on, Talato. Let's find our way out while we still have a chance."

General Sako led the way up the staircase, with Lieutenant Talato, Taka and I following closely behind.

18

General Sako seemed to know his way around. He took us through a network of narrow corridors, flanked with heavy brass doors that were sealed shut. After a while, we arrived at a much larger set of double doors.

"You should see this," he said. "They marched me through here after I'd been captured."

And he opened the doors, revealing a gigantic room containing zigzagging conveyor belts that trundled over a complex arrangement of whirring cogs and gears. Out of the right side of the room, a conveyor belt carried incomplete automatons, each with two enormous feet, bulky bodies, and Gatling guns four times the size as those on Velos' armour. Their arms looked like they could knock down walls. Further along the assembly line, hooks lowered down from the ceiling, attaching heavy plates on to their bodies and installing various components.

Also, those cables that Ratter had pulled out of the automatons back must have been a design flaw. Because, further down the line, a hook lowered thick metal guards onto each automaton. It placed them with precision over each machine's visible cables. A little further still, a huge gear spun on the ceiling, attached to a welding tool on a pole.

This moved in a tall and precise elliptical motion to secure each shield-guard in place.

"Faso was wrong," General Sako said. "It looks like they have developed a new type of technology. They look a bit like ogres."

And I thought Ogres a rather apt name, given their clumsy but brutal appearance, as if they'd be able to crush anything that got in their way.

Though the factory was running like clockwork, it was also under construction. A steel walkway passed overhead, on which I could see bare human feet scurrying around. They belonged to the slaves, who wielded spanners, hammers, and screwdrivers, which they used to repair and install equipment on the roof. Others hefted great mechanical arms – the kind that attached to the claws and soldering irons – on their shoulders, in lines of three to five.

There were redguards up there too, though none of them looked down at the floor below. They carried green syringes in their hands and watched the slaves vigilantly.

And each slave moved with a noticeable lack of vigour. None of them paused to rest – even to wipe their brow or take a breath of air. They applied themselves to the job at hand, be it hammering a rivet in place, adjusting a screw on this massive factory machine, or hooking a component onto the railings. They just didn't seem human anymore, and that thought caused a shiver to travel down my spine.

When the Tow Observer had referred to this place as an automaton that produced automatons, it wasn't talking about anything specific, but a concept. As this place grew, the automatons would no doubt take more tasks upon themselves, and the slaves could work on other things until their services and lives weren't needed at all.

They weren't regarded as people, but fleshy dehumanised automata, cogs in a larger machine.

King Cini would go to any means necessary to achieve what he wanted, even if that involved drugging his own population into oblivion. And he wouldn't stop using methods like this until the Southlands was under his control and he had destroyed every single dragon alive.

"We need to save them," I said. "The way they're being treated... It's terrible." Some of these were from my homeland. Others lived on the same continent. Many would have come from the Sovereign States, such as the country of Orkc which we were now in.

"But this is the nature of war, Dragonseer Wells," General Sako replied. "You can never save them all."

And my heart sank as we turned away.

We continued down the corridor, Velos' and the dragon automaton's roars and the booming of machine gun fire getting louder as we progressed.

"This way," General Sako said, and led us down a narrower corridor. Ratter soon met up with us – he'd been on a little reconnoiter, it seemed. The automaton scurried ahead, as if it knew of a safe route. It took us past corridors of non-operational war automatons, and Rocs lined up on either side in their own alcoves. Then the corridor widened into a room as large as Fortress Gerhaun's courtyard with perhaps a hundred Mammoth automatons arranged in neat rows, facing a massive closed door at the front that was even wider than the chimney to Gerhaun's treasure chamber.

"Blunders and dragonheats," General Sako said. "These things are ready to march."

And as we rushed past one, I looked up at it in horror, wondering what would happen when it activated. It was eerie to see one of these terrible automatons so lifeless and so close. I'd never truly got a scale of the Mammoths when we'd attacked them from a distance or passed them so fast in flight.

The two tusks it used to toss secicao into its jaws were at least four times the height of me. And if they charged using those heavy legs, I could see them breaching great gashes in Fortress Gerhaun's walls. I honestly wasn't sure which was a more terrifying weapon, the great tusked mammoths, the spear beaked Rocs, or the heavily armoured Ogres we'd encountered before.

198 | CHRIS BEHRSIN

But one thing was for sure – King Cini was building an army of giants, and it was only a matter of time until he sent it south.

We picked up pace and left the Mammoth room moving into another narrow corridor, this time containing traditional war automatons. Then we passed through another hallway, with tiny compartments inset into each wall. Some of these contained Hummingbirds. Others contained the fast-moving hornet automatons, usually equipped with sedative or light venom, that King Cini deployed when he needed crowd control.

Finally, the corridor swung to the left, emerging at an open door, behind which a battle raged. We rushed to the entrance, taking cover behind the door's wide steel frame. I felt the chill hit my bare skin, Talato and I still dressed in threadbare rags. But I had enough adrenaline in me to charge outside in my bare feet, despite the danger from the cold.

Outside, war automatons had gathered in small squads of five or six, and they had their shielded heads turned up to the sky, which they fired into with their double Gatling-guns. Velos and the dragon automaton wheeled around above, wisely keeping their distance.

The war automatons supervised groups of slaves, who still worked away at the low boulders, oblivious to the battle raging around them. In the distance to the left, trains of them carried iron girders on their shoulders in groups of three, unloading them from a trailer attached to a Mammoth further south. Wisps of fog swirled around the legs of the Mammoth, concealing its feet.

Slightly to the west of this, stood a stack of logs so tall we couldn't see the landscape behind. That seemed the best place to sprint to for cover, and once behind them we could work out what to do next.

But between us and those logs stood four of those terrifying Ogre automatons. Unlike the other automatons, they had their gaze focused on the perimeter, not even trying to track the fast moving dragons with their bulky weapons. Two of them looked out to our left, two of them looked out to the right. If we tried to pass in front of them, they'd flatten us with their shoulder mounted Gatling cannons. And they were so close together, that they'd crush us with their feet if we tried to dart between them.

They were the more immediate danger, but I also knew that we couldn't get close to any of the clusters of smaller war automatons. Although these were currently focused on Velos and the dragon automaton, if we passed too close to them, they'd turn their guns on us.

I sang to Velos, to instruct him to keep his distance. Not just because he was vastly outnumbered, but also because I didn't want his flames to do any damage to the slaves. Then I turned to Talato, who was vigorously scanning from left to right, looking for an opening.

"Can you see a way through, Lieutenant?" I asked.

"Not yet, Ma'am," she said.

"Blunders and dragonheats," General Sako said. "We need to take a risk here. Taka, stay close."

Meanwhile, Ratter had his own plans. The automaton leapt off my shoulder and onto the ground. I put up my hand to stop General Sako charging forwards, as Ratter scurried over to the huge automatons in front of us. He drew their attention, causing them to swivel their guns towards him and open fire. This gave us an opening to our right.

Usually, I'd augment before facing off against any kind of automaton. But we weren't only just unarmed, but also bereft of our secicao flasks. Which meant we had to rely on our natural instincts alone.

"This way," I commanded. As I rushed towards the back of the automatons.

We passed the giant machines, just as they kicked up the snow and gave chase after Ratter. They were surprisingly fast, and they seemed to want to pancake the ferret automaton into the ground. But what they gained in speed, they lacked in manoeuvrability. Ratter darted underneath one of their undercarriages. The automaton responded by raising its bulky fist and bringing it around in a sweep that knocked one of its brothers back by several metres.

That's all I registered as I picked up speed and focused on the logs straight ahead. Out of the corner of my mind, light flashed, and Velos' shadow passed over me. Then there came the roaring of fire and the sensation of heat from the left.

Meanwhile, my lungs were burning, both through exertion and the intense cold. We swerved close to another cluster of regular war automatons, currently unleashing their ordnance into the sky. As we entered their perimeter, they swung around on their spindly legs, and pointed their guns in our direction.

Fortunately, the logs were only seconds ahead. Talato dived behind the cover first, followed by Taka. I was next, followed by General Sako. The war automatons unleashed their bullets, splintering the logs in front of us, cutting into them at the edges.

I waited for the volley to abate, then scrambled over to the end of the logs, and was just about to peek out from cover, when there came a screeching sound from the sky. Ten Roc automatons had joined the battle, flying in from the west. They had their missiles equipped – the same kind that had almost taken out Velos at the Battle of East Cadigan Island.

The flock split into two divisions, so they could pursue Velos and the dragon automaton individually. A swarm of Hummingbirds accelerated past these – green and secicao powered – so many of them that I couldn't see the clouds behind them. A thin line of hornet automatons also followed a lower line, beelining in our direction.

"Dragonseer Wells," Lieutenant Talato said.

I pivoted, sensing the alarm in her tone.

Travast Indorm's voice came before I saw him. "Enough of this tomfoolery," he said.

And there he stood, right behind me, framed by a red cloak and standing on his hovering platform. And this time, I knew I wasn't looking at a hologram but his true form.

Just behind him, we'd completely missed the Mammoth automaton looming just a little taller than the stack of logs. It had its jaws and tusks lowered to the ground, and it looked ready to charge. It also had its four side-mounted guns trained right on us.

Travast Indorm crossed his arms. A scowl marred the upper half of his face, as his bandana whipped violently in the wind. The front-mounted gun on his platform was trained on a point just between my eyes.

"I ask you for one simple thing, and you have to defy me. Why can't you just cooperate? Don't you value your lives?"

And before I could say a word, I felt a sting in my neck. A dart had buried itself in there, and the drowsiness of sedative rushed to my brain. My legs wobbled, and I fell onto the soft snow, knowing there was no point in trying to resist.

The last thing I saw was some slaves scattering away from the dragon automaton just before it crashed into the ground. Then, I blacked out.

PART VI

CINI

"Those who claim secicao will take over the world truly underestimate the power of industry and human endeavour."

— KING CINI III

19

This time, Travast Indorm had had the courtesy to put beds in our cells, rather than plonking us down on hard wooden chairs and trussing our hands behind our backs. In a way, it was a blessing, really. After everything I'd been through the last couple of days, I'd needed somewhere to lie down.

The mattress beneath me was cardboard thin, and I could feel the hard wooden plank underneath it against my shoulder as I lay there. As if to punish us for trying to escape, Travast had also turned the furnace down low, and I only had those threadbare rags to keep me warm. I kept waking up, shivering, and grappling at bedclothes that weren't there. So whatever sleep I got wasn't good sleep.

I didn't understand his logic, really. Treating me this way, certainly wouldn't put me in the best of moods when Travast wanted me to display my utmost respect before the king.

Eventually, I thought it better to get up and take stock of my surroundings. A little movement would, after all, bring a little warmth. And there was enough light coming from the flickering torches upstairs that I could see around me.

I was back in the same holding area as before. This time, all four cells had been filled, and I had a cell to myself. Opposite me, Faso and

206 | CHRIS BEHRSIN

General Sako sat on their beds staring at each other, but not saying a word. Travast didn't seem to have liked Faso too much, and what better way to torture him than to stick him in the same holding cell as his ex-girlfriend's father.

Taka shared the adjoining cell with Lieutenant Candiorno. The boy stood at the back of the cell, throwing bits of stone and other rubble he found on the floor against the wall, almost as if he believed they'd help him tunnel free. Candiorno sat on the bed, watching him, without saying a word.

Talato and Winda were in the other cell. Talato lay on the bed fast asleep, while Winda sat watching her beloved with an expression of scorn, perhaps a little jealous that Faso was paying General Sako more heed than her.

"Well, fancy seeing you all here," I said.

General Sako jerked his head around. He seemed relieved to have someone else to look at other than Faso. "Dragonseer Wells, you're awake. We were staying quiet, to give you as much sleep as possible. It seems you have quite an ordeal ahead of you."

I nodded. "Thank you, I guess. But I need to know. Faso, what the dragonheats happened? And how did you end up getting captured too?"

Faso turned his head slowly. He looked ashamed, and I saw much of the likeness between him and Taka then. He'd been bested, I could see that. "I had it under control," he said. "We'd found a little hole in the rock. A cave, if you like, that tunnelled down into the earth. I planned to use the helmet while Winda and Candiorno kept watch. If I had Ratter, then he would have seen them coming and sedated them before they had a chance. But, of course, I had to send out Ratter to rescue you, and Lieutenant Candiorno went outside to scout the terrain."

He stood up and paced towards the wall, then back towards the door and reached out to hold on to the bars.

"The problem came," he continued, and he gave his girlfriend an unpleasant look, "when Winda let her gaze drift off for too long. She started daydreaming or something, and so the troops somehow got through the entrance, waltzed up behind her, and took her hostage. Then, just as I was bringing in Velos to attack one of those massive war automatons, one of Travast's guards yanked the helmet off me and threw it across the cave. It hit the wall, and goodness knows what condition it's in now."

I turned to Winda, half expecting her to have something to say about this. I'd known Faso so long, that I doubted it really was all her fault. It sounded like they would have got captured regardless. And if she had made a mistake, so what? We were all human. She lowered her head. She looked as though she'd been crying. But she didn't seem ashamed, she seemed angry.

I turned back to Faso to give him a piece of my mind and stick up for Winda a bit. But I was interrupted by footsteps coming from the stairs. Travast limped down them, two standard issue war automatons looming in his wake.

He posted the automatons at the bottom of the stairs, and traipsed over to my cell, keeping his gaze dead set on mine. He had that same scowl on his face as he had when he'd sedated me. But I would not back down. So, I met his look with an equally acerbic frown of my own. Meanwhile, anger surged within me. Literally, if he opened that cell door right then, I would tear him to shreds.

"Wells," he said. Clearly thinking he could make me feel inferior by neglecting my title and first name. "The first time I met you, I truly hoped that we could be friends. But your recent actions have shown you to be a wild animal, not capable of friendship. You're a true disappointment to your kind, and I don't know how anyone can possibly think you a dragonseer."

Wild animal… I'd show him. I bared my teeth at him, hissed, and then rushed at the door. I tried to yank it open, as if I had the strength of a thousand men.

But he didn't flinch in response. Instead, he stared me down, and then turned slowly towards Taka and walked up to his cell door. Taka kept as far away from the door as possible, shrinking away against the wall as if Travast were some kind of shade to fear in the night.

"And you, boy," Travast said. "I had truly great plans for you, and you have also proved an utter disappointment. Imagine what you could do with all that power inside you? But yet, you instead follow this beast." He swung his arm around in a wide arc towards me.

Taka didn't move from his position and looked up at Travast with a defiant stare. "I trust those who treat me well," he said. "And do good in this world. Much like *Chantell* did. And your kind killed her."

Travast shook his head. "I had nothing to do with your mother's death. That was all part of Alsie Fioreletta's plans."

"You're all the same," Taka replied. "You work for the king."

Travast chortled. "Oh, it's so much more complicated than that, believe me. Now, while here I was thinking that I could get you to do my bidding willingly. It now appears I have to use other measures."

He turned to one automaton near the base of the staircase and gestured for it to come forward. The machine jolted upright, cocked its plated head like a bird, and then took a few steps forward. It turned to me and trained one of its Gatling guns right on me. I looked down the barrel, drained of any fear I should have felt.

"What are you going to do, shoot me?" I asked.

Travast walked up to my cell. "I don't think I'll need to. But I must take precautions, understand." He reached into his pocket and took hold of a vial of liquid. For a moment, I thought I'd see Exalmpora, and I began to salivate. But instead, I saw that same green drug that we'd caught Taka with back at Fortress Gerhaun. Patterns of dark swirled within it. A sense of disappointment emerged in my chest.

"What's wrong?" Travast asked. "You look so sad. Almost as if you wanted Exalmpora. But this is Exalmpora, see." He took off the bung from the vial, and the metallic scent of the drug wafted into my nostrils. I wanted it, but only for a second, until Travast replaced the bung. "We merely coloured it differently so you wouldn't recognise it. Oh, and there's some extra magic in there. Although, I'm sure Mr Gordoni behind me would rather refer to this as science."

Travast's cloak stretched out so wide that I couldn't see Faso and General Sako's cell behind me. But the door there clanked loudly, causing me to recoil in shock.

"You get that stuff away from Dragonseer Wells, you hear?"

General Sako bawled. "I've heard all about how the king forced that stuff down my daughter's throat, and I will not let you do the same to her."

"Oh, pipe down, old man," Travast replied, without even turning to look at him. "I don't want to have to shoot you now. Not in front of the boy…"

The door rattled again, and then General Sako fell silent. I turned to see Talato now sitting up in bed, eyeing Travast as if wanting to take him down. But she had no means of getting out of the cell and she'd have to wrestle two war automatons, even if she did. I gave her a reassuring glance, to let her at least believe I had this under control.

"You know, maybe the old general's right," Travast said. "We should take you and the boy somewhere private. But be warned, if you defy me again, I will cut you down and tell the king we had an accident. Remember, this factory is much more valuable to King Cini than your own lives."

He clapped his hands, and the war automaton stepped forward and unlocked the door. Its side mounted cannons remained trained on me, and I had no doubt that if I fought back, it would unleash carnage first into my body, then turn around to annihilate everyone else in the room but Travast. To try to wrestle down a war automaton would be absolute folly, anyway. I could take them down with guns, when augmented with secicao, but it had taken me a lot of training to learn how to do that.

Travast moved around the back of the automaton towards the stairs. "So come," he said. "Let us have a party. I'll have wine and you can have Exalmpora. It will be a ball."

Despite his limp, he somehow managed to skip up the steps. I looked again at the fierce automaton, then at Faso, General Sako, Winda, and Talato, who all looked out from their stations at their beds as if wondering what I would do next.

But I had no choice. I followed Travast upstairs, the automaton's gun-barrel stuck into the small of my back like a clockwork key unwinding me towards my fate. Taka and another automaton followed closely behind.

THE WAR AUTOMATONS led us down corridors walled by inactive automatons, into the training room. The door was already open, and the room looked like a traditional classroom with a blackboard, stand-up desks arrayed in front of it and a lectern at the front.

But Travast didn't seem intent on giving us a lecture. Instead, the automatons shoved us towards the back of the room, sectioned off by a high wooden screen. Behind this stood a round table, with four upholstered seats evenly spaced around it. Travast sat on one of these, with a tall-necked glass half filled with red wine. He had put two smaller glasses on the table, both containing that green Exalmpora, with black specks floating around within.

The sudden sensation came again – the thirst. It drew me towards the glass, as raw steak does a dog. I sat down mesmerised, watching it in awe. Hypnotised, as if part of a sacrificial ritual. Taka did much the same.

But neither of us reached out to drink the concoction – we managed to at least show some restraint. At this point, I'd kind of expected Finesia to be in my head, willing me to take the stuff down in one go, telling me I needed it, and that it would complete me. Her absence seemed rather odd.

Was the cyagora blocking her out? I couldn't possibly still have it in my system, could I?

Though his smile wasn't visible underneath his bandana, mirth danced in Travast Indorm's eyes. He wasn't watching me at that moment, but Taka.

"You know, you dragonseer types are meant to be so sophisticated. I've seen Alsie, Charth and Francoiso, and I knew well Hastina, who eventually became Wiggea's wife until he lost her in the Cadigan hills to the coyotes…" He paused a moment, and I detected a very slight sadness in his voice when he mentioned Hastina.

"Then there was Sukina," he continued, "and now you. All of you have such grace. And yet all it takes is a drop of the blood of a dragon queen, and you're reduced to animals. It's fascinating."

I clenched my teeth. "What do you want, Travast? Something tells me that this isn't just about the king." He most certainly had an agenda of his own.

"That is for me to reveal on a need to know basis," Travast replied. "After all, I am the one with the upper hand. All I can say is that the battle in the Southlands before did an excellent job of convincing him he should divert additional funds towards this factory. Now, he's coming to visit the very stars of that battle in person."

"You won't win," I replied. "We have a much larger force than we sent inland, and they will come to rescue us."

Travast let out a raspy laugh. "If you're referring to that flotilla of archaic ships and icebreakers you sent towards Ginlast, we've destroyed them already. Such an idiotic plan of your admiral to send them into a location without an escape route. Ships aren't meant for travelling through ice."

"I don't believe you," I said. Faso had said it himself – the automatons would have to be heavily modified to have a chance of crossing the ice. They could send the Hummingbird, Hornet, and Roc automatons against Sandao's ships. But these hadn't been designed to battle ironclads, and only the missiles from the Rocs could pack a punch against a heavily armoured ship. But those missiles could equally well be torn to shreds by shrapnel-flak. Battles against ships were best fought by ships.

But then I remembered the automaton sharks that had attacked us before. If Travast had more of those, they could find their way under the ice-caps, and Sandao wouldn't have stood a chance. Dragonheats, we should have left the dragon automaton with him. Or at least, we shouldn't have charged in so fast.

Travast watched me discerningly, as if he could hear my every thought. I lifted up my gaze from the table and scowled at him. He responded by raising his glass to the air.

"Let's raise a toast to King Cini," he said. "And everything that he stands for." His words almost sounded sarcastic, but I dismissed that impression as nonsense.

In front of me, Taka already had his glass cupped in both hands, his cheeks glowing as if he was relishing in the slight warmth the cup gave off. He stared down at the Exalmpora, his eyes wide, his mouth slightly agape. But once Travast lifted his drink and put it underneath his bandana without revealing what was behind it, Taka smiled and lifted his glass to his lips.

I also raised the glass, while eyeing the two automatons in front of me. They had their guns trained on me, and I didn't doubt they'd use them if I took one false step. I sighed, touched the glass to my lips, and let the metallic warmth wash over my tongue. I swallowed on instinct, and the familiar sensation I'd yearned for so long returned.

Sheer joy. Sheer power. I could transform into a beast and rip out Travast's heart. Then, not even a single bullet could graze my skin before I tore his automatons into shrapnel. What a fool Travast was. Did he realise how much danger he was putting himself in?

No, I told myself. I can't let myself succumb to Finesia. I must not claim her gifts. But where was she? Exalmpora was meant to open up my connection to her.

I also found my spirit soften towards Travast. No longer did he seem a menace who would soon take our lives if we didn't do what he wanted for the king.

He wanted what I wanted – at least while under the influence of Exalmpora...

To unify the lands. To eliminate the dragons. To feed the growth of secicao in the northern continent. To create a better world for all.

I didn't really want this. These thoughts were the Exalmpora's doing. They were what Finesia wanted. And I remembered what Sukina and Gerhaun had taught me – how to still my thoughts; how to keep myself in control.

"I can handle this," I said to myself.

"Yes, you can, Auntie," Taka replied in the collective unconscious.

The collective unconscious. Taka... *"The cyagora has worn off,"* I said. *"Finally, we can talk."*

But that was the last cogent thought I heard from the boy, as his mind went wild and his eyes glazed over. *"She's here, Auntie. And she'll visit you soon. The wolves roam the night, and the bears stalk during the day. But none of them can beat the shades, Auntie, can they?"*

"Taka... Don't let it take control. You must fight it. Remember our training. You are separate from your thoughts."

"Oh, I am here all right. I'm here in my purest form. This is my natural state, how I was raised. And the shades, don't you see them, Auntie? You mustn't be afraid..."

It seemed I'd lost him. But I also had to put on a front so I would make Travast think his drug was having more of an effect on me than he realised. I stood up and walked towards the window. I tottered a little as I moved so as to give the impression of not quite being in control of my senses.

Outside, I could see the slaves working at the rocks. They had so much energy, despite it being so cold and them wearing so few clothes. The greenness pulsing underneath their skin, would have provided extra warmth. This, of course, was the work of secicao. And so, it took a lot of strength to look upon this despicable scene and keep acting my role at the same time.

"Wow..." I said, drawing the word out long, flat, and slow. "It's beautiful."

Travast giggled like a nine-year-old boy who'd just heard a joke about breaking wind. "You know, I'm one of the few scientists in high circles who acknowledges magic exists in this world. There's no scientific reason Exalmpora should work so well on you, and yet it does."

I remained silent after that, purposely swaying from side to side on my two feet. The room was spinning a little, admittedly. But I had my mind under control, and I kept my thoughts distant.

Meanwhile, Taka's thoughts babbled like a kettle boiling in my head. I didn't listen to the words, so much, only acknowledged the repeated motifs – the shades, the dragons, the wolves, and the bears. The slave that had visited us in the camp had spoken about similar things in his delirious state.

Soon, I heard footsteps scuffle on the carpet from behind the screen. A redguard appeared and raised a salute. "Commander Indorm, sir, the king has arrived."

Travast immediately stood up and brushed the dust off his clothing with his hands. "Took his time," he replied. "Well, tell him we'll be there in five minutes, I just want to make sure our subjects will make a good impression. Dragonseer Wells, sit down."

I turned back around, ambled over to the table, and plunked myself down on the seat, as Travast poured more Exalmpora into my glass from a fresh vial. Dragonheats, I'd hoped that I'd only have to deal with one, as each shot would be harder to resist.

"One more for the road," he said. And he poured a glass for Taka, and then topped up his wine.

This time, I raised my glass before he'd even led the toast. "Here's to the king," I said, slurring my words and focusing on a distant point behind Travast's head to make my eyes appear glazed.

Shortly after, I poured the second glass of Exalmpora down my throat, as I planned what I'd finally do to the king who was largely responsible for Sukina Sako's death.

Our meeting was a long time overdue, for sure.

Travast left Taka and I waiting in a spacious dusty room. We sat on two low foldable wooden chairs at the end of a long oblong table furthest from the door. The other seats in the room were tall, upholstered, and looked soft. Travast had gone to greet the king outside, but he'd posted two redguards and two war automatons to stand guard over us.

Taxidermied animals on plaques and pictures of the entire Cini line of the Towese monarchy, leading back several hundred years, adorned the three inner walls. Light came into the room from a long line of stained glass windows, again with royal depictions, such as the circular insignia of the four sabres cutting at the air like a propeller blade, and King Cini III himself resplendent in his white fur coat and felt crown.

I could taste a dusty dryness on the air, indicating it wasn't used very much. Probably, it only saw action when the factory received visits from important officials. And King Cini was the most important of them all.

Taka had stopped babbling in my mind by this point, and so all I could hear was the swishing of the wind outside, punctuated by an occasional cough or sneeze from the guards.

216 | CHRIS BEHRSIN

"Taka, are you there?" I asked in the collective unconscious.

"Yes, Auntie, I'm here... " He paused a moment. *"What do you think they're going to do with us?"*

It surprised me that Taka had regained control of his mind, since he'd seemed long gone in the training room. But that might admittedly have been an act. Or was this all the work of Finesia? I didn't know. But then, apparently, children could break down Exalmpora much faster than adults could. So it might have just been his natural metabolism.

"I don't know," I said. *"But right now it's important that we go along with their plans. We'll find a way to escape and save everyone."*

Taka let off an audible sigh. *"Will we really, Auntie? From what I can see, it seems like there's no escaping this."*

"We escaped the palace, didn't we?" And as soon as the words came out, I regretted them.

Taka lowered his gaze to the table and drummed his fingers against it. *"We did..."* Both Taka and I knew that such an escape had been at a huge cost – Sukina's life.

While Taka seemed ready to bend to the king's wishes, I couldn't help but worry what I might do. I'd driven a knife into the slave at the camp, without being in control. Then I almost killed Talato. How did I know that Finesia wouldn't also take control of my mind at such an apt moment?

If I lost myself to her and transformed into a dragon, I could end his life here and now. And he wouldn't even see it coming.

But then, there was another way out. Another way to end this danger.

They said I was the last dragonseer, but I wasn't. We had Taka, and if I forfeited my life before the king, just as Sukina had, then Taka might live. I truly believed that he could become the greatest dragonseer in history. Even if he wasn't a woman.

But if I sacrificed myself, who then would look after Taka to help lift him up towards such greatness? Given his recent rebellious streak, I somehow doubted he'd get there himself.

Yet, there was always a chance King Cini would execute me on the spot. Last time I'd encountered him he had tried to kill me. And back then, he had also demonstrated that he didn't particularly care about preserving Taka's life either.

"Taka," I said. "*If I don't get through this, I want you to promise me something. Don't let Finesia in... You are stronger than her, and you must never let her take control.*"

Taka looked up at me and blinked hard a few times. "*Auntie, you must get through this. Without you, I'm alone.*"

"*You have Gerhaun.*"

"*She won't last for much longer...*"

And I paused a moment as I let that truth sink in. Gerhaun hadn't long left in the world, and without her and without me there would be no one to mentor Taka.

"*I'm only saying this just in case,*" I said. "*Yes, I think I'll get through this. But we need to prepare for every eventuality.*"

Taka's eyes moistened. "*You will survive, Auntie. There is no other way.*"

A pompous voice coming from the other end of the room interrupted our conversation. I turned to see the alabaster powdered face of King Cini, who now stood at the doorway. Travast stood behind him, blending into the background by leaning against the wall.

"Well, well," King Cini said, "when we met again, I thought it would be head to head on a battlefield, not in a conference room. While it seemed, regrettably, that I would have to kill you, Dragonseer Wells, now I hear you're ready to join my side."

I stared at him, saying nothing, biting my tongue to stop myself screaming out abuse.

Sukina had had a diary in which she'd written of this man's crimes towards her. This king had thrown her mother's severed head in the bin after she had died at Cini's father's hands. He and Captain Colas had drugged Sukina during childbirth, so they could steal her baby – Taka – away from her. And he'd almost killed her by drowning her underneath the Costondi sea, just south of the Southern Barrier. After that, King Cini had changed Taka's gender, and masqueraded him around the palace as his nephew.

Later he'd taken me and Sukina hostage, drugged us and forced us into marriage with the two dragonmen – Francoiso and Charth. He had also ordered my home in the Five Hamlet's razed, destroying everything that my parents had built for themselves over the years, driving them off their own land.

He wasn't a good man, and I hated him to the bottom of my heart.

These thoughts, as they built up inside my head, caused anger to build at an unnatural level. It was almost as if I was being puppeteered by an invisible force. But then, wasn't that how rage worked? Taking control of your faculties, until you later emerge from your blind actions to feel the regret...

"I have to admit," Cini continued as Taka and I watched him silently, "I'm sceptical. You see, I want to believe you. Commander Indorm here tells me he's used drugs to suppress you. But the last time we tried that strategy, I almost ended up dying at a dragonseer's hands." He lifted his head, took a deep and loud breath, and drew a sword from a sheath on his back. "Come forward, get down on one knee, kiss the blade, and swear your fealty, and I'll believe it for myself if I see it in your eyes."

By this time, my tongue must have been bleeding with me biting it so hard, and the rage continued to build in my chest. He wanted me to bow beneath him, so he could demonstrate his absolute power. If he wanted to kill either of us, he'd only need to turn the blade sideways and slice mine or Taka's face in half.

King Cini looked at the guards at the back of the room, now standing behind us. "Start with the boy. Come forward, Prince Artua. It's been so long and look how much you've grown."

Taka kept his gaze distant and swayed on his short legs as he edged forwards. He placed himself on one knee, just above the blade that King Cini rested by its tip on the ground.

"I offer you my loyalty, Uncle Cini, you never lost it and you never will." His words sounded rehearsed, as if he'd had to speak them before. Probably, someone like Alsie or Charth had trained them into him to stop him getting into trouble with the despotic and volatile king.

All this time, my heart was hammering in my chest. I really wouldn't put it past this king to turn his blade on Taka right that moment.

Taka leaned over and placed his lips on the blade that glinted in the soft light. He rested them there for a few seconds, and then he stood up slowly. He wobbled a little as he did, and I wasn't sure if the drug still affected him or if he was putting on an extremely convincing act.

Cini watched the boy with a cold gleam in his eye. "Look at me," he said. "And tell me you love me."

Taka paused. "I love you with all my heart. You are the guardian who raised me, and my birth parents mean nothing to me."

And for a moment, a chilling silence cut through the room.

"Okay," King Cini said with a discerning nod. "I believe you." He raised his head to me. "Dragonseer Wells, it's your turn to convince me of a good reason I shouldn't kill you right this moment."

My legs felt like jelly as I stood, adrenaline pumping through them and my heart pounding fast. I approached my quarry, with such fast and long strides that I could see out of the corner of my eye how my guard had to rush with arrhythmic steps to keep pace with me. King Cini turned a shoulder away from me, as if entering a fighting stance.

I forced myself down on one knee. "King Cini. You have asked me for fealty. You have asked me to join your cause. And to that, I can give you only one response. You are a swine and you are scum!"

Before he even had a chance to react, I thrust myself upwards, and placed my body between him and the sword. I kneed him in the groin, and then I went for his throat. I ripped out his Adam's apple first, and I clenched my hands around his windpipe. His sword clattered to the floor as I flattened him against the wall. Then I spat in his face.

At the same time, I felt myself willing to change into a dragon. Scales crawled under my skin, tearing it apart. I was about to transform. I was about to give King Cini what he deserved...

But then I remembered Charth, and how he'd lost himself to Finesia. I couldn't claim her gifts. I couldn't let the dragon gain control.

I had nothing to defend myself against the blow that clubbed the back of my head. The butt of the gun hit me once, and I managed to keep the stance. But the second swing from the guard sent me reeling away from Cini. Travast hastened towards the hyperventilating king, and he popped his Adam's apple back in place.

The guard held me at gunpoint, and he had such rage in his eyes that I knew if I even budged, he'd shoot. What the dragonheats had compelled me to be so stupid? Where had that rage come from? I had thought I'd been keeping myself under control. But clearly, I'd been wrong.

I looked up into the wild and cruel eyes of King Cini III, as he wiped my saliva off his face with the purple handkerchief that Travast had given him.

"You are a fool, Dragonseer Wells. I offer you a place by the throne in exchange for your fealty, and I had hoped you might take Alsie Fioreletta's place. But, like her, it appears there's no changing you." He turned to the guard – the same one who had hit me with his rifle. "Take her to the firing chamber. Travast bring a Hummingbird and set it to record. We'll execute her now and have done with her."

"As you wish, my liege," the guard replied, and he clapped handcuffs onto my wrists and pushed me towards the door. As he stopped to open it, I turned my head to see King Cini looking down at Taka who stared back up at him with wide and tear-rimmed eyes.

"Don't look at me like that, Artua," the king said. "We have to make hard decisions in such tough times, and this woman has been doing you no good."

And I saw no more of the exchange because the guard jostled me out of the room.

I didn't end up taking a direct route through the factory. Instead, our path wound through the corridors, as if I was being punished by being shown the absolute power this factory held within its walls. I must have passed thousands of automatons, some of designs I didn't even recognise. Enough, in other words, to annihilate Fortress Gerhaun within hours.

Eventually, we stepped out into the open, onto a field of snow lit golden by the waning sun. The guard pushed me over the hoary ground. I still walked barefoot, and pain shot up through my legs with each step. The guard led me to a boarded platform, on which gallows stood at the back – their ropes gilded with streaks of blood.

The sun shone into my eyes as the guard pushed me up the steps, and it admittedly felt good for my feet to touch a warmer surface. Still, the wood hadn't been heated by anything, and after a moment I realised such warmth was relative. I wore only rags, and so I couldn't stop my teeth chattering as I moved.

I thought the guard would lead me to the gallows, but instead he led me towards two poles sticking out from the platform in front of them, with two metal rings on each one – one at the base and one at head height. These had thick and rusty iron chains hanging from them, with manacles at their ends. The guard pulled my arms out and secured the manacles around my wrists. Another guard moved forward, with his rifle trained on me in case I tried anything.

Slightly behind them, a Hummingbird automaton pointed a narrow camera lens at me. Part of me wondered if I should try to fight the guards. I'd get shot down on the spot. But that might have been better than a formal execution recorded by the Hummingbird for Tow and its Sovereign State's civilians to watch over cups of secicao in their city halls.

Still, I thought it better to use the time to formulate a plan for my escape. But no ideas came to mind. One thing I had to do, though, was to keep my fears away from Taka. He'd already witnessed his mother's death, and I didn't want him to witness mine too.

"Auntie, what are they doing to you?" He called out in the collective unconscious. *"What you did was stupid. Auntie, please... Answer me!"*

I knew it was cruel to say nothing in response. But I felt whatever I said would hurt him even more. And so, I kept my mind calm and distant from both his and my own anxious thoughts.

I took a moment instead to take stock of my surroundings. They had led me to some kind of open courtyard, with only a narrow gap in the rock face separating the factory from the open world. Several doors led back into the rock. One of these opened from my right with an ingratiating creak. King Cini stepped out, followed by Travast, trailed by one of those massive war automatons – the ones General Sako had called Ogres.

This time, King Cini kept a few arms' length between me and him, much further than I could spit. He carried no rifle, or even a pistol and I wondered for a moment what he planned to execute me with. Until I remembered the massive Gatling guns on the shoulders of the Ogre.

King Cini looked up at the automaton, and then at me with a grin on his face. "Our previous conversations told me of how much you hate automatons," he said. "So, it's only fitting that you should get executed by one.

Travast was looking at me with creases at the corners of his eyes.

The delight evident in both men caused a wave of nausea to rise inside me. I swallowed down bile, rather than letting myself retch. I didn't want to give these men the pleasure of watching me suffer.

"Gag her," King Cini said to one of the guards. The next thing I knew, I had a cloth in my mouth. Rough hands tied the ends of it tightly behind my back, causing my head to throb in pain. I could feel my pulse beating there – heavy and fast. Then, I felt light-headed all of a sudden. The gag tasted funny, like something similar to grass.

Then I realised. They'd soaked it in a drug. They wanted to sedate me a little. They didn't want me to struggle before the camera. King Cini wanted his citizens not to see me as a fighter, but a weak-willed individual. He wanted to communicate that any resistance against him was futile.

"Auntie," Taka said once again in the collective unconscious. "I must do something. I can't let them hurt you... I just can't..."

And then a sense of horror washed over me. Could Taka turn into a dragon? Could Finesia gain control over him and force him to lose his mind? But I'd never seen him transform, and I could only hope he'd never gained such an ability.

King Cini observed me for a while through narrow eyes. I could only barely make out his expression with the sunlight streaming into my vision. The king strode forwards and pulled back my head. A gob of spit landed on my face, causing me to jerk my head away in revulsion. But that only caused his grip to tear at my hair, and I grimaced in pain before he let go.

The spit dripped down the crevice between my nose and cheek and crawled past my top lip before falling off onto the floor. King Cini turned back to the Hummingbird, and the lens rotated towards him.

"This is an example of an enemy of the state," he said. "Her name is Pontopa Wells. Down in the Southlands' resistance, they call her a dragonseer. It's a name that suggests great power. But look at her now. Do you see her calling dragons to her aid? Do you see her summoning fireballs from the sky, or any of the other nonsense I've heard spoken about her? No. And do you know why? Because she is as human as the rest of you. But despite that, she rides dragons and tries to use them to destroy our civilisation.

"Here we found her trying to infiltrate an automaton factory. She knew that we have a mechanical army ready to march on them, and she knew that we know of their base's exact location. But she didn't seem to realise the limits of her own mortality. This woman who stole away my nephew and tried to topple the throne. Now, witness the execution of one of your beloved empire's most dangerous enemies. And when you do, applaud, because your loyal king, your protector, is watching out for all of you."

He bowed to the camera, clearly imagining the uproarious applause coming from the audience as they watched it on high screens – the recording projected by Hummingbirds, and his voice spoken out by other Hummingbirds carrying massive loudspeakers. The king stepped off the stage, keeping a hard stare trained on me, as he continued to back away. The Hummingbird automaton pivoted around a little, and then it moved in for a closeup.

"Remove the gag," King Cini said.

"Yes, sir," the guard said from behind me. Though, his voice came kind of muffled now with the side-effects of whatever chemical they'd put in the cloth floating around in my brain. But I could still feel pain, and they'd stretched my arms and legs so that my chest and groin felt as if they would tear apart.

There came the sound of someone drawing a knife from a sheath behind me, and I felt a sting of a blade against the nape of my neck. The gag came free in my mouth, and I unclenched my teeth to let it fall to the floor. I tossed back my head and snarled at King Cini.

"Oh dear, oh dear, Miss Wells," he said with a chuckle. "Please behave, will you? Remember you're on camera. And we will only display the highlights, and not the bad parts, so there's no point trying to manipulate the show."

I rattled at my chains. "You will never get away with this, Cini."

"And here, I was going to ask you if you wanted to say any last words? Any expressions of love to your parents? Or maybe a plea to your dragon queen to fly over and help?"

"You want to hear my last request? Curl up and die."

I don't know where my last words came from. They didn't feel like my own. And strangely, I didn't feel afraid. I felt empty. I felt fulfilled. As if this was my destiny, about to unfold.

And then I remembered the dragons on the carrier. I sang a song to call for their aid, and their spirits rose in the collective unconscious in response. Maybe they'd come in to save the rest of us, but for me it was certainly too late.

King Cini shook his head. "Always such a disappointment, Miss Wells. I never thought you'd live up to the legacy of Sukina Sako."

The cloth returned to my mouth, and this time it was tied so tight that it took an exceptional amount of control not to scream out in pain. The drug entered my head again, and I went all bleary-eyed so I couldn't even focus on the machine-gun barrel that would soon riddle me with bullets.

This was it. I had truly reached the end.

"Prepare," King Cini said and raised his hand, and then he lowered it in a vigorous cutting motion. "Fire."

There came a great roaring sound from the guns on the Ogre automaton. I closed my eyes, and I prepared to die.

But nothing pierced my body. I felt no pain. I opened my eyes and raised my head to see a volley of twelve-inch bullets edging towards me at a snail-pace, a white swirl visible behind them. King Cini, Travast, and the Hummingbird automaton were completely still, their faces skewed with active expressions as if posing for a painting.

How the dragonheats could this have happened? Was it magic? Or was this what you saw before dying – the last seconds of your life playing out in agonizing motion.

"Well, well, Acolyte Wells." Her voice came finally in my head. *"Welcome to death. "* She'd been gone for so long, I'd almost missed her.

"Finesia," I replied. *"What do you want?"*

"To save your life, of course. Or would you rather I didn't?"

"Yes, I would rather die than succumb to your will."

"And what good will that do for the world? Are you prepared to let these lesser mortals defeat one who has the power of a god?"

"I've kept you from controlling my thoughts," I said. *"And things will stay that way."*

"Oh, but have you? The way you behaved before the king, do you really think that was your doing? I have much more control over your mind than you think. And now it's time to show these imbecilic mortals your true power."

A rush of air came into my ears, and I felt the clarity of time restoring itself. The bullets hit my body, as if hitting a bag of meat. It felt like someone had hit my chest with a sledgehammer.

But then an even more excruciating pain emerged. The sensation of thousands of scales tearing apart my skin. The screams segued into a roar that caused the ground to quake in front of me. I tossed my muzzle to the air and craned my head over a long growing neck. My shoulder blades lashed apart, and two massive wings shot out of them. My wrists and ankles widened, and all four manacles snapped off at once.

Some bullets fell to the ground in front of me. Many more ricocheted off my leathery skin, causing Travast Indorm and King Cini to dive for cover. I beat my wings as I gnashed at the guards who had rifles raised against me. One of these guards, I lifted into the sky, then I dropped him from high above.

Then, my consciousness became no more, and I entered that frightening place between dreams and oblivion.

The land beneath me doesn't belong to Orkc, or at least not the country that I'd entered a few days ago. It isn't covered in snow, but secicao resin. Here, secicao clouds roil around the bare roots and branches that have cut into and consumed the planet.

Here I am, a servant of Finesia scouring the world to rid it of our enemies. The demons who want to strip away the gifts of immortality. Those lesser mortals who are so consumed by their own petty lives. They fear death, and so they try to defy it. But they can't do so forever.

I open my mouth and roar out, and a black dragon joins me. It flies alongside me, and we swoop across the sky in brilliant aerobatic patterns. If swallows still existed, they would stop to watch in awe.

I turn my head to look at the dragon. *"Rastano?"* I ask. My beloved has come back to join me at last.

"Yes, darling," he replies. *"I'm here, and I'm yours, always."*

"And Alsie Fioreletta? Where is she?"

"You know, Pontopa, that it's our duty to vanquish her together. Me and you, we shall live until eternity. You as the master, and me your loyal slave who you can do with as you please."

My mouth curls up in a reptilian smile, and I swoop down to get a

228 | CHRIS BEHRSIN

closer look at the earth beneath. There it is – the Tree Immortal, the source of all life and the place where I shall one day claim my dominion as Finesia's right hand. Its roots dig down so far into the soil, and come up again so sharp, that it's hard to tell them and the secicao apart. Its branches twist through the sky, rising above the secicao clouds. Around it, the clouds eddy as if the tree is singing out to the world.

The melody is haunting. It resonates out through what once was the collective unconscious. The channel that once thrummed with the echoes of life, is now filled with the screams of regret of the dead.

It's the most beautiful song I know.

I fly down below the Tree Immortal's branches and focus on my enemy. There they are, concealed beneath the secicao. A covert force of shades who have come to take it all away. They approach the tree with their daggers because they want to peel off its bark and eat it to claim some power for themselves.

Inside that tree lives the spirit of Finesia. She claimed its power herself ages ago, and I helped her plant its seeds again. Now, I shall not let our work become undone.

The shades reach the tree and hack away at it with their knives. The bark is tough. It will take them hours to extract even a slice. But still their actions are insults to Finesia and the world we have created. I cannot allow these creatures to roam.

"This is your destiny," Finesia says in my head. "To rid the world of those who oppose us. To wipe the planet of our enemies and create a new and beautiful race of dragonmen and dragonwomen. Your kind, secicao, and the Tree Immortal are the only things this world needs."

Her words fill me with exultation, and I toss my head to the sky and let out a thunderous roar. My voice reaches out over the land, sending out a command to the very corners of the world. It orders those in power to come and join us, as we wreak destruction. And, as my call resounds over the land, I swoop down – Rastano trailing slightly in my wake – and I unleash my flames upon the shades.

And there are other trees around us – replicas of the Tree Immortal – with other shades chipping away at their bark. The shades only have their knives, which are useless against airborne dragons. One by one, they go down in the brilliant flames that lick their tongues over the land.

This is the way it was meant to be. The beginning of the end of the world.

Another wave of men rises over the horizon. These carry swords – as if such weapons will give them a better chance. They charge as one. But their slashing blades can't reach us, as we continue to spray the land in a brilliant display of fire.

Meanwhile, another presence is drawing nigh. My cohorts have answered my call.

"Join me," I say to Rastano. Then I climbed back up into the sky.

A line of black dragons emerges through the secicao clouds. *"Hooooiiieeee,"* one of them cries. *"Your wish is my command,"* another says. And I wheel around to join them, so we can destroy the charging army en masse.

This time, the shades have weapons that they can use to defend themselves. But they are only sticks and stones that glance off of our tough hides.

Meanwhile, we are one. A coordinated, awesome force that nothing in this world stands a chance against. But my energy is fading. I haven't yet adapted to the life of a dragonwoman.

"Come, Rastano," I say. *"Let us leave this battle for another day."*

"As you wish," he replies. And we leave the flock of dragons alone to wreak havoc upon the shades.

We fly over a wonderfully barren land, bereft of all life but secicao. Not a fox, or hare, or hawk, or squirrel, to be seen. Only yellowness stretching out so far that it's hard to make out where the secicao clouds end and the sky begins.

This is our world now.

We find a brown river, flowing wildly. It splits off into two tributaries which converge around an island and then meet again to become one. Rastano and I land on this island, and we laugh and transform back into our human forms. A shroud of black dust rises around us – our very own private curtain. And because the cold cannot affect us, we cannot wait to strip off our clothes.

We are naked, we are nearly impervious in this form, and we can breathe the secicao here. I gaze into Rastano's eyes and then I beckon him forward.

He nods with a grin – one that didn't belong to the old Wiggea. But I prefer this version. Finesia has made him a better man. A wild creature with passion and allure.

He takes hold of me by the waist, and I flatten him down onto the ground, for I have more strength than he does. Our bodies meld as the yellow clouds boil around us, and the sounds of destruction and death linger upon the stale air.

Then, my memories become lost to roars and screams of passion...

And wonder...

And pain...

Anguish for those who I have lost – and the soul I have sacrificed.

I collapse, my energy spent, not caring anymore about Wiggea. And it's no longer a ground rife with secicao, but a cold, hoary and barren ground. As I lie there shivering, thoughts rage in my head that Finesia has betrayed me.

It's only a matter of seconds until I black out.

23

I woke up with my eyelids stuck tight together, feeling surprisingly warm, given I'd just gone to sleep naked on the snow. As I came to, I realised I was wrapped in a blanket, lying in a bed, with people milling around me. Human voices – and a sense of dragons being there in the collective unconscious.

The dreams, what had they meant? Had they been real?

Velos. Yes, I could sense Velos. And a voice, one so familiar and close to me. It stopped a moment as I forced my eyes open.

Then, I realised I wasn't outside, but surrounded by a white canvas that rose to a central point. Some marines worked away adding firewood to a pit in the centre of the tent. But they hadn't had time to light it yet, and so I couldn't have been here long.

"She's awake."

The man's footsteps moved towards me, and I looked up into that gentle face. He had a tidy beard, a calm expression, and a polite manner.

"Admiral Sandao," I said.

"Dragonseer Wells… You made it. We feared we'd come too late, and we'd heard that they'd already shot you. But we couldn't find the body, so we thought they'd incinerated it or something. And then we find you lying out here, naked in the cold."

"You came to rescue us?" My voice was weak, and my brain found it hard to find the words."

"Aye," Sandao said. "Our dragons heard a call from you and got alarmed, and so we immediately knew you were in danger. So, we brought in the dragons and the marines. But we had no idea how outnumbered we were. And we would have lost, if we hadn't had other help."

I shook my head, remembering. "But Travast... He said that he sent out an army of automatons against you."

Admiral Sandao smiled. "That he did. There were Mammoths and giant things General Sako has started calling Ogres, and there must have been hundreds of them. They marched out over the ice, and for a moment we didn't think we had a chance. But they were so heavy, that we only needed to send out the dragons to melt them into the water. And the rest is now history."

I propped myself up on my elbow, taking a moment to look underneath the blanket. Someone had clothed me in a shirt and some trousers, but my hands and my feet were bare and looked bruised and scratched.

"You mentioned reinforcements at the factory. Who were they?" I asked Admiral Sandao.

"A black dragon. No, actually, two of them. But they were ruthless. We watched them for a while, and they not only wanted to melt down the automatons but scorch the slaves. We're not sure a single man or woman there survived. Then more dragons came, and we took advantage of the distraction to free our people from the cells."

A wave of repulsion rose in me as Admiral Sandao spoke. Could those two dragons have been me and Wiggea?

"And what about Taka?" I asked. I'd abandoned him, because I'd let a blind rage build within. And then Finesia had used that rage to wrest control.

Sandao lowered his head. "We couldn't find the boy," he said. "We saw an airship fleeing from the factory towards Ginlast, and we suspect Taka was on board."

I raised an eyebrow. "But you don't know for sure?"

"No, we don't," Admiral Sandao admitted.

I nodded. *"Taka,"* I said in the collective unconscious. I thought it was worth a try. But there was no reply.

"The dragons?" I asked.

"Velos made it out alive, and Faso also managed to fix the dragon automaton on the way out to get it flying again. They're waiting with the other dragons outside."

I heard some more footsteps approaching. I looked up to see Lieutenant Talato holding a cup. She reached out and offered it to me. "Cup of tea, Ma'am?"

I took it, trying hard not to drop it as its heat seared my fingers – my hands still tender from the cold. "Thank you."

"It's not a problem. I was so worried that we'd lost you, Ma'am. A guard came down and told us they had sent you to your execution and that we would be next. Then, he went away. There was some commotion from outside, the sounds of dragons and rifle fire. Then, the next thing we knew, we were being broken out by the marines, and then we found you lying naked on the ground."

I shook my head. "Those weren't normal dragons." She hadn't seen what had happened at East Cadigan Island, before the battle against Cini. How the volcano had erupted, and we'd escaped through the billowing ash after which the black dragons arose from the earth. Finesia had called them mine to command when I first encountered them. Alsie had been there, and Charth. And we'd had many of the king's airships barring our escape. Then Finesia had appeared in my head and instructed me to call my minions. And I'd refused, much to Finesia's dismay. But in my head, she then promised me I would one day command them.

Now, it seemed, I finally had. Destroyed innocent lives, through my powers, without even being in control of my senses.

It was me. I had attacked the slaves at the factory. I'd scorched them out of existence. Wiggea had been there as well. And the other dragons had come at my call.

If Finesia could gain such power over me, did I have any chance at all?

Sandao's marines added the last log to the fire pit. They then poured on some oil and set it aflame. I relished the heat coming from it, even though it stung my face a little. I mustered some energy from somewhere to swing my legs around on the bed and sat up, still keeping the blanket clenched against me to protect me from both the heat and the cold.

"Blunders and dragonheats! Dragonseer Wells, you're alive." I turned to see General Sako had just entered the door, the flaps billowing out in front of him. "And you're not in a coma. You looked so blue when we found you, I wasn't sure you'd make it through."

I shook my head. "Me either," I said.

"What the dragonheats happened? How did you end up getting from the firing range to lying naked on the ground? They said that they'd shoot you, but what they did seems an even crueller way to make you die."

"I don't know," I lied. "I blacked out, and then I was here in this tent."

"Are you well enough to get up? Because we have to fight back. Alsie, or someone, is up there with those same black dragons she used to take down Cini at the Battle of East Cadigan Island. They caused so much destruction, that this is our opportunity to march in and burn down the place, so it never sees the light of day again."

"I can stand," I said. And I put my feet on the floor and eased myself gently onto them. I started teetering a little at first, and Lieutenant Talato reached out to catch me. But I put up my hand to stop her, and I waited a moment to endure the pins and needles that stabbed at my feet and ankles.

I looked around at the men and women who had gathered at the fire pit, then at Admiral Sandao, then General Sako, and finally Lieutenant Talato. I wondered if they could have any inkling of what had just happened. What I had just done.

But then, the only person in the room who knew I could turn into a dragon was Talato. And she still seemed to trust me. "Lieutenant, may I have a word?" I asked, and I beckoned her over to the other side of the tent. I led her far out of earshot of everyone else.

"What is it, Ma'am?" Talato asked.

"I need to know, have you still got cyagora?" Even if I could no longer control the dragons on the march, even if I lost my connection to Velos, I couldn't risk having Finesia take control of my mind again.

"No, Ma'am. I'm afraid Travast confiscated it in the factory. Do you need them?"

I shook my head. "I don't know..." And I watched her for any suspicion from her that I was part of that flock of black dragons that had attacked the slaves. But I detected nothing. It was no surprise, really. She'd found it incredibly hard to believe in Finesia and the power she had over us. And it was probably better that it stayed that way.

But even so, my chest felt heavy as the gravity of Lieutenant Talato's information weighed down on it. Without the cyagora, I had no way out. Finesia could do what she wanted with me whenever she pleased.

I nodded and Talato and I walked over to General Sako and Admiral Sandao, who were discussing the situation from besides the bed.

"The problem is," General Sako was saying, "that Taka could still be in the factory. I don't want my grandson to get caught in the cross-fire. I know you have good marines, Sandao. But they still need to proceed with utmost caution."

Admiral Sandao scratched at his beard. "You don't think he's on the airship? From what the guards told Lieutenant Talato, the king wanted to take him back to the palace and return him to his life as Prince Artua."

"And the king didn't care if Taka died at East Cadigan Island, for wellies' sake. I heard him say it over the loudspeaker myself."

"I think the king must have taken Taka," I said. "He forced us to swear fealty to him, and Taka accepted, and... I refused. That's why they wanted to execute me. But now, King Cini thinks Taka is on his side."

"You did what?" General Sako's face went purple.

"I'm sorry," I said. "I acted on impulse, and I messed up."

General Sako nodded, but he said nothing else.

"This isn't what we need to focus on right now, General," Admiral Sandao said, and he reached out and put a hand on the general's shoulder. "Taka is in danger, and if he's in the factory, we'll rescue him. But if not, we'll send Dragonseer Wells, Lieutenant Talato, and the marines to Ginlast to retrieve him. He can't have gone far."

I nodded my affirmation. I was glad that we had Admiral Sandao here with a level head, because both General Sako and I were incredibly emotional at this point.

"Very well," General Sako said, and the colour had started to drain from his cheeks. "Dragonseer Wells, promise me you'll do whatever you can to get the boy back."

"I promise," I said.

And I turned away, no longer able to hide the guilt for everything that I'd done.

PART VII

ALSIE

"Who wouldn't want to gain the power of a god?"

— ALSIE FIORELETTA

24

This time, Sandao's marines set up the screen outside to prepare for the briefing, while others packed the tents away, ready for us to spring into action.

It was now mid-afternoon, and the sun shone the brightest we'd seen since we arrived, melting the snow to slush and preparing the land for spring. This was one of the reasons we wanted to get to the factory fast. We not only wanted to take advantage of the chaos caused by the previous day's attack, but we also knew that the slush would freeze to ice overnight. This wouldn't make marching easy, and could give those huge automatons, with their massive feet, the advantage.

The troops latched the screen onto two high pine trees. No one sat – it was far too cold to be doing so. Instead, we stood in lines, Lieutenant Talato and I at the front as usual, while Ratter dangled from a helium balloon behind us and projected images of the carnage onto the screen.

That was the first time I experienced for real the extent of the damage I had caused, and it hit me hard. I saw so many slaves lying on the snow – their skin burned red and brown but still with that unnatural green tint underneath it. They were distributed in circles around the rocks, with their pickaxes scattered around near them.

What had they done to deserve this? Convicts of the king destroyed by the mad will of Finesia and a dragonwoman who couldn't control her own mind. In the picture, I could see the melted automatons. Those immense beasts that Travast had developed hadn't stood a chance against the black dragons. The barrels of their Gatling guns were warped, as if a giant had marched over and bent them in half. Claws had ripped the shields protecting the power cores right off their back. And the hole, where the power core would have been, was surrounded by charcoal black char marks.

General Sako stood in front of us, so he could give his briefing. This time, Admiral Sandao stood next to him, though he remained quiet. It seemed rather odd, to be honest. General Sako had lost his commandos and the marines were the admiral's troops to command. But the more mild-mannered man didn't seem to mind the general taking charge.

"This is perhaps the easiest mission you've ever embarked upon," General Sako said. "The work has already been done for us by that mysterious dragonwoman, Alsie Fioreletta. None of us yet know what she wants, but it's the second time she's rushed in to aid us. So, I guess we should be grateful. But don't be tricked into thinking she's on our side."

Of course, I didn't tell him it wasn't actually Alsie Fioreletta controlling those dragons, but me in dreamland. They wouldn't have believed it, anyway.

"Also," the general continued, "although I doubt you'll encounter resistance, you must still be vigilant. I saw many deactivated automatons inside the factory when I escaped, which didn't look ready for battle. Though, blunders have been made on assumptions before, and we have to expect Commander Indorm might get some of them operational. So, keep your weapons loaded and ready at all times.

"We have forty Greys at our disposal. They will provide support from the air while we charge in and plant explosives in the factory. I've indicated the best locations –" the image on the screen changed to an overhead blueprint of the factory, with red crosses on it "– here, and here, and here. Just remember, I want all rooms checked before the explosives are clear. My grandson might still be in the factory, and he's far too valuable for us to lose him."

"I can communicate with him in the collective unconscious," I said. "And so, I can check if he's still in there." As long as I wasn't on cyagora, I'd at least have that ability.

General Sako's moustache twitched. "And you can do it if he's sleeping? Or in a coma, wellies forbid."

"I'll be able to sense him. As long as he hasn't purposefully closed off his mind."

"And why would he do that?" General Sako asked.

"I don't know. Hopefully, he won't."

But I was pretty sure Taka wouldn't be in the factory. He was on the king's royal airship to Ginlast. And this was another reason we had to storm the factory as quickly as possible. I needed to get Velos and the other dragons chasing after him.

"General Sako, if I may." Faso had stopped tinkering with the dragon automaton and walked over to join us at the back. And perhaps something about what had happened had changed him, because it wasn't like him to be so polite. "Shouldn't we go in and reconnoiter before we charge in?"

"Blunders and dragonheats, Gordoni, boy, we don't have time."

"But if Travast activates more automatons, we need to know what we're up against. We don't have to lose any time doing so. Pontopa and I can go ahead of the troops as you march. You can keep the dragons nearby, and if we encounter unexpected resistance, Pontopa can call the rest of the dragons in ready for battle."

He was making sense, I guess. But I didn't want to go ahead of the marines. I wanted them to be there, so they could shoot me down if Finesia tried taking control of my mind again. That way, this world would be a little safer. At least for a while.

I looked back at the blueprint on the screen, noticing the rocks where I'd seen those slaves working. Many of them were my country-men. Perhaps important figures convicted for crimes such as trying to resist a despotic king. Perhaps people whose causes weren't so different from my own. And I'd roasted them under my flames without a care in the world.

"And is your dragon automaton ready yet?" General Sako asked Faso. "And also, what about Velos, he didn't seem in too great condition when I last saw him?"

"Velos is recovering fast," Faso said. "The armour really does help heal him. And I'm almost there with the automaton. I also recovered the helmet in a lot better shape than I thought it would be in. Anyway, you can journey ahead while Pontopa, Winda, and I finish up here."

"Very well. So, we march now. Is everyone ready?"

From around me came the calls of, "Yes, sir."

"Then commence this operation."

General Sako took hold of a flag and waved it in the air as he marched ahead of everyone. Admiral Sandao also took hold of a flag and did the same. The rest of the troops quickly got in formation, arranged by Candiorno and the other officers, and followed the two leaders.

Some of them towed sleds behind them, with various supplies. There was one large sled in particular, covered by canvas, and I wondered what was underneath.

Meanwhile, I sang out a dragonsong to call the Greys into the air to escort the march. If the troops met resistance, then the dragons could provide maximum support. The Greys launched into the air, snow crumbling underneath them. They circled the company as they marched forward.

I watched them for a moment until they became small enough to become part of the scenery. As they went, I remembered the dream I'd had, and the carnage that I'd wrought, and I prayed that I wouldn't end up annihilating Gerhaun's troops as well.

FASO ALREADY HAD the dragon automaton laid out in front of him and was working hard on repairing it. It looked different in the snow, and the white reflections on the metal gave it an almost angelic quality. Faso was making a racket using a welding torch on a plate that had lost a rivet and had sprung out of place.

Meanwhile, Winda worked at the automaton's head – earplugs in, as she tightened some screws. She had this ferocious scowl on her face, which didn't suit her too well. I guessed that Faso hadn't yet apologised to her for his behaviour before.

Velos stood tall next to Faso, with his helmet lying beside him on the ground and his head craned over the inventor, as if supervising his work. When I looked up at his scaly face, I could see curiosity in his eyes. And I felt it too.

Finally, I was at one with Velos' emotions again. Yet, with the sacrifices I'd had to make to get there, I still couldn't help but question if it was worth it. I walked up to Velos, and he turned his head to me and lowered it. I wrapped my arm over his muzzle and stroked him on the cheek. He let off a soft crooning sound.

Faso turned to me and cut off the noise from his torch.

"Almost there," he said. "Then we can put the helmet back on Velos, and we'll fly in."

"We can't just augment?" I asked. "Must we really use that ugly helmet?"

"Yes, we must." Faso stood up and put his hands on his hips. "That's how we're going to see the heat signatures inside the factory, remember. We might save some marines' lives if we spot an automaton moving towards them. And the signatures might even help us find Taka in there." He shook his head, and he shuddered. "Dragonheats, I want to know he's safe."

All this time, I'd been thinking of my guilt and how bad I felt about losing Taka, I hadn't even considered Faso's emotions in the equation. "Yeah, me too," I said.

Faso lifted his head and gazed off at the horizon. "I just can't stop feeling that I've failed him as a father. I should have been there for him. And now, I could have lost him forever."

I turned to Winda to see if she could hear any of this. But she seemed absorbed in her work, and the earplugs were working well.

Shame, though, because Faso was displaying a rare expression of his humanity.

It was definitely behaviour to be encouraged. So, I walked up to him and put my hand on his shoulder. "You know, you can't blame yourself. Cini wanted Taka back, and he took him. We'll get him back, you have to believe that."

Faso looked up at me. The bottom of his eyes were wet. They must have really stung in this cold, but he didn't wipe the moisture away. "And what if we don't? I never thought, until Sukina, that I'd have a son. And then I finally had someone to pass my legacy on to. And now he's gone."

I stepped back and placed both my hands on my hips. "Is that what Taka means to you, Faso? An opportunity to pass on your *genius*?"

Faso recoiled. "I –"

"For wellies' sake, Faso. You just don't get it, do you? He's your son, and you've got to accept that his interests and your interests might not align. My father and I are such different people, and yet we share something above the relationship. That's what it's about. Not moulding him into the person you want him to be but helping him to survive the world and build a life for himself. That's what you're here for, Faso."

Faso opened his mouth as if to say something, but instead his bottom lip trembled, and he closed his mouth again as if to protect his lungs from the frigid air. He held my stare, and for a moment I thought he was going to do a typical Faso and argue back, and we'd have one of our spats. Instead, he broke off his stare and his gaze trailed off into the distance.

"I guess you're right," he said after a moment. "I haven't been the greatest father to him, have I?"

I shrugged. Sometimes, when Faso showed his soft side, I just couldn't help feeling sorry for him. "There's time to change all that. We'll get him back and you'll work out how to be a better parent."

"I hope so," Faso said. "Well, I guess I should get back to work." And he wiped his eyes with the back of his mitten and then turned back to the automaton.

"You know," I said. "You can start making up for other things today. You've got to treat the people you care about well, otherwise they'll just push you away."

Faso looked over to Winda. "Yes, I guess I do," he said.

Winda raised her head and looked at Faso, who returned an apologetic smile. He stood up, walked over to her, and crouched down to talk with her.

I thought I should give them a little privacy, so I moved back towards Velos and tousled his scaly head. Then, without thinking, I sang him a song in the collective unconscious. It was my way of saying sorry to him, because I'd neglected him too. I'd cast my own needs above the responsibility I had to keep a connection with him, and with all the dragons for that matter. That was my role as a dragonseer. And just as Taka relied on Faso to be a father, that's what everyone relied on me for.

Yes, I had done terrible things. And I wanted to blame Finesia, and secicao, and the whole world for being so cruel. I wanted to be a victim, to say it had happened to me, and I had no control.

But that's when I realised if I adopted that philosophy, I might as well give up now.

I had to believe I had control of my mind. And I had to believe I could overcome Finesia, without cyagora.

"You really think you have control?" she said to me.

Gerhaun and Sukina have taught me how, I replied. *I've prepared for this, and I know how to keep my mind whole.*

"Fool! You really think mere mortals can defeat a god?"

"You are no god," I reminded her. *"The Gods Themselves left us, and you tried to take their place. But you are just as flawed as the rest of us."*

My mind went silent for a moment. I took that time to listen to the rhythm of my heart, and my breath resonating with Velos'.

For the first time in a long time, I felt completely in control.

25

Velos sailed through the sky. The wind whipped at my hair as I sat in place at the front, with Lieutenant Talato on the back seat. Faso had refuelled the armour with secicao, and so we could move fast. My helmet dangled at one side of my body, and I'd secured my hip flask to the other side. Faso flew besides us, wearing his helmet. Winda sat behind him, her hands gripping the bars of the turret in front of her.

"Testing," Faso said over the speaker system.

"It works," I replied.

"Good. We need to make sure we coordinate everything well. And why the dragonheats don't you have your helmet on, Pontopa?"

"I prefer to see things with my own eyes. That strange heat-sensing vision messes with my secicao blend's capabilities. Surely, it's better for me to have the augmented reaction speed in my blend of secicao oil, rather than the helmet's thermal-sensing capabilities."

"And if we need to see inside the factory? What if I miss something?"

I sighed. "We've not even caught up with our own troops, Faso."

"No, but we're almost there now. I can see much more through the helmet than you can through your eyes, even augmented."

"Then, until we're truly in danger, I want to relish the wind rushing against my face and be able to see things as they truly are."

Soon enough, we caught up with the rest of the company. I watched them trundle along from my high vantage point, as the Greys wheeled above them. Admiral Sandao, General Sako, and the other marines were on the ground, towing the heavy weaponry and crates of explosives on their sleds. There was also that huge sled with the long object laid out covered by a thick canvas. I still hadn't worked out what it could be.

The factory was only a few hours away on foot, but it would take Faso and I only around fifteen minutes to get there once we flew ahead. Particularly with the secicao pulsing through the armour, which generated a refreshing warmth at my feet. That, together with the sunlight, abated the wind chill factor somewhat.

As we passed over the marching army, the dragons let out a cry to welcome me, and Velos joined in their roar, sending a tremor up my spine. I clutched at my ears to keep the noise out, and then I reacted instinctively by singing a harsh staccato dragonsong to berate them.

"Dragonheats, can't you keep them under control?" Faso said from the talkie.

"They're wild animals, for wellies' sake," I replied. "They're going to make a noise sometimes."

Velos whimpered underfoot, and I changed the notes in my song to calm him.

"Come on," I told him. "We'll be there soon."

And it wasn't long until we left the company behind and started speeding towards the factory.

"Pontopa, put the helmet on now," Faso said, once again over the speaker system. Dragonheats, he could be annoying sometimes.

"I thought I said–"

"No time, Pontopa. It looks like we've met resistance."

I sighed, unhooked the helmet from my hip, and placed it over my head. I didn't notice anything different from normal, so I flicked the switch to turn on heat-signature mode, and I found the dial to adjust the zoom.

At first, they were tiny specks on the horizon. But it wasn't long before I saw them to be those massive Ogre automatons, the red heat signature against the glacial blue of the rock face showing they were active and dangerous.

The wind beat against the sides of my helmet as I watched the automatons scan the sky. Whether they were looking for us or Alsie Fioreletta's black dragons, I had no idea. As we drew closer still, I made out the shapes of a Mammoth automaton hiding near the log pile, and another that had been previously concealed from view behind the rock face. Several Rocs also patrolled around the edges of the rock, their sharp pointed beaks spearing into the sky.

"We should go back and warn the troops," I said.

"I've already spoken to General Sako over my communications system, and he thinks we should take a closer look. We've not yet got a full scan on the perimeter."

I swallowed cold air. I didn't want to go closer. Not so much because I feared the automatons, but because I knew what was coming next.

And soon enough I saw them. The dead slaves were lit up in my display as cold blue corpses on the ground. Yet they still had a trace of heat coursing through them, as if the secicao still lived there. My stomach lurched, and I wanted to vomit, but I held it in.

"You did well, acolyte." Finesia said in my mind. "And I will reward you in due course."

But, no. I wasn't meant to be listening to her. I was stronger than this. I had to fight her in my mind. Whatever the consequences, I had to accept them. And I had to keep myself sane.

"What the dragonheats is that?" Faso asked.

"What?"

"Coming from the bodies. They're emanating some kind of warm gas."

I hadn't noticed it at first, because it was so faint. But when I looked for it, I could see the gas ever so slightly pink in my helmet's vision. It drifted out of every single body and then diffused into the air. There was a warmth to it that drew the eye towards it. And so, I stared mesmerised at the way the patterns danced in the air.

I lifted my visor, so I could at least see the colour. And, as I'd expected, it was green, just like the bodies that had lost their red pigment and had that same sickly colour pulsing beneath their skin.

That drug that Travast had given them, had had secicao in it for sure. And now, it was trying to dominate the land. To find its roots in the ground. But then that's what secicao did. It crept its way into its consumers' digestive systems and then leached back out into the soil through urine. Eventually – according to Gerhaun Forsi's book, Dragons and Ecology – it would make the soil so acidic, that no plant other than secicao could grow there.

When that happened, secicao would take the opportunity to spread across the world.

I felt something then. Another presence. Not human. A flash of black darting above the rock face. I'd seen him in my dreams, and I didn't know the difference between what had been a dream and what had been reality. Now he was here. "Wiggea," I said out loud, without realising.

"Wiggea?" Faso replied. "You've got to be kidding me! He's here?"

"It doesn't matter," I said. "We should retreat. We need to meet up with the rest of the company so we can take this place full force."

"No," Faso said. "We need to get even closer. If they're going to set that place alight, I need to know if Taka's in there. You should be able to sense him, right?"

I sighed. But I guess Faso was right. "Not from this distance. But if I get close enough. Yeah, I'll know if he's in there. But the automatons…"

"There's an opening in the centre, there. We just need to fly close to the rock face, let's just do one pass, and then get out. I'll look out for a sign of Taka's heat signatures behind the rock. Just make sure you focus as much as you need."

"Who put you in charge?" I asked, a slight element of mirth in my voice.

"I'm just doing what needs to be done, Pontopa. Sometimes, you need to focus on the objective above your own ego."

Huh, that was rich coming from him. "Okay, I said, let's go in."

"Your helmet, Pontopa…"

But instead I took hold of my hip flask and unscrewed the cap. I needed my reactions more than I needed to see what was inside the factory, which Faso said he could do himself. "Best to pool our resources."

I took a swig of secicao, and the world ghosted into speckled green. I felt clarity of mind return to me. Everything was now moving incredibly slowly.

I hadn't augmented for a while, and I'd forgotten how good it felt.

"Yes," Finesia said. "This is my world."

"No, you will not take control."

"But I already have, dear. I already have."

I pushed her away from my mind. Meanwhile, I raised a hand forward to signal us towards the rock face. There was an Ogre automaton on the left, another on the right. Both were a few hundred metres away, and my heart skipped a beat when I saw them turn their massive bodies towards us in sync. But this was just part of their programmed routine, and they soon turned back away without noticing us.

I pushed down on Velos' steering fin, to get him closer to the rock face, and then I veered him sharply to the right. I reached out in the collective unconscious.

"Taka," I said. We slid so close to the rock that I could feel the cold emanating off it. "Taka, I'm here. Auntie Pontopa is back, Taka."

But there was nothing. Not even a sign of him trying to push away the collective unconscious.

"Oh, he'll come back soon enough," Finesia said in my mind, "once he bends to my will. You shall see."

"Shut up!" I said in the collective unconscious, and I felt something building inside me. It was a power that had been used on me by Alsie before, and I wanted to unleash it. The scream could disable dragons and stun any secicao powered automatons on the field.

"That's it, my acolyte. Use your powers, claim your gifts."

But instead, I balled my fists by my side, so tight that my nails seared pain into my palms. I centred myself and let the anxiety and the frustration leave my body, before Finesia took control.

"He's not here," I said over the speaker system. "Taka is nowhere to be found."

"Then we should return," Faso said. "General Sako, the place is clear."

There was a pause and a little static on the line, before General Sako's voice bawled out of the speaker system. "Then that's it. We shall set the explosives. Come back and we'll charge in together and take this place down."

"But what about Taka?" I asked. "Every minute we lose here, he's getting further away. I should go after him alone."

"Blunders and dragonheats, Pontopa. You will do no such thing. We need to take this one step at a time."

And I realised, as much as I hated it, that he was right. Taka was on the airship, and the sooner we got rid of this factory the better. Then I would take the dragons, finish off the king, and finally get vengeance for everything he and his father had ever done. I could finally liberate Tow.

"That's how it starts," Finesia said. *"Such beautiful thoughts of glory and conquest. We shall make fine partners."*

But I ignored her and turned Velos back towards the marching company. It was time to get this show on the road. And it was to be a grand spectacle indeed.

26

By the time we returned to the company, the sun had begun to set low in the sky and would soon sink below the horizon. The latent warmth that it had brought to the land was dissipating with it, and soon the cold would set in once again. Then, the melted slush on the ground would freeze and become slippery, making marching difficult. We could have sent the marines in on dragons. But we planned to use the dragons as a distraction, drawing the automaton's fire into the air as the ground-based marines sneaked passed them with their explosives.

I didn't even bother to land. Instead, I sang out to the dragons to coordinate them. And I continued to work the spell in my voice, commanding them into a long V-formation, so we could sweep across the sky in a broad swathe.

"You're looking good and ready, Dragonseer Wells," General Sako said over the speaker system.

"Better than ever," I said, keeping my sentence short, so I didn't interrupt the song.

"By the way, we have something for you," General Sako said. "We thought you should be well equipped."

"And you brought two of them I trust," Faso said.

"Of course." General Sako turned around and raised his hand to halt the march. "Troops, reveal the cannons."

The marines by the large sled saluted, then the ones on the right-hand side took hold of the tarpaulin and tore it away to reveal two long weapons. These attached to the underbellies of Velos and the dragon automaton and could punch a hole in the largest of automatons, taking it down in a single shot.

"Oh, goodie," Faso said. And from behind me he clasped his hands together. He was lucky his harness was buckled, because without it he would have fallen off. "We'll pick it up first."

Soon after, the dragon automaton swooped towards the ground. Faso had lined it up perfectly. His automaton let off a loud clanking sound as it connected with the target, then emerged from the swoop with a massive cannon sticking out of from beneath its belly. Now, the dragon automaton truly looked like a machine of war – more terrifying than any I'd seen in King Cini's or Travast Indorm's arsenal.

"Our turn," I said. And I glanced over my shoulder to check that Lieutenant Talato was buckled in. I brought Velos around in a broad circle and then pushed up on his steering fin and sent him sharply towards the ground.

When the marines on the right saw my aim was off a little, they scattered. But they didn't have to, because I quickly corrected my course. We hit the target, the cannon clanked onto Velos' underbelly, and we lifted it back up into the sky.

I felt a triumphant roar build inside him, and I let out a dragon-song to admonish him before he roared and encouraged the other dragons to do the same. There was something strange about the way they were behaving. They were almost mischievous, as if in the presence of something trying to control their minds.

"That went smoothly," General Sako said over the speaker system. "Why can't every operation go that way?"

"I wish it could," I said. I flew Velos around to meet up with Faso, flying within the protection of the Grey's V formation. But we weren't going to cower at the back. With our powerful weaponry, it made sense that we should take the vanguard. So, I sang out to instruct the flock to part, and I signalled Faso to join me at the front. He did so without complaint or any sign of annoyance.

Behind me, Talato controlled the distribution of secicao in the armour. Velos didn't need much of it, only enough to compensate for the extra weight of the cannon and stop it dragging him down. But we were going pretty slowly to keep up with the troops marching on the ground. So most of the flight was a casual soar, with each dragons' wings turned against the air stream slightly to slow us so we didn't end up abandoning our company.

Fortunately, the troops below were also augmented, and hence they marched unbecomingly fast.

Eventually, the first automatons came into view. Two Rocs faced us head on, their sharp beaks looking like they wanted to skewer us in flight, and their missiles primed, ready to fire.

"Pontopa, put your helmet on," Faso shouted.

"No, Faso," I said. "Remember, I'm the one in charge here, and I'm going to do this my way." The effects of the secicao from before had already worn off, and so I lifted the hip flask to my lips and took another swig. The greenness washed over my vision, and time slowed.

Each Roc had missile launchers hanging underneath their wings. These were currently pointed at the ground, as if they expected to attack the troops first. But they soon pivoted upwards, until they were pointed right at us.

"This will take some aerobatics," I said.

"That's for sure," Faso replied. "But we're well equipped for it."

A warmth pulsed underneath my feet and I looked down to see that Lieutenant Talato had directed more secicao into the armour. Meanwhile, there came a screeching sound from ahead, like a flock of crows in intense pain, and the missiles detached from their launchers on the Rocs, plumes of smoke trailing in their wake. Twelve approached in total. Six headed directly for Velos, the other six for Faso's dragon automaton.

"Talato, get the cannon fired up," I shouted back.

"Yes, Ma'am," Talato replied. And a white light glowed from beneath Velos' neck. I knew it would be tight, and I narrowed my eyes so I could focus on the missiles directly. At the same time, I kept my hands clenched around Velos' steering fin, so that I could make sudden movements on impulse. I didn't have time to turn to see what Faso was doing, but I could see out of the corner of my eye he was also charging the dragon automaton's cannon.

"Fire," I screamed, and the blast came straight out of Velos' cannon, bucking us upwards a little. A brilliant beam of white light seared through the cold sky, and it hit our Roc target right in the belly.

I still had the missiles to contend with. They were only metres away now, wailing out as they approached. I noted their location and speed, then veered Velos into a sharp barrel roll. The missiles shot past us, did a one-eighty, and approached from behind.

Last time we'd dealt with these things, we'd had to duck underwater to shake them. But there wasn't any water here. However, we had dragons surrounding us, and so I sang to them to instruct them to chase the missiles. Several of the dragons at the tips of the V-formation were far back enough that they could reach the missiles in time. They coated them in flames, knocking them off target. The missiles veered downwards slightly and then passed underneath us.

They continued away from us, glowing red hot, and they slowed again and turned in the sky to track us. This time, I thought they would take us, and I watched in horror, out of ideas.

But the heat got to them, and the missiles eventually stuttered, fell towards the floor, and exploded before they hit the ground.

I reacted quickly, singing a song to get the dragons as high as possible. We passed above the explosions, the heat brushing against my calves.

I released a deep breath I hadn't realised that I'd been holding. Then I took stock of the surroundings. Both Roc automatons had clean holes punched in them – Faso and Winda's shot had been just as effective as mine. They plummeted and crashed into the snow, sending out a massive shock wave that caused the troops down below to cover their ears.

Still, there were a load of automatons on the ground to deal with.

Those massive Ogres, and the war automatons, placed around the men and women that I'd killed.

I led the dragons down low enough that we'd draw their fire, but high enough that they couldn't hit us. The automatons rose to our bait, and they turned their guns upon us. Our Greys coated them in flames, slowing them somewhat.

Meanwhile, General Sako, Admiral Sandao, and the marines took advantage of our diversion and charged into the factory without issue. It would take them time to set everything up, and we didn't want the automatons to cotton on to our plans. So, I continued singing my dragonsongs to manoeuvre the dragons around the battlefield. They dived, and they swooped, and they unleashed carnage.

But we had to perform difficult motions in the air to dodge the bullets, and the dragons didn't have infinite stamina. Eventually, I felt their energy fading, as the roars they let out into the sky diminished. And I also was losing control, in my voice. I hadn't used my abilities like this for quite a while.

The first dragon got shot down. A bullet from a war automaton clipped its wing, and it screamed out, before plummeting to the ground and tumbling across the snow.

It tore at my heartstrings to see such a brave soul go. The Grey writhed on the ground and it would suffer before it died. I sang a song to thank him for being brave, to tell him he would join a better world as he transcended into the collective unconscious.

Meanwhile, several more dragons got shot out of the sky, left to struggle to their deaths in much the same way. And I kept muttering under my breath for the marines to hurry and set their explosives in the factory. If these automatons eliminated us, the marines would have nowhere to run when they emerged from their mission. Yes, we might successfully destroy the complex, but we'd also lose many men, including General Sako and Admiral Sandao.

And so, even though I was tired and wanted to just fly Velos away, we soldiered on. Meanwhile, Faso brought down the dragon automaton down towards one of the Mammoths. Not far away, another Mammoth was ripping fire into a group of three Greys in the sky.

I turned Velos and instructed Talato to charge up the cannon. Then I took Velos down and approached the Mammoth from its flank. The machine rotated slowly, while a cluster of Ogres provided support from nearby by firing at us with their Gatling cannons. I pushed on Velos' steering fin, and he entered a barrel roll. Meanwhile, the guns on Velos' armour turned on the Ogres, and unleashed such force, it managed to flatten one to the ground.

I turned my attention to the Mammoth automaton right in front of us.

"Fire!" I shouted. The cannon unleashed a massive beam of light, and I guided Velos into a loop-the-loop. We turned upside down, and then I executed a half barrel roll to get us upright again. I looked over to the Mammoth to see the massive hole punched right through its body. Its weapons had gone slack, and it stood there dead to the world.

Beneath us, there came a cheer, and the marines filtered out of the factory. The automatons, who still were directing fire into the air, paid them no heed as they made their retreat.

General Sako's voice came over the speaker system. "The charges are all set. No sign of Taka. Everyone, fall back!"

And as I turned the dragons away from the battlefield, a sense of dread washed over me. This had been far, far too easy. And my heart lurched, as it dawned on me, in vivid flashes... Suddenly, I understood Travast's plans.

Back at East Cadigan Island, Captain Colas had given drugs to the tribespeople. And he'd devised a ritual, where they would combine my blood into the drug. Exalmpora – the blood of a dragon queen – mixed with the blood of a dragonseer, mixed with secicao, heated with intensity. That specific blend of ingredients had birthed drag-onmen and dragonwomen from the tribespeople after the volcano had erupted, and the magma had passed over them and stripped away their mortal lives.

Travast... He'd already been feeding the slaves with a mixture of secicao and Exalmpora. All he needed to do was add dragonseer blood to the mix. And the guard had taken a sample of my blood in the prison cell.

This had all been orchestrated. And now, the factory was about to blow.

I swallowed a bubble of air and clenched my teeth. "General Sako," I said. "We must stop the explosives. They can't be allowed to go off."

"Blunders and dragonheats," General Sako said as he ran. "We can't stop the explosives now. They're set and primed. What's this about?"

"They wanted us to blow up the factory. Because, just like at East Cadigan Island, they've created perfect conditions here for the dragons to arise from the fires."

As we spoke, the automatons cut off their fire. But there was movement. A floating platform, with a man on top, his cloak billowing out behind him. I swore, then put on my helmet, zoomed in, and turned on the heat-signature display for a better look.

Travast stood on the platform, with a loudspeaker pushed up against his purple bandana. I felt compelled to take Velos in there and then and shoot him down on the spot.

"Oh, you don't want to do that, my acolyte. Don't you want to learn what he wants?"

Dragonheats, she was right. I levelled Velos into a hover so I could watch him.

"I just wanted to thank you," Travast said. "For your brilliant help in this operation. I wanted to blow up this factory myself, but then I thought it so much better if you witnessed our power. For this isn't the work of science, as King Cini thought, but the work of magic. The work of Finesia." A thick black cloud rose around Travast that looked almost like crow feathers swirling around his platform.

The man continued to speak in the collective unconscious, and clearly his words were meant for me alone.

"Yes, Dragonseer Wells, we've all been watching you with such interest. You try to fight Finesia, and you end up aiding her plans. Well, it's about time I revealed my true identity, because that is Finesia's will. My name is not Travast Indorm, but Indira Trastino.

Alsie Fioreletta, Chartha Lamford, Francoisa Lamford, and I, we were the Famous Four who the public thought were executed by King Cini in the gas tower. And we might have been, had it not been for our father, Captain Colas, who decided which of us dragonseers would be most loyal to Finesia."

General Sako and Faso couldn't hear Travast's, or Indira's, voice in the collective unconscious, as they didn't have a connection to it. And so, they talked obliviously amongst themselves over the speaker system. But I was so interested in this person's words, I didn't register what they were talking about.

"Your father..." I replied. *"You mean to tell me you are Charth's and Francoiso's sister."*

Indira chuckled in the collective unconscious. *"Oh, he birthed eight of us. Captain Colas was a genius, and he still lives as a dragonman – Finesia's gift for his service. And you don't realise, do you?"*

I felt the anger rising in my chest. Because I kind of suspected what she was about to tell me. *"I don't realise what? Tell me..."*

"Your true mother, Sukina's mother, and the mother of the other two dragonseers whose names have been wiped from history. They were all my father's daughters. As I said, he was quite a womaniser. And he was also the first and only man in history to think of having all eight dragonseers as his offspring."

Colas... My grandfather? It couldn't be.

"I only had to get one man to be loyal to me," Finesia said in my head. *"All this time, I could use him to manipulate the minds of the dragonseers, so I'd be born within them. I am a part of your family line. I'm innate inside you. And that is why you cannot escape my will."*

Dragonheats, I couldn't believe what I was hearing. This hadn't just been planned over the last couple of years. Finesia had orchestrated it over generations.

I took a deep breath, as the whole gravity of this situation sank in. Soon, the clouds around Indira's platform subsided, and from it a black dragon shot into the air. She spiralled upwards and then dived back down towards the ground. *My sister will be here soon. I believe Alsie Fioreletta has become famous. And Charth, and Wiggea – who I believe was once one of your own. And even my father. I thank you, Dragonseer Wells, for giving them immortality.*

Then Indira spoke once again out loud, this time not needing a loudspeaker to cut through everyone's voice.

"My daughter is out there, somewhere," she continued. "And we shall find her. And we shall ensure both her and Dragonseer Wells convert to Finesia's cause."

And, before anyone had a chance to say anything else, the explosion came.

27

The factory exploded with a terrifying green hue. It filled the sky with ugly light. But we hadn't added any secicao to the explosives. Which meant there must have been something else catalysing this strange explosion. The gas that had come off the men, perhaps, and a kind of magic seeping through the ground.

I knew already what had happened. The secicao had taken root in the soil, and it had just been waiting for a catalyst to grow. As the green smoke segued to yellowish-brown, the first shoots of secicao sprung out of the ground. Then she spoke in my head. Not Finesia, but another almost as bad.

My arch enemy…

"*Dragonseer Wells,*" she said in the collective unconscious. "*We keep rubbing shoulders under such strange circumstances.*"

"*Alsie Fioreletta… I might have known you were behind all this.*"

"*Can you never just say, 'Hello, how are you?'*"

"*You are not my friend.*"

"*I guess not. Friends aren't usually destined to battle to the death.*"

"*We can duel now, if you like?*"

"*Oh, you'll finally take Finesia's gifts. Because she's been waiting for you* to convert to her cause. She almost had you, I believe. But you're not loyal and that shall be your undoing."

"I can defeat you without Finesia," I said. "Just let me battle you in your human form."

"You think that will be enough to defeat me, wench? I'll never let you have access to my throat, and you are not yet mature enough for such a battle. Meanwhile, I brought your friends. Charth, why don't you say hello?"

And I heard a groan come back from the collective unconscious. It had the same dryness and the same emptiness as the man I once knew. But he wasn't there. His spirit had been completely stripped away from him. It was as if an automaton had been put in his place. But this time, it wasn't cogs and gears, but the will of a mad goddess that controlled it.

"He's not very talkative nowadays," Alsie said. "This is what happens to disobedient subjects of Finesia. They end up with existences not worth having at all."

Something flew overhead, and the troops below tried aiming their rifles at it. But it was too fast, and its massive form blocked out the sun momentarily, casting a shadow over the land. "Charth?" I said again. "Are you in there somewhere?"

I had hope, but there wasn't much of it. He'd sacrificed himself to Finesia so we could live. And, somehow, I knew I'd never speak to the man again.

"You know," Alsie said. "Perhaps it should have been you and he that were lovers. But I believe you chose another. And here he is now."

Another smaller black dragon shot out of the clouds emerging from the factory. He did a barrel roll, and then a loop-the-loop, almost as if trying to court me. "Come and join me, darling," Wiggea said inside my mind. "I promise I'll make it worth your while."

But the last thing I wanted to do was succumb to Finesia's will. "Wiggea, there must be some trace of you somewhere. You were always so loyal."

"I still am. I'm loyal to you and I'm loyal to Finesia."

"Those two loyalties contradict each other."

"I don't think they do. You are closer to her than you realise."

His voice clicked out of the collective unconscious, and then he stopped his circus tricks and vanished back into the unfolding secicao clouds.

"Oh, and there's one more who I thought we'd bring to join the show," Alsie continued. *"Taka, introduce yourself in your new form..."*

And those words brought even greater dread to me than anything she'd said before.

"Taka..."

"Auntie Pontopa, I'm here."

"Go on," Alsie said. *"Show yourself, boy. Don't be shy."*

"Taka... You drew on Finesia's gifts? I told you not to..."

He emerged from the clouds, the smallest and rattiest of dragons I'd ever seen. Yet what he didn't have in size, he made up for in agility. Someone down below had had enough of these black dragons, and let off a rifle shot, but he darted out of the way.

"Don't shoot," I said over the speaker system. "That's – That's Taka."

"Blunders and dragonheats," General Sako replied. "How is it possible?"

"It just is..."

"Taka," Faso said. "No! What did that freak, Travast, do to you? It can't be..."

"It wasn't Travast," I said. "It was Finesia... This is the danger I've been trying to tell you about all along..."

"Auntie Pontopa," Taka said in the collective unconscious. *"I know you're angry, but I really had no choice."*

"I wish you'd stayed with Cini," I said. *"We would have come to rescue you."*

"But King Cini is dead," Taka said. And, although Taka had grown up with the king all his life, I didn't hear a hint of sadness in his voice. *"These dragons, they took down his airship in Ginlast, before he grouped with the others. They left so many flames burning around me. And I was trapped, and I thought I would die. But now, King Cini is dead. No one survived except me. Finesia gave me a way out. She saved my life, Auntie. Like she saved yours..."*

"No!" I screamed out loud. *"Alsie, you could have killed him. He's a child, for dragonheats sake. What were you thinking?"*

"Oh, he wouldn't have died," Alsie said. *"No child would ever neglect their own survival for spiritual and pointless goals. And he already had a way out. He just needed to be prompted to take it. Much like you were, I believe, in East Cadigan Island."*

I could feel the rage boiling in my chest. My heart was pumping incredibly fast, and adrenaline coursed to my arms and legs. I wanted to leap into the sky and take Alsie down. I wanted to turn into dragon form and battle her here and now. I would rip out her throat, much as she had done to Francoiso.

"That's it, my acolyte," Finesia said. *"Use your powers."*

But then an image of Sukina came into my head. She was there, somewhere in my mind, looking out for me. Present in the collective unconscious, ready to appear when I needed her most.

I'd promised her I'd look after Taka. She'd sacrificed herself so he and I could live.

"Taka," I said. *"You must keep Finesia out. Get on the ground, get back to human form, and never convert again."*

Taka flew towards the troops below, unnerving the Greys who circled close to him. I sang a quick dragonsong to remind them that Taka was Taka, and not our enemy. "He's going to land," I said to General Sako. "Make sure that no one even raises a rifle against him. And trust me, General Sako, this is your grandson."

"Blunders and dragonheats!" he blustered. "I guess I have no choice. I just hope you're right Pontopa..."

Taka roared out, extended his claws, and came in to land just in front of the company. A black dust cloud came up from the ground as he landed, and this subsided to reveal the sandy-haired boy in his jerkin and frilly white shirt. He ran towards General Sako, who opened up his arms and then held him tight.

"That's it, boy," Alsie said. *"Go to them. I'll come back and get you when you're ready."*

"You will pay for this, Alsie," I said.

"Perhaps," she replied. *"But you'll need to give a lot more to Finesia,*

before you'll truly have the strength to battle me. One massacre is nothing in the grand scheme of things. Anyway, the show is about to start. The fruits of our efforts shall now be reaped. Behold our new dominion, for tomorrow we immortals shall rule the Northern Continent.

And her words were cut off by another explosion, this one much larger than the last. It filled the sky with a tremendous white light, with such a thunderous roar that every human present clutched their hands to their ears.

"From this earth, immortals shall rise," Finesia said. *"These men and women were wrongfully convicted by an errant king. Now, they can have the immortality they deserve. You sowed the seeds for this, Acolyte Wells. And you can claim your reward later, once you're ready."*

The air filled with a thickening smoke. It brought with it the acidic smell of secicao. It wasn't enough yet to stop us breathing, but it would be soon. Although there were gas masks in the armour and in the dragon automaton, the men below hadn't brought them inland. Thus, we had to get the troops out, otherwise they'd die.

"General Sako," I said. "I need to bring the dragons down to pick you up. We must get you all out of here."

And before he could respond, I sang to command the Greys into action. They swooped down and took up the men in their talons. We had to leave the extra equipment that we'd brought behind. None of the weaponry we had here would do anything against these black dragons, anyway.

One Grey took hold of Taka, and under the command of my dragonsong hovered over Velos and deposited the boy in the central seat. Taka quickly buckled himself into his harness, without me asking for him to do so.

"I'm so glad you're alive," I said to him in the collective unconscious. And I turned to see that tears were streaming from his eyes.

"Are you angry?" he asked.

I shrugged. How could I be angry? *"I also had to use Finesia's gifts to save my life at East Cadigan Island. You didn't have a choice. But you must be even more vigilant now. Because she wants to trick you into getting closer to her. And we cannot let her gain control."*

"I know, Auntie. And she said some horrible things to me. She wanted me to join her cause for immortality. But it's just stupid. I just want to be human, Auntie. I don't want her to take away Velos and the other dragons."

We were interrupted by a third explosion. This one was smaller, but had an intense pitch like a thousand snare drums sounding at exactly the same time. Then, out of the ground emerged the first dragon. *"I'm finally free,"* came its voice in the collective unconscious. *"And Acolyte Wells, you are my master."*

"And I," another said. Another black dragon shot out of the ground. *"All I did was steal a loaf of bread, and it eventually earned me immortality.*

"What the dragonheats is happening?" Faso said. "It's impossible."

"But you saw the same happen at East Cadigan Island," I replied over the speaker system. "Alsie is taking control of this land."

"But what about the king?" he asked. Of course, he hadn't heard any of the conversation in the collective unconscious, so he had no way of knowing.

"King Cini is dead," I said through clenched teeth.

"What? How?"

"The black dragons killed him."

More dragons continued to emerge from the smoke. They claimed to be my minions, and asked me to command them. But I didn't give them an answer. Alsie, once again, could have them. Because to accept control of them would be to surrender a large part of my will to Finesia. And that, I couldn't do.

There came a whirring sound, and the ground beneath us parted. Out of it shot heavy strands of secicao, and war automatons popped out of the land, their rifles raised to us. The secicao shoots continued to twist up around them, faster than any plant could naturally grow. Soon, the stuff would take the land, and with it the gas would snuff out all life here.

"Ah, my automatons," Indira said in the collective unconscious. *"By employing me as his chief scientist, the late King Cini appointed me in command of them. We shall set up more factories like these, and we shall make more dragonpeople and automatons ours. And those who don't join our cause shall die."*

"*And, we shall take our armies south,*" Alsie continued. "*And use them to destroy all mortal dragons on your precious continent. Then this world will become our own. Are you still sure you want to be on the wrong side?*"

I took one glance at the war automatons, and the secicao spreading across the land, its branches and roots spreading outwards, tearing apart the ground. This was Sukina's hometown. And now it was being taken over by the force she'd battled to protect us from.

Ginlast would be taken first. Tens of thousands of citizens having their lives choked up by a virulent and unforgiving species they had no idea could live here. "We need to go," I said over the speaker system.

I directed Velos up into the air, just as the war automatons fired upon us. My dragon roared, and the Greys followed his call, crying out mournfully into the blue sky above the rising acrid clouds. We'd all been fighting to prevent this – humans and dragons alike.

Faso took the dragon automaton down for one last pass, spraying the war automatons with bullets and flame. The automatons returned the fire, but neither side seemed to hit their targets or do any damage. The dragon automaton came up to join us, and we rose ever higher.

"*You need to return home now, Dragonseer Wells,*" Alsie said to me, just before I was out of reach. "*Because someone you love dearly is on her death bed. Indeed, I've received reports that Gerhaun Forsi will soon draw her last breath.*"

Dragonheats. I'd been so consumed by my own problems, and more recently this carnage, that I'd neglected to listen to the more subtle echoes on the collective unconscious. And when I pushed Finesia and Alsie, and the fear, and hate, and guilt away, indeed I could hear Gerhaun singing out from afar into the void.

I needed to get back to Fortress Gerhaun to say my goodbyes.

"*And remember,*" Wiggea then said. "*That I love you, and I always will.*"

And that was the last I heard before I caught sight of the ice caps and I left the dying Northern Continent behind. The catastrophe Gerhaun had been warning us about for so long had started. And there was nothing I could do to prevent it.

PART VIII

GERHAUN

"Those who live to help others, will never truly die, for their legacy will remain eternal."

— GERHAUN FORSI

28

As we approached Fortress Gerhaun, the clouds felt heavier than normal. Usually, I'd get a sense of them easing off as we approached the fortress. But now, they felt as if the secicao was trying to push in. As if it knew Gerhaun's death would give it the opportunity to swallow up all human life.

It was just Taka and I on Velos's back. We'd escorted the rest of the fleet to Port Szutzko, and when we'd decided we were clear of any Towese forces and dragonmen, we left them to travel the journey alone. We kept Velos as light as possible, so I let Faso refill the tank on his armour while I took out all unnecessary luggage, keeping only a few snacks and the water we'd need to make it back.

If someone had told me before this day that I could make that journey in twenty-four hours without landing once, I wouldn't have thought it possible. But necessity has achieved much more unlikely things in the past and would in the future.

I could already feel Gerhaun's spirit waning in the collective unconscious as I brought Velos in to land. We had only taken a small force up north, and so numerous soldiers awaited us in the courtyard. They stood at attention in their olive drab suits and then saluted us in unison as Velos touched down. My parents were with them, and Papo stepped forward first. Meanwhile, Velos lowered his back so Taka could rush down his tail. I followed the boy down to the ground via the ladder.

"Pontopa," Papo said. "You made it back. A Hummingbird scout came back to us with the news of King Cini's death, and we worried so much. They blew up the factory, Pontopa. How did you survive?"

"Papo," I cut in. "We've not got time." I could already feel Gerhaun's life force dissolving. She was mumbling in the collective unconscious, something about this being the end of the good life, repeatedly.

Mamo strided up to me and hugged me quickly, then took hold of my hand. "Gerhaun has been wanting to see you." She looked me in the eye, seemed to notice something, but said nothing. She turned to Taka. "Both of you... It's good that you made it in time."

"I'll go," I said.

Mamo nodded. "We'll be right behind you."

"No, please, wait outside. This is something that Taka and I need to handle alone."

I took hold of Taka's hand and we rushed through the empty corridors. They were even dustier than usual, and I let off a sneeze as we walked. We passed the tapestries of dragons in battle, torches that had failed to be lit, even Mamo's tearoom with a sign on the door – 'Closed Until Further Notice'.

Then we were outside the double doors to Gerhaun's treasure chamber. I pushed them open, and saw Gerhaun lying on the floor, wrapped around the golden egg. Her head was flat against the ground, and her warm breath buffeted against me as I stepped forwards, Taka trailing only slightly behind.

I remembered Velos and I knew that he would also want to join us. So, I sang to him, to invite him down the chimney, thinking Gerhaun wouldn't mind.

"There's no need," Gerhaun said. *"I've already extended the invitation."* Even in the collective unconscious, her voice came across as fragile.

There came a rush of air from above, and Velos came down the massive chimney, and landed just a few metres away from Gerhaun's back. He let out a groan, and pushed forwards, nestling his muzzle into the gap in front of Gerhaun's neck.

"Gerhaun," I said in the collective unconscious. "We came as soon as we could."

"And how glad I am that you did. Dragonseer Wells, I am proud of you. As I am of you, Taka."

I turned to the boy who had remained silent up to this point, both physically and in the collective unconscious. He had his head bowed to the ground, his sandy fringe covering his eyes as if hiding away his pain.

I didn't know whether I should tell her. Not on her deathbed. She'd banished Charth for crimes like mine, and I didn't want her last thoughts to be those of despair. But she'd been my trusted advisor, my mentor for several years after Sukina's death, and a friend. I owed it to her, whatever the cost.

"Gerhaun," I said, and opened up the channel to make sure Taka could hear me too. "I need to tell you something, and I'm sorry it comes at such a late hour. But I'm no different than Charth. Both Taka and I, we ended up taking dragon form. But while he took it for his survival, something happened to me. Finesia took control of my mind in my sleep. Out there, I lost it. I massacred, and I destroyed the lives of innocent men and women. I couldn't keep Finesia out."

Gerhaun shook her head slowly and gently. "We all have regrets. Had I not had banished Charth from here, we might not have lost him. And when you told me what happened at East Cadigan Island, I privately resolved that I'd help you through it whatever the cost."

"But when you pass on," I said. "You won't be there..."

She paused a moment and regarded me with her great yellow eye. "You've come so far, Dragonseer, and you've learned how to be good, like Sukina. None of us can stay on this world forever – none of us, that is, who remain true to ourselves."

"But you can fight it, surely, Gerhaun. I – I – I can't do this alone. Finesia wants to control my mind, and I need your help." I had tears welling at the bottom of my eyes now. Taka reached out and took hold of my hand and squeezed it a little. He also had tears in his eyes, and he looked lost.

You can, Gerhaun said. *And you will. Because you are much stronger than you think...*

I shook my head. Her words comforted me somewhat, but I still couldn't truly believe it, not after everything I'd done. *"How long do we have before the secicao swallows this place?"* According to convention, the dragon queens should come to the funeral, and they'd help keep the secicao away for some while. But when they left, we would all have to relocate.

"A day or two. But at least one of the dragon queens should arrive before that time elapses."

"And then I'm alone..." I said. The sense of emptiness crashed down upon me like a tidal wave coming ashore.

"You will never be alone, Dragonseer Wells. Sukina and I, we'll be there to help you in the collective unconscious, in the most profound ways."

I took a deep breath, and I held the silence for a moment. I felt empty, and I felt afraid.

Gerhaun turned her head slowly, and she moved a little closer. *"Sing with me Pontopa, we need to make the call."*

I looked up at her. *"What do you want to sing?"*

"Just follow the notes. We shall rally the dragon queens, and this time they must come. They cannot refuse a dying dragon queen's call, even if they've refused my invitations before."

And so, she sang.

It was the most beautiful thing I'd ever heard. With notes like wind chimes against a soft breeze, a stream swishing by underneath them. Each note twinkled, like sparkles from the sun reflecting off the water. Like all dragonsongs, it had no melody to it. But still it had in it a sense of completeness, designed to calm anyone who could hear it.

My heart latched on to the song, and the notes flowed out of my mouth, though with slight variations on the primary theme. Taka also joined in with his own improvised cadence. And even Velos crooned a counterpoint to Gerhaun's song.

The song reached out to the edges of the Southlands, and with every note we sang, I felt a new dragon out there joining in. Some of them were on Sandao's ships. Some of them in distant fortresses I'd never visited. Some of them were wheeling around Fortress Gerhaun on patrol, scouting for automatons. This was the voice of the collective unconscious, and it only existed because souls united in this world to fight the good fight.

That day, the whole of the Southlands sang. And for a while we could forget about the danger that loomed, the lives we'd lost and the lives we'd have to lose.

We came to the end of the song, our harmonies converging into a powerful whole – a held note that pushed the secicao clouds upwards for just a moment.

And then, Gerhaun died.

She didn't go with a scream. Nor did she whimper. Simply, her life was there one moment, and then snuffed out the next. The subconscious didn't lurch, like it had when Sukina died. We'd prepared her passage, and so she transcended naturally.

After which, a long silence fell.

The first to wail was Velos, with a high pitch that I didn't even think could come from his vocal cords. I moved forward and wrapped my arm around his snout. I would always be there for him. He was the father and now the sole protector of the unhatched dragon queen. No female dragon egg had been born for centuries, and so this one was incredibly precious.

When I'd moved to Velos, I'd left Taka standing there, and now he stood with red-rimmed eyes, staring straight at Gerhaun's lifeless head. "Come," I said, and he walked over to me, and I embraced him with my free arm.

"It will be okay," I said. "Everything will be okay."

"But, Auntie, without Gerhaun, we're nothing. I didn't even say goodbye. I didn't know what to say…"

I tousled his hair. "You didn't need to say anything, Taka. She knew how much you cared, and she knew that, above it all, you're a good person. And a fine dragonseer."

276 | CHRIS BEHRSIN

"But without Gerhaun, how can we stop that horrible woman and keep her away from our minds?"

I took a deep breath. Part of me didn't want to believe all this. Dragonheats, five years ago, I didn't even acknowledge the existence of the collective unconscious, and the power that existed within. *"Gerhaun's still there,"* I told Taka. *"She's somewhere in the collective unconscious, and she'll find a way to reach us when we need her. Perhaps we'll see her in our dreams. Or perhaps she'll appear suddenly when we need to find the courage to do a brave thing."*

"But she's not really there, is she Auntie?"

I turned down to Taka, and I smiled, despite the tears stinging at my eyes. *"I believe she is. And if you believe the right things, you can accomplish a lot. Finesia preys off a lack of hope. But we won't let her win anymore. Okay?"*

He looked back up at me and blinked some tears out of his eyes. *"Okay."*

I left Taka in the room because I knew he wanted to mourn a little longer. But on the way out, I took the effort to close Gerhaun's great scaly eyelids. Then, I stepped out of the door.

Mamo and Papo were waiting outside, and Doctor Forsolano was just rushing down the corridor with a massive briefcase in his hand. He looked at me as if wanting to acknowledge I was there, but also to signal he really didn't have time to talk.

"It's too late," I said. "She's left this world."

That stopped Doctor Forsolano in his tracks, and he pivoted around. "What? You're kidding? Are you sure?"

"I just felt her go, doctor," I said.

He feigned a step forward, as if he wanted to reach out and hug me, but then he noticed my mother hovering nearby. "I'm sorry," he said. "I did everything I could."

"I know. But it was time, and she was old." And the last words barely came before I found myself weeping again and then wrapped in my mother's arms.

No matter your age, there's something about your mother's embrace that soothes even the greatest of despairs. I wondered then, how much longer my parents would also be on this world. Would they die first, or would I? Before all this, they'd wanted me to settle down and find a nice husband and have a good life under the control of King Cini. They also wouldn't have ever thought we'd end up here, in a barren land where we can't even breathe the air outside.

I left my mother's embrace and turned back to Doctor Forsolano, who was peering around the doorway, almost as if he didn't believe Gerhaun was dead.

"Doctor Forsolano," I said. "Do you mind if we have a private word?"

He nodded, and I led him aside down the corridor where we wouldn't be able to be heard. I turned back to see Taka was now in my mother's arms.

"I'm sorry," I said. "But I lost the cyagora. And I wasn't able to get more."

He turned back to me. "Oh dear," he said. "Were you okay? Did you have any repercussions?"

I shook my head. "It was hard to come off it. But I think I'm finally okay. I'll try to go out with Velos to get the herb as soon as I have the chance."

"You've got other things to worry about right now," the doctor said as he put his hand on my shoulder. "Don't worry, I'm sure I'll convince Candalmo Segora to bring out a shipment soon. By the way, is it true? I heard news around the fortress that King Cini has died."

"Taka saw it with his very own eyes," I said.

"That must have been hard for him. How has he been since?"

"I think we'll both need a checkup. But I don't think he's going to go back to those drugs. Not after everything that's happened."

"I understand," Doctor Forsolano said. "And I truly am sorry... About Gerhaun, I mean."

"It's okay," I said, and I turned back to look at my parents. "I should go."

"Of course, you'll probably need this time with your family." Doctor Forsolano gave me a warm smile before he left, and then he strolled back down the corridor.

I walked back to my parents, and this time Papo took the chance to give me a hug. Not long after, there came the call of a bugle from outside, and a guard came rushing down the corridor. She was a young woman, not much older than I'd been when I'd left the Five Hamlets to become a dragonseer.

"Ma'am," she saluted. "There's a great golden dragon approaching from the air. We're not sure we can trust it. I wanted to ask Gerhaun…"

I sighed. None of the troops would have had a chance to find out yet. "I'm sorry to say that Gerhaun has passed on," I replied. "Please inform the rest of the troops. And also, tell them not to show any resistance, for this is one of the dragon queens and she comes in peace."

The guard saluted one more time and then she rushed back off towards the courtyard. I turned around, nodded to my parents. Then, I marched through the corridors as I wiped the tears away from my eyes.

29

"Ah, there you are, Dragonseer, I wondered when I'd finally get the chance to meet you."

While Gerhaun had never come across as patronising, the first dragon queen's voice in the collective unconscious had an undertone of contempt.

I stood with the troops lined up neatly in Fortress Gerhaun's courtyard. Behind them stood every single Grey that remained at Fortress Gerhaun, and Velos too. Taka stood beside me, his posture rigid.

A gust of wind came from the dragon queen as she brought herself down to land. It was so strong that I worried it might knock us off the ground. It wouldn't look great if she saw we employed troops that couldn't stand upright.

But I looked over my shoulder and saw the troops were holding their ground. The wind subsided, and the dragon touched down, sending up a cloud of brown dust around her. I let it settle and then stepped forward.

"Keep your distance, dragonseer." The dragon queen said. And I recoiled, more than slightly taken aback. "Oh, don't look at me in that sulky human way. I sense a presence in you. I might have known Gerhaun *would be harbouring agents of Finesia. Much as she did with that fool, Charth. She was never the best judge of character."*

Now I wanted to pull a rifle off my back and take a shot at her. How dare she say such horrible things about Gerhaun. *"I am not an agent of Finesia."* I said. *"Nor is Taka."*

I looked down at the boy, and he smiled.

"The dragon queens shall be the judge of that. When they arrive, we'll have a council and decide what to do with you. We need to know that this place is safe."

"Taka and I are the last dragonseers alive," I pointed out.

The dragon queen raised an eyebrow. *"Are you now?"*

"Of course, I am. Francoiso and Sukina are dead," I said. *"Alsie, and Charth, and"* – I hesitated – *"Indira, are now under Finesia's thrall."*

"But I sense you have the same abilities as them. And yet, you seem to think yourself different."

"We are different..."

"How can you be so sure?"

And that was the question that I'd been asking all this time. How could I be sure of who I was when I had Finesia raging through my mind? Part of me wanted to admit myself as a traitor, after what I'd done. But, like Gerhaun had reminded me, I had to put that all behind me now.

"Answer me! How can you be so sure?" And with that question in the collective unconscious, she let out a massive roar that caused the ground to tremble in front of us.

But I would not let her scare me.

"Because I have my own will," I said. *"And I will never surrender that to Finesia. Also because I care about the fate of this world more than I care about my own.*

The dragon queen paused a minute and then lowered her head as if assessing me. I affixed my gaze on one of her eyes, and I held the stare, not letting her bully me. Gerhaun had been nothing like this.

"Oh, don't be so harsh on the woman, Tarinah. She has just lost her dragon queen." I looked around for the source of the voice and saw another massive golden dragon approaching from the sky.

"*Yol,*" Tarinah replied. "*You're late, as always. Where are the remaining dragon queens? And what happened to the other woman?*"

"*They're coming, and they'll be here in due course. It's not like we can start the funeral before Admiral Sandao and General Sako get here, anyway. Their boats are still a long way away.*"

The two dragons continued to natter away, like two elderly rivals. They hadn't put their feuds behind them, it seemed, and so their conversations diverted Tarinah's attention away from her threats, at least for the time being.

While they argued, the third dragon queens came into view. This time she landed silently without a word to the other two dragon queens. They also ignored her, seemingly more interested in their own conversation. The third dragon queen turned to me.

"*Ah, the young dragonseer,*" she said. Her voice sounded younger than the other dragon queens I'd encountered before. "*You must forgive my comrades, for they know not how to behave in front of humans. I am Castlonth. And you, I believe, are Dragonseer Wells.*'

Castlonth.... She was the dragon queen we were meant to trust. I stepped forward slightly so I could bow to her. But the dragon tossed back her head and roared to the sky. I stumbled backwards.

"*Don't be so hasty, Dragonseer,*" Castlonth said. "*We've all agreed to not let you get too close. We need to know where your allegiances lie.*"

"*Auntie?*" Taka asked. "*Why are they being so unfriendly?*"

"*I guess we have to earn their trust.*" I said. I hadn't expected the other dragon queens to be so hostile towards us.

The next three queens came in from the sky in a group of three. They landed in unison. One was shorter, one thinner, and one more stout. They touched down behind the first three dragon queens.

"*Ah, there she is. The traitor.*" One of them said, though I don't know which one.

"*Heard she made a whole volcano erupt,*" said another.

"*Heard she torched her own village, and almost destroyed a covey of dragons in rage,*" said the third.

Dragonheats, this wasn't going well at all. All these dragon queens had it in for me. And this time, they didn't even seem to want to tell me their names.

"*Silence!*" A voice boomed out in the collective unconscious. The six dragon queens turned their golden shiny heads to the sky, and I looked up in the same direction. She was like a whirlwind coming through the clouds. I couldn't see her yet, but rather what looked like an approaching storm. The air started to smell of ozone, and the sound came of gigantic beating wings.

"*One of our own has died,*" the voice continued. "*And it seems your spirits have devolved into chaos. Show some respect for our order. We need to stick together now more than ever before.*"

"Bassalhan," Castlonth said. "*It's been so long...*"

A hole opened up in the clouds, and something massive plummeted down through it. The dragon queens scattered, and it landed right between them, where the mosaic depiction of Gerhaun lay on the cobbles on the ground. The force of her landing sent up so much dust that it took me a while to be able to see her.

When the dust subsided, I saw not one dragon but two.

There was the queen I presumed to be called Bassalhan, as spectacular as the tallest of statues. She had long teeth that passed over the top and bottom of her mouth, and eyes that looked so rugged they displayed both age and wisdom. She must have been a good head taller than Gerhaun had been – and much more muscular too.

The second dragon was a coloured dragon just like Velos – a splendid citrine with scales like early autumn leaves. He was slightly larger than Velos, and I could sense in the collective unconscious he was much older too.

But what surprised me the most was a red-haired woman in a one-piece leather suit, who carried a double-headed spear on her back. She sat bareback on the coloured dragon, and I cast my mind back to the days before Faso installed the armour on Velos, when I'd ride him that way too.

The woman slid down the dragon's tail, and then lifted herself back up to an upright standing position, one tip of her spear plunged into the ground. I then noticed her right leg shining in the light. It was metal, but still she walked on it as if it were made of flesh.

Meanwhile, the golden dragon queen called out loud to both humans and dragons alike. Her voice was loud and could cover massive distances with ease.

"I am Bassalhan," she said. "The strongest of all dragon queens, and hence the most suited to take leadership of the fortress. From now on, you shall answer to me, is that understood?"

Confused murmurs came from the troops from behind me. They answered to me, General Sako, and Admiral Sandao. But Gerhaun left tactics down to us, while she managed strategy and morale from the top. This, suddenly, seemed quite a different arrangement.

"Is that understood?" the dragon queen roared again.

I glanced over my shoulder and nodded. Best to let her have command until we had a better handle on things. The troops noticed my signal, and out came a cry of, "Yes, your highness," from them. I noted that it wasn't, 'yes, Ma'am', or 'affirmative', almost as if they'd been trained what to say in this situation.

As I turned back to look at the massive dragon queen, I saw the woman sprinting at me at a speed I wouldn't have expected given her artificial leg. Before I had time to react, she stopped herself and extended her spear at my throat in one swift motion. She stopped it just short enough to pinch my skin without nicking it. I looked down at it, my heart thumping, and then I looked up into the woman's assessing stare. Those cold cornflower eyes told me that if I budged even one inch, she'd end my life here and now.

"Auntie Pontopa," Taka called out.

I put up my hand carefully to stop him doing anything stupid. "It's okay..."

"Don't hurt her, please." Taka said. "She means you no harm."

The woman didn't even look at him. Now I could see her up close, I noticed three jagged scars that ran down from the corner of her left eye to her right cheek. It looked almost as if she'd been clawed.

"I'll be the judge of that," she said. And she twisted her spear slightly, tugging at the skin on my neck.

"Who are you?" I asked.

"I'll be the one who'll ask the questions, Dragonseer Wells," she said. Then her voice came again in my head. *"And you'll talk to me on this channel, where no one else can hear."*

She could talk in the collective unconscious... How was that possible? *"Fine,"* I said. Without daring to flinch. *"What is it you want?"*

"To prove to us that you're not an agent of Finesia.

"How am I meant to do that?"

"Pledge allegiance to Bassalhan right now. Say it out loud and look me in the eye as you say it. If you're a traitor, I will know."

I wanted to swallow but doing that might cause that sharp tipped spear to rip out my throat. It looked so well sharpened that it would cut through cartilage like a scalpel. And the woman held it there with surgical precision.

All this while, the voice of Finesia was running circles in the back of my head. Trying to get me to transform into a dragonwoman and run rampage around the fortress. But I didn't pay her any heed.

"Have it your way," I said. "I, Dragonseer Wells am loyal to Bassalhan, and Castlonth, and Yol, and Tarinah, and the other three dragon queens here whose names I do not yet know. I serve dragons and I serve the good of humanity, and I have done so since I was a child. Yes, Finesia is in my mind. But I will not let her have dominion. Is that enough?"

The woman paused. She narrowed her eyes, as if trying to scare something out of me. And I stayed silent and calm, much as Sukina had taught me.

"That will suffice," Bassalhan said in the collective unconscious, and the woman stepped back and lowered her spear.

"I warn you, though," the woman said. "If I see even a hint of treachery – of you going over to Finesia's side, I will end your life without question. Is that understood?"

"I understand."

She then turned to Taka and stared him down. He backed off from her, clearly afraid she'd also raise the spear to his throat. "The same goes for you, Taka Sako. Don't think because you're a child I'll go easy on you."

He nodded, looking back up at her with wide eyes.

I crossed my arms. Her threats on Taka hit home a lot harder than those directed at me. "You still haven't told me who you are?"

She looked away. I could only see her face in profile, but it was enough to see the bitterness that washed over it. "My name is Hastina Wiggea, a dragonseer. Like my mother, Indira, the world has thought me dead for a long time."

Hearing those words caused a pang of sadness to surface within. Hastina was Wiggea's wife... He'd mentioned her when he was a good man. He'd loved her, and for most of his adult life he'd regretted losing her to the coyotes.

But she'd survived.

"This isn't a time for discussion," Bassalhan said. "But a time for mourning. Return to your chambers and stables until the army and navy arrives, and then we shall perform the funeral rites."

I took hold of Taka's hand and led him inside before we had any more potential trouble. My parents were waiting at the northernmost courtyard entrance. I looked at my father as I approached. "Best do as they say for now. Return to your room, and we'll talk after the funeral."

Papo nodded, and Mamo touched my shoulder. They walked off without another word. I watched them go, hoping that the political situation here in Fortress Gerhaun wouldn't turn into a dictatorship.

Because no man, woman, or dragon here had signed up for this, that was for sure.

SUKINA'S STORY

Want to learn more about Sukina? You can download a full-length novel about how she came to be a dragonseer by signing up to my email list.

I send emails approximately twice a month. You can subscribe at http://chrisbehrsin.com/sukina/.

If, at any time, you want to shoot me an email, you can reach me at: author@chrisbehrsin.com.

DRAGONSEERS AND EVOLUTION

The story will continue in Dragonseers and Evolution, coming in 2021.

ACKNOWLEDGMENTS

I'd like to first thank my father, who keeps up reading my work, providing valuable input, and continually helping me to improve my craft. Also, thank you to my mother for keeping up the emotional support.

Also, a huge thanks to Wayne M. Scace for his help editing the manuscript and all the incredibly valuable advice. Plus, a big thanks to Carol Brandon for helping get rid of those niggling typos.

Thank you furthermore to all the talented people at Miblart for another awesome cover.

I'd like also to thank my good friend, Patch Willis for all the motivation, advice about art, and help with the blurb.

And a big thanks to everyone on my ARC team, for being patient with me, reading my work, and providing awesome feedback and encouragement.

Finally, thank you most of all to my dear wife, Ola for everything she does.

ABOUT THE AUTHOR

Chris Behrsin is a British fiction writer who is pursuing the digital nomad lifestyle, hopping from pond to pond and working remotely he goes. Fiction-wise, he writes in multiple genres, but mainly science fiction and fantasy.

He's also a working freelance copywriter and he co-runs the Being a Nomad (beinganomad.com) travel blog with his wife. In his spare time, he enjoys reading and playing the piano, whenever he has access to one.

He's travelled extensively, having lived in France, South Korea, Poland, China, Spain, and Vietnam. He has a passion for exploring off-the-beaten-path destinations and infusing pieces of them in his work.

CPSIA information can be obtained
at www.ICGtesting.com
Printed in the USA
FSHW010444070821
83853FS